GUARD MY HEART

ALSO BY SABRINA FEDEL

All Roads Lead to Rome

All Paths Lead to Paris

GUARD MY HEART

SABRINA FEDEL

Delacorte
Romance

Delacorte Romance
An imprint of Random House Children's Books
A division of Penguin Random House LLC
1745 Broadway, New York, NY 10019
penguinrandomhouse.com
getunderlined.com

Editor: Wendy Loggia
Cover Designer: Christina Chung
Interior Designer: Cathy Bobak
Production Editor: Jamie Johnson
Managing Editor: Tamar Schwartz
Production Manager: Shameiza Ally

Library of Congress Cataloging-in-Publication Data
Names: Fedel, Sabrina author
Title: Guard my heart / Sabrina Fedel.
Description: New York : Delacorte Romance, 2027. | Audience term: Teenagers | Audience: Ages 12 and up | Summary: Seventeen-year-old Ryleigh dreams of being a D1 ice hockey goalie and strikes a deal with a new hockey player at school in order to boost her skills, breaking her no-dating rule in the process.
Identifiers: LCCN 2026001394 (print) | LCCN 2026001395 (ebook) | ISBN 979-8-217-11813-7 (trade pbk.) | ISBN 979-8-217-11814-4 (ebook)
Subjects: CYAC: Dating | Hockey goalkeepers | Hockey | Romance stories | LCGFT: Romance fiction | Sports fiction | Novels
Classification: LCC PZ7.1.F418 Gu 2027 (print) | LCC PZ7.1.F418 (ebook)

The text of this book is set in 11.75-point Maxime Pro.

Manufactured in the United States of America
1st Printing

The authorized representative in the EU for product safety and compliance is Penguin Random House Ireland, Morrison Chambers, 32 Nassau Street, Dublin D02 YH68, Ireland, https://eu-contact.penguin.ie.

Random House Children's Books supports the First Amendment and celebrates the right to read.

For the hockey girls, especially my Goalie Girl

Chapter 1

Frozen Hearts

THE RINK IS WARM. SCORCHING AUGUST HEAT JUST BEYOND THE metal walls is doing its best to put the air conditioners through their paces. Which would be great if they were athletes instead of machines on the verge of breaking down. The ice is so soft that you'd think we were in Florida instead of Connecticut. It's hard to get a good grip with my blades when the ice is watery, and my legs ache from the effort as I slide from side to side. I yank my helmet off and grab a water bottle from the top of the net. Cold water cascades over my cheeks as I squirt my face, which must be as red and shiny as candy apples right now.

Matt yells to me from the other side of the ice. "Ryleigh, pickup game?"

I'm the only goalie at stick time this afternoon, so all that really means is offense against defense. They'll sit on the bench and take turns, three on three, and me. There are only nine skaters: seven guys, ranging in age from twelve to twenty-something, and two other girls, who play on the fourteen-and-under in-house league. Matt and I are seniors at the same high school outside Danbury. We should all be at a swimming pool or the beach, but if you love the ice, it's a kind of addiction. Matt only plays on the high school team, though. He's more into the investment club than hockey.

I wave my glove to tell him yes, and he gathers some extra pucks so we won't have to stop to retrieve them every shot.

The scoreboard clock counts down the last twenty minutes of stick time. Sometimes the rink lets us go over if it doesn't need the ice right away, and today there's nothing scheduled until later. It all depends on whether Earl is running the Zamboni. He opens those gates exactly on time as if the whole world might collapse into anarchy if he's one second late.

We start playing, but the only shots I need to worry about are Matt's and Otto's—he played club hockey in college. I dump the shots I catch with my glove back out, and they start all over again so we never stop unless I call for a break. My chest is tight from the humidity despite the two puffs I took from my inhaler before I came on the ice. We're a few minutes in when the familiar clang of a door opening and closing rings through the rink from the far side.

A tall guy wearing an orange jersey slides onto the ice. He drops a puck and takes shots on the empty net at the other end while the rest of us stop and stare. This kid can skate. Even out there completely alone, he shines. The smoothness of his turns, the way he angles himself on his blades, it's like watching a work of performance art or an eagle soaring.

Matt rolls to a stop beside me. "Whoa," he practically whispers.

I glance at him and smile.

"He's better than you, Ryleigh."

I should be annoyed, but the awe in his voice is a total compliment.

"I would hope so. He's wearing a Danbury Junior Hat Tricks practice jersey," I say.

Matt nods, his gaze still fixed on the wonder before us.

The girls pull up beside us. "Who is that?" one of them asks.

Matt and I shake our heads as the kid sends a slap shot to the net from the blue line with so much force, I'm surprised the net doesn't dislodge.

"Wait," the twelve-year-old boy says, "look at his jersey. Is he really in the NAHL?"

"Looks like it," Otto says as he rolls to a stop next to me. We're clustered now, like a gaggle of fans.

"What's the NAHL?" one of the girls asks.

"North American Hockey League," Otto says.

"Tier Two juniors," I add. "There's only one tier and the farm teams between him and the NHL."

"He's practically guaranteed a D1 college slot," Matt says. He skates down to talk to the kid.

We all wait, watching the precious seconds of stick time wind down. But my lungs could use the break. The kid shakes his head, and Matt skates back to us.

"I asked him to join, but he said he didn't want to shoot on a girl." He shrugs at me.

"Whatever," I say. "Let Mr. Miracle-on-Ice enjoy his half of the rink. We're losing valuable time." I replace my mouthguard and clamp down on it.

Otto and Matt laugh, and we start back up. But we're all trying a little harder now, as if we have something to prove to the hotshot misogynist across the ice who doesn't think I'm good enough to waste his stick time on. Although the way I played last year, he could probably make me look like a squirt player up against prime-time Sidney Crosby. I should be grateful, I guess, but it stings like that moment you realize you've met a wasp. This year is my final chance to get a D1 scholarship. I can't blow it like last season. I've already promised myself that I won't let anything distract me from my goals. Operation No Distractions, as my dad and I call it.

The buzzer sounds and Earl bangs open the Zamboni doors. Everyone taps my helmet to say thanks as my chest heaves trying to get enough oxygen. The younger kids skate off, but Otto, Matt, and I gather pucks and wait for the Zamboni to make its first pass at the edge of the rink. We move the heavy net against the boards so it's out of the way. Across the ice, the hotshot moves the other net. The three of us skate off from our side and he skates off from his.

The younger girls chatter in the locker room as we change.

"I can't believe he wouldn't shoot on you, Ryleigh!" one says.

"I bet you could shut him down with one eye closed," the other chimes in, and they laugh in agreement.

I smile. It's nice that they think so highly of me, but maybe that kid was afraid of hurting me. He's not your average player. He's an elite player destined for big-time hockey. Still, it bugs me that he assumed I wasn't tough enough to take a beating.

When I emerge into the late-afternoon sun, I stop and squint while my eyes adjust. My leg pads are tied together and slung over one shoulder, and my hockey bag hangs from the other. My giant hockey bag that's big enough to curl up on when we are stuck at rinks waiting for locker rooms. My right hand holds my keys and my left holds my stick. To my left, someone leans against the building at the edge of the automatic doors, one foot up against the wall. Dark hair falls around his face as he stares at the phone in his hand. A hockey bag with the Jr. Hat Tricks logo rests at his feet. Two top-of-the-line Bauer sticks lie across it. He stops scrolling and looks at me with eyes the color of a strong Americano.

I step off the curb.

"Hey," he says, "you were really good out there." His voice sounds like a Coke slushie, cool and crisp. I stop and look at him. It didn't seem like he even knew we were on the ice with him. He pushes off the wall and stands straight.

Based on my reflection in the glass door, I'm still beet-faced and my once neatly braided hair is a halo of wispy, dark frizz.

His gaze takes in my size and then the logo on my bag, the Connecticut Polar Bears. There aren't the same kinds of junior leagues for girls. I'm as high as I can go before college. Most guys like him will play juniors for two years after high school before they start college so they can get bigger and faster first.

"What level do you play?" he asks. He has a slight accent. I can't place it, but the words sound softer and more melodious than typical English.

"Triple-A," I say. A lot of my teammates will go D1 or to a high-end D3, though not as many as his teammates.

He tilts his head. "U16, right?"

I take a breath. "I only look twelve. I'm seventeen."

He laughs, though I didn't say it to be funny. Everyone thinks I'm younger than I am. Mostly because I'm built like the flyer on a cheer squad, not a goalie. My head barely rises above the crossbar, and even with the bulkiest pads, I hardly block any of the net just with my body. But my face looks more fourteen than seventeen, too.

"You're solid," he says with a grin, dimples flashing like tiny stars on his cheeks.

I purse my lips together and nod thanks and walk to my car.

The back of my beat-up Rogue opens with a click, and I use all my weight to toss my heavy bag into the cargo bay. Then I layer my pads and stick on top.

"I'm Jett," he calls from behind me. I swivel halfway as the hatch slowly closes. I contemplate him for a moment. He smiles like he's never known a day of worry in his life. It must be nice to have your dreams already in the palm of your hand.

I give him a vague wave. Then I climb into my car and drive away.

Chapter 2

We Meet Again

A WEEK AND A HALF LATER, SCHOOL STARTS. THE FIRST DAY OF any class with a lab is key. If you sit down too quickly, then you get chosen by your lab partner, and that's a total lottery. But if you wait too long, then all the good partners are taken. I really can't afford to be paired with a slacker since I miss so much school for hockey. Or someone who's worse at science than I am. I've been thinking lately that I'd like to go into scientific research for alternatives to the toxins we pump into our lives, so I definitely need to improve my chemistry and biology skills, not weaken them.

The problem is that everyone else in honors chemistry also knows this information about finding a lab partner, so they're milling around the room like it's a reality dating show.

Some kids partner up and a few brave souls take a seat at the two-person black stone tables. I let out a breath as seats fill up. Halfway across the room, there's an empty spot by Danny Ayers. He's kind of a creep, but he'll do his share of the work and let me have his notes when I miss class. I'll just have to listen to his immature innuendos. I glance around one more time to make sure there isn't a better option. People are settling in as we inch closer to the bell, so I step toward Danny. A tall kid in a red T-shirt jostles my arm as he brushes past me straight for the only open seat left with a partner, the one next to Danny. My dad would throw one of his favorite proverbs at me: "He who hesitates is lost." I turn and grab a chair at the empty table by the door. I'll have to take my chances with whoever sits beside me.

I drop my book bag at my feet. When I look up, the red-shirt kid is at the edge of the table.

"Is this seat taken?" he asks, and slides into the empty place next to me without waiting for an answer.

It's the hotshot from the rink.

I look at him and blink as my brain processes what just happened.

"Weren't you about to sit with Danny?" I ask.

"That kid over there?" He points at Danny. "I was, but then I saw you."

He leans in and smiles. A perfect, dazzling smile complete with those unnecessary dimples.

"You're Goalie Girl, right?" he says. "You look a bit

different . . ." He trails off but uses his hands to gesture like he's trying to hold a misshapen basketball. There's a laugh in his eyes as he implies that I looked like a hot mess that day at the rink with my flyaway helmet hair.

"I tend to sweat less at school," I say as the bell rings. I guess this misogynist thinks girls should leave the rink looking like they've been to a spa instead of hockey.

He laughs and elbows me like we're old friends sharing a joke. I move my elbow in and open my notebook.

Mr. Gobbledygook, our chem teacher, starts class. His name isn't Gobbledygook, obviously. It's Polachuk, but he's had the moniker for so long that even some of the teachers call him Mr. G. It's also apparently well earned. His rep is that he'll answer any question with a five-minute recitation that sounds like it's straight out of an academic journal.

Hotshot makes a *schweet* noise. When I look over, he mouths, *Do you have paper?*

He can see my new notebook. I look around the class to check if there's anyone who might switch seats with me, but everyone is focused on our school's version of Professor Snape as he tells us there won't be any accommodations for "unnecessary absences."

I rip out a page from my notebook and hand it to him. He searches the empty table as if he's expecting a pen to magically materialize if he looks hard enough.

"Here," I say, and hand him mine. I pull another pen from a pouch in my backpack.

He smiles and nods his thanks.

I go back to taking notes. Leave it to me to get a lab partner who can't even bother to bring a pencil to class. So much for improving my science skills.

Mr. G. takes roll. When he calls, "Jett Robitaille," everyone turns and stares. Our school isn't huge, so we pretty much know each other by name and sight at least. Girls nudge each other and giggle. I get that he's cute, or more accurately, six degrees past are-you-even-serious-right-now, but I highly doubt this ace is skating on sharp blades.

"Here," Jett says, raising his hand.

Mr. G. marks his attendance sheet and keeps going. He calls my name last.

"Ryleigh Vento?"

I raise my hand in a little wave as Jett watches me. Mr. G. nods and puts his pen down.

"Ryleigh Vento," Jett says under his breath, as if he's placing my name into his memory.

I don't look at Jett the rest of class. Instead, I focus on taking notes on how we're supposed to handle the equipment and what all the rules are for the supplies and class in general. I shouldn't be in honors chem, but it's the only chemistry offered in the mornings, which means I'll miss it less for hockey absences.

As soon as the period ends, I shove my notebook into my backpack and get up to leave.

"Hey, Ryleigh, wait up," Jett says. I stop.

He's instantly swarmed by every girl in chemistry who isn't shy, which seems to be most of them. I turn and plunge into the bustling hallway, filled with first-day-of-school reunions.

As I serpentine my way through the crowd toward my locker, there's one thing I know for sure: I am totally screwed in chemistry.

I roll the dial on the lock I've had since middle school and open my locker. I shove my chemistry notebook onto the top shelf. Imani, my best friend since second grade, has taped a paper heart the width of the locker to the back wall. "Best Year Ever" is written across it in beautiful calligraphy. I smile.

"Hey, Ryleigh," Jett says as he jogs up beside me. "Did I do something wrong?"

I raise my eyebrows and stare at him.

"What?"

"Of all the people in that class, why would you sit with me?"

Jett shrugs. "You're the only person I know at this school?"

"First of all, you don't know me. Second, and more importantly, we both play competitive hockey."

My new chemistry nightmare studies me. "We can be hockey buddies," he says, breaking into his model smile.

The guy who wouldn't shoot on me now wants to be hockey buddies. Right.

I count to five in my head before I answer. "Explain to me,

please, who is going to complete our labs and take notes for us when we're both traveling?"

Jett's dark eyes go wide. Finally, he gets the problem.

"I hope you're as big a hotshot with chem as you are on the ice, because I'm not. I'm only in honors chem because regular chem is in the afternoon every year, and I'd have to miss it too often to keep up."

"Sorry," he says. He bites the corner of his pretty lip.

"It's too late now." I close my locker. Mr. G. made it very clear there would be no changing partners. Period. "And just so you know, Mr. G. hates student-athletes. He won't do anything to accommodate us. The only game that guy has ever played would be *Tetris* when he was a pimple-faced fourteen-year-old."

Jett laughs. "Got it. It'll be fine. I'm good at science." I hope he's not exaggerating.

The warning bell dings. "I need to get to calc. Please tell me you aren't in that class, too?"

Jett shakes his head, looking more like a guilty puppy than a guy running the world. "I'm headed to English. Do you know where Mrs. McKinnon's class is?"

I walk him to his class since it's mostly on the way to mine. We get a lot of stares and whispers as we go, especially from girls.

"In there," I say when we reach Mrs. McKinnon's room. Then I turn down the hallway to calculus. I barely survived last year. I've been hoping for a reset. But as I trudge the hall, I'm wondering if all this is actually a bad omen for how heart-breaking the rest of my senior year is going to be.

Chapter 3

It's Good to Have Friends

I'VE JUST OPENED MY LUNCH CONTAINER WHEN IMANI SLIDES into the seat opposite me.

"What's up, my ice queen?" she says.

"Please don't ever say that again."

Imani laughs, completely unfazed by my reprimand. Her curly dark ponytail swishes behind her, the only part of her that seems to belong on the cheer squad. And yet, she is. She's friendly with the rest of the squad, but she doesn't hang with them the way they stick together. Imani is one of those rare people who can't be pinned into a clique. She cheers, plays lacrosse, and sings in the chorus. She moves between those groups effortlessly. But mostly, she's a thrift store quirk master, pulling off looks that would be impossible for most people.

"Rye," she says, "I have news. Big news."

I glance up. Her slightly lopsided smile makes me laugh.

"Yes?" I prod when she stares at me.

"You aren't the only D1-bound hockey player in school anymore." She pops open a can of lime sparkling water and wiggles her thick eyebrows.

I unpack my lunch into a neat little square.

She frowns. "You don't seem surprised."

"Oh, I'm not. He's my lab partner in chemistry." I take a bite of the avocado-and-cucumber sushi I brought.

She studies me. "And you're not happy about this?" Imani does not believe that opposites attract, which may explain why she's dating Lewis Graham, the jazz band's answer to a thrift store queen, totally quirky but somehow fascinatingly cool, too.

I shake my head. "Who is going to cover for us when we're both traveling? It's already hard enough for me to do honors chem. Plus, he seems like he's way too used to having anything he wants just magically fall into his lap. Not to mention the whole 'I don't shoot on girls' thing."

"Wait, that was him?" Imani's face scrunches up. Her master plan to see me date just hit a huge snag. She probably thought she could talk me into dating a serious hockey dude. Next to getting into Pratt or the Savannah College of Art and Design to major in fashion, Imani has no bigger life goal than to have us double-dating.

I nod. "Now he's my chemistry nemesis."

Imani laughs. "Your chem nem. That's what I'll call him from now on."

Matt slides in beside me, while Lewis climbs over the bench to sit beside Imani.

"I'm glad you think this is funny," I say.

"Well," Imani says in her annoying look-at-the-bright-side way, "he's a work of art. There's that at least, right?"

"Who?" Lewis asks. He crinkles his freckle-spattered nose as he waits for an answer.

"The new guy who plays for the Hat Tricks," Imani replies.

Matt and Lewis scoff.

"Oh, he is," Imani says, swirling some spaghetti on her fork. "I caught a glimpse of him in the hall." Lewis glowers at her.

A few other friends show up and fill the table just as Jett appears in front of me. His glance roams the group and settles back on me.

There really isn't enough room, but that doesn't stop Matt from scooching over to make space, which pushes everyone else down the line. "You can join us," he tells Jett, who is turning away.

Jett stops and looks at me.

I press my lips together and give Matt a side-eye but move into the space he's made so Jett can take my end seat. The two of us squash together like spectators leaving an arena, both of us trying not to touch while still being able to move. More than once, I let my other elbow knock into Matt.

"I'm Imani," my traitor best friend says, and then proceeds to introduce everyone else at the table.

My chem nem nods politely. "I'm Jett. Thanks for inviting me to sit with you."

Well, some of us invited him. I feel rude now. And, whether I like it or not, we are chemistry teammates. I need to get along with him. Still, it's not like I have anything to talk to him about. I'm certainly not going to bring up hockey when he wouldn't even shoot on me. The cafeteria rings with chatter, including our table, as everyone catches up on what they did this summer.

"You bring lunch, too, huh?" Jett says after a few minutes.

"It's way healthier than anything they have here."

He nods. His lunch looks like a nutritionist packed it, from the wrap with grilled chicken and veggies down to the pistachios. "Do you want some?" he asks.

Matt coughs while Lewis nudges Imani.

"I'm good," I say.

Lewis turns to Imani. "Do you want my fruit cup, I.?" Imani bobs her head yes and Lewis slips it onto her tray. "I need to keep my muse well fueled," he tells us, with just enough self-awareness to make it funny instead of gross. We all laugh while Imani fans herself dramatically.

"So, Jett, where are you from?" Matt asks. His watery-blue eyes study Jett.

"Montreal," Jett says, which explains his slight accent, soft and round like all the French Canadian hockey players sound in their interviews. He must have grown up speaking French.

"Did your family move here so you could play with the Jr. Hat Tricks?" Matt asks. He should be a journalist. He's always the curious one who asks lots of questions.

Jett shakes his head. "I'm living with a host family. Their kids are in middle school."

"Let me guess: They're big hockey fans and their kids play," I say.

Jett laughs. "Yeah, they're always asking me to play roller hockey in the driveway or go to the rink for stick time."

He's more good-natured about it than I'd be. I wouldn't have time to mess around entertaining a host family's kids. But I guess he can afford to be generous with his time. He probably already has a college commitment. That thought is barely through my head when Matt asks him.

"I'm committed to Cornell." He's not full of swagger over it like I expected. The Ivies may not send as many kids to the National Hockey League as the big schools like Boston University or Michigan, but it's still a big deal. I'd be thrilled to commit there. Now I'm slightly curious if he's been drafted.

"Wow," Matt says, "mad hockey skills and smart. You should definitely hang around this guy, Ryleigh. Maybe he could help you."

My mouth drops open, and Imani kicks him under the table.

"Ouch," he says.

"You're not committed yet?" Jett asks as he watches me.

My face burns like I just finished a full overtime period. "No," I say. "Not yet."

Jett bobs his head as if there's no rush, but the sting at the edge of my eyes makes everything a little out of focus for a moment. I shove a baby carrot into my mouth and try to forget what a disaster last year was. There aren't many goalie spots left for next year among the D1 schools. Between now and when either I get a commitment or the last spot fills up, I need to spend every moment on the ice as if my future depends on it. Because it does.

"Ryleigh is amazing," Imani says.

"She really is," Matt chimes in, and then the whole group erupts into telling Jett what a hockey virtuoso I am. As if they would know. Still, it's nice to have them support me. I'm just not sure I deserve it. Sports are all about playing through adversity, but last year I let everyone down. Especially myself.

Jett holds his hand up to stop them. "You don't have to sell me. I saw her. At the rink a couple weeks ago. She was fire."

I want to look at him, but I can't. Did I even hear him right?

"I'll have to come see you in an actual game," he adds.

"I forgot water," I say, and squeeze out of my spot to go to the vending machines along the back wall of the cafeteria.

Imani is beside me faster than my shadow. "Rye, are you kidding me?"

I dig the five-dollar bill my dad slipped into my hand this morning from my pocket. "Since you always forget your water bottle somewhere," he'd said.

Imani gives me a soft shove.

"He couldn't have been that impressed with me, or he would have been willing to shoot on me."

"He probably said that because he thought you were twelve when you guys were on the ice in all your gear," Imani says, "since you're about as short as you can be and still play goalie in your age group."

"Maybe," I admit, remembering how he asked if I played at the sixteen-and-under level. "Anyway, it doesn't matter."

"Look, Rye," she says as I pull a chilled bottle from the vending machine, "I know how important getting a D1 slot is to you, but don't forget to have some fun, too. You're only going to be a high school senior once in your life! There's more to life than Operation No Distractions."

I hand her my water and then grab her shoulders and stare into her eyes, searching them. She's one of the few people in my life who are shorter than I am, even if it's only by an inch.

"What?" she says, pulling back. Her long, slender face challenges me.

"I'm just wondering how my dad got in there," I say, pretending to be bewildered. My dad is always worried that I've grown up too fast because of my mom's illness.

She laughs and pushes me off her, then hands me the water. "Very funny. But your no-dating rule until you have a D1 spot secured is going to be pretty hard to keep with that kind of temptation sitting beside you in class. Chem nem or not." She drops her jaw and smirks at me.

I turn her around and push her back toward our lunch table. "Not happening," I say. "There's no way in this universe that I'm losing a D1 spot over a guy like Jett Robitaille."

Chapter 4

Rules Are Rules

PRACTICES HAVE BEEN RUNNING HARD SINCE THE BEGINNING OF August and tonight will be no different. We skate onto the ice, and my goalie partner and I go to the far side and begin stretching. Girls' hockey isn't a big world, and my teammates have all grown up crossing paths, sometimes playing with each other and sometimes against. My goalie mate, Hailey Shipman, and I have known each other since I started in developmental, back in fourth grade. But she'd already been playing for a couple of years and has always been a standout, while I've always had to reach every year to make a better team than the year before.

Hailey and I stretch and then take a slow skate around the blue line to the net. The fluorescent lights are bright tonight, the steady rhythm of everything about ice hockey flowing around us. Some girls from the younger team lounge on the bleachers, waiting their turn for practice, alongside some of their parents. The rink manager walks around to the Zamboni cave to check on the air conditioners or something. Other coaches gather and watch us as they wait for their teams to clear out or start after us, debating our chances to go to nationals. Their heads bob in the direction of the girls they talk about.

"Ryleigh," Hailey says as we sway on soft blade strokes, "I hear you have a guy from the Jr. Hat Tricks at your school." Hailey goes to a different school in another suburb of Danbury.

"Mmm," I say.

She looks over at me. "Everyone says he's Dark Knight beautiful."

I nod, but not enthusiastically.

"What, you don't like him?"

"He's okay," I say. "He's committed already. He seems like he takes life on the downhill too much, especially since he's my chem lab partner."

Hailey laughs. "Well, once you've got your commitment, you're pretty well set."

I glance over and she realizes what she just said. Hailey is going to Boston College next year.

"Sorry," she says, "I didn't mean it like that. You'll get committed for sure this year."

I give the obligatory nod. These days, it feels like half-hearted nods and yeses are all I have in my vocabulary.

"It wasn't your fault, what happened last year," she adds. Hailey and I have never been friends exactly, but we've always gotten along.

"You heard?" It's so great that everyone knows my junior year was a complete dumpster fire.

She laughs. "We all heard. Coach Blackmon is such a narcissist. If he decides you aren't trying hard enough, then he'll do anything to punish you for ruining 'his' team. That guy totally lives through his kids. I bet he wants to win nationals way more than his daughter does. Did you ever notice how his family does whatever he wants? It's definitely not normal."

I laugh. "Thanks," I say, "but that doesn't change my situation. I have a lot of ground to make up." The laugh fades, replaced with the nagging fear I've been carrying for the past year.

"You've got this," she says with a grin, and taps my pads with her stick as she skates backward and sets up in net. "You're a Polar Bear now!"

We alternate taking shots and running drills. Coach Kaitlyn pushes us hard, but I don't mind it. I love being on the ice. Well, I didn't last year. Last season I thought about quitting. Everything, some days. But my dad convinced me to hang in and see what team I made this season. Coach Kaitlyn seems cool. I just hope she stays that way. Coach Blackmon didn't seem that bad at first, either. Until he singled out me and three other girls to berate on a regular basis.

I feel pretty good tonight. I'm able to keep up with the shots that are coming my way, although no one really tries to take high shots toward their own goalie's head. No one wants to lose their goalie to a concussion just from practice. My legs are strong since I skated all summer, even if it was just at stick time. My blades are a little too soft. I should get them sharpened.

By the end of practice, I need my inhaler, but I stay and collect pucks. My dad taught me early to be the first one ready to go on the ice and the last to skate off. That's what leaders do, he says. I kind of miss the days when he was one of my coaches.

"Good job tonight, Ryleigh," Hailey says as she heads to the locker room.

"Thanks, you too." I pick up the puck bag and turn to skate off, but Coach Kaitlyn calls me over as the Zamboni starts its run. She seems no-nonsense, and she has the credentials to take this team all the way since she's played D1 and on Team USA. I don't know why she's singling me out, though. That can't be good.

I pull up and hockey stop. "Yes, Coach?"

"I just wanted to check in with you. How's it going?"

"Good?" I say, on my guard.

"So, do you like being a Polar Bear?"

"Yes, I'm really happy here." There are other girls new to the team, but I seem to be the only one she's asking. At least I can be enthusiastic about being with the Bears. Although men's beer league would be better than what I went through last season.

She nods. "I ran into Coach Blackmon yesterday. He had a lot to say about you."

My heart drops. I squeeze my blocker hand around the puck-bag strap and my stick. Then I wait to hear how many ways my former coach trashed me. All the anger I felt last season rushes through me. It's easy to blame everyone but yourself, but even my coach from the year before and my teammates were asking why Coach Blackmon bullied me so much. I have a lot of improvements to make to get where I want to be, but I didn't deserve the way I was treated. There seem to be a lot of narcissistic dad coaches in hockey, because he's not the first I've met over the years. They always play the kids whose parents are on the board or coaching with them and pick on the kids whose parents mind their own business. My dad says corporate America is the same way. The narcissists surround themselves with people who will go along with whatever so long as they're protected.

"He thinks you don't put out the effort it takes to be a winner," Coach Kaitlyn says.

Every detail about last year flashes through my mind. The way he always compared me with my goalie partner, the way he'd tell me that she'd have stopped the shot even when she told me she didn't think she would have, the games he benched me for no reason, the way he hated me so much that he'd only speak to me at practice through another coach. He didn't even let me play at nationals against the team we were sure to beat, only offering me the third period when the score was so high that even I couldn't blow it in his mind. My mom was proud of me because I told him no. It was better to not play at all than to take his handout as if he were doing me a favor. The way he hammered my confidence down and limited my ice time, maybe I wouldn't have played well even in a game that would normally have been easy for me. My mom ranted so much about beating him up in the parking lot, I almost believed she might.

My chest tightens. My hands are sweating more than they already were. The last thing I need this season is for Coach Kaitlyn to think I'm weak. Of course she would know Coach Blackmon. The coaches are on the same circuit we're on.

"I promise I'll try my hardest, Coach. All I ask is that you judge me for yourself and not on what Coach Blackmon says about me." My voice sounds shakier than I'd like. It's hard to breathe and I don't think it's my asthma at this point.

She studies me a moment, and then she smiles. "I've known John Blackmon a long time. He's a real bastard."

My mouth drops open, but I'm not sure how I should respond.

"You want to go D1, is that right?" she asks.

The Zamboni inches closer and Coach motions with her head for us to skate off, so we do. When I bounce onto the soft rubber mats surrounding the rink, I turn to her.

"Yes, Coach. More than anything."

She purses her lips together. "I heard you had a lot going on last year."

"I guess." She's probably heard more than I'd want to tell her anyway.

"I hope your mom is better now?" She raises her eyebrows with the question.

I swallow and nod.

"Well, you just keep putting in the effort I've seen over the last few weeks, and I think you've got a real shot at making D1 happen, despite your size."

"Honestly?" It seems too good to be true that she believes in me after what I went through last year.

"Honestly. But it's not going to be easy. You have some weak zones, and some of that you can't do much about because of how small you are. Do you think you can go full tilt? No distractions?"

I nod. "I know I can. Thanks, Coach Kaitlyn!" This is exactly what I need, a fresh start. I let out a breath that takes the weight of last season with it. Now I just have to prove myself.

She laughs and chucks her chin up. "Go ahead and get changed. I'll see you next practice. Come ready!"

"I will, Coach! I promise!" I turn and practically run down the hall to the locker room. I know Imani is going to be upset with me for not soaking up my senior year, but nothing about high school is worth missing this chance for. She can think my rules are pointless all she wants. Operation No Distractions has just been fully activated.

Chapter 5

You've Got to Be Kidding Me

MY CHEM NEM SAUNTERS INTO CLASS EVERY DAY SURROUNDED by girls. Not that this is surprising since his red-and-blue Canadiens T-shirt hangs on his lean, muscular frame in a way that makes it impossible not to think about how nice it would be to have his arms wrapped around you. If you're into life coasters who are just a little too full of themselves, that is. Slim jeans, dark blue Converses, and a black backpack slung over his shoulder complete the look. His dark hair is short and layered in the back, and just long enough on top and in the front to fall into his eyes when he looks down. It's so thick that it curves just a bit as it frames his forehead. The layers are like a perfectly balanced waterfall, with a hint of red highlights to them. He should be going to some future actors' school in New York, not our school.

At least he's finally bringing his own supplies, though. I thought I was going to have to hit Target and buy him some so that he'd stop using mine.

"Happy Thursday, Ryleigh Vento," he says as he peels away from his fan club and slides into his seat. He shoots his dimples at me like laser beams. "How was your practice last night?"

"How do you know I had ice last night?" Three weeks of this and I still can't get used to him.

Jett loses a tiny bit of his composure. "You mentioned it at lunch the other day."

I pinch my eyebrows together. Then I remember that he asked how many times a week we practice, and I told him usually Monday, Wednesday, and Thursday, with games on the weekend. I should have just said two to three times a week. I don't know why everything about him irritates me so much, but it does. He contemplates me as he waits for my answer.

"It was good?"

"If you ever want to hit stick time together, let me know. Here," he says, and holds his phone out, "give me your number."

"Oh, that's okay," I say. "I wouldn't want you to have to shoot on a girl."

Jett raises his brows as if what I said didn't make any sense. Apparently, he's forgotten he's a misogynist. I have not forgotten.

"Well, we're going to need to exchange numbers anyway for chemistry." His smile twitches into a frown.

I take his phone and put in my contact information. When

I hand it back to him, he immediately texts me. The message pops up on my screen as Mr. G. calls the class to order. I turn my phone over without looking at it.

As soon as the bell rings, I slip out of my seat and head for the door without even putting my books in my backpack. Jett calls my name at the same time a chorus of "Jett" erupts from his gaggle of followers, and they surround him. I keep going. The girls follow him because he belongs on the cover of a magazine, and the guys follow him because the girls follow him. He's like the freaking Pied Piper of our high school and he's not even from here. I glance back down the hall and laugh when I see Jett trying to weave his way through the crowd that surrounds him like some K-pop star in a television comedy.

I stop at my locker and exchange notebooks for my calc class. Imani has made a Polar Bear fan page of me and taped it to the inside of the door, complete with my official hockey picture from the team's website, my biography from my NCAA recruiting page, and a quote by me from my first year playing AAA. She must have dug around in our text messages for a long time to find that. I sound like a complete baby: "I know there will be challenges this year, but I'm ready to work as hard as I need to so that I can play for a D1 team someday!" I was only fourteen, but it's still cringey. It's kind of funny, too, though. And naïve. I was so young and innocent back then.

"Why is your face so red?"

I look up at my chem nem.

"Nothing," I say, and try to close my locker, but Jett stops the door and peeks inside. When he sees the poster Imani made, he laughs.

"Oh wow, that's awesome. Did you make that?"

"God, no!" I shove his hand off my locker door and slam it closed. "It's just Imani's idea of a joke." It's not a joke, but I am not telling Jett that it's Imani's cheesy way of cheering me on.

"I think it's sweet," he says, leaning against the lockers with his shoulders flat against them.

I scrunch my face and stare at him. "Did you want something?"

"Oh, yeah," he says as he pushes his hair from his face. "I have to travel next weekend, so—"

I cut him off and nod. "I have to do the lab by myself." I turn and head toward calc class. And so it begins. At least this time, one of us will be here to do our lab.

Jett jumps into step beside me. "Well, you'll have to do the physical part of it, but we can video-chat about the results. I can help with that part. I just might be a little hard to reach, between the bus and practices and games. Coach has a strict no-phone rule at the rink. And sometimes it's hard to get service on the bus in the more remote places."

I stop. "Yes, I'm familiar with hockey travel."

Jett pivots toward me. "Oh, right, sorry."

I start walking again and he follows. "This is only the first lab. It shouldn't be that hard. I can manage it myself," I say.

"That's not fair to you, though. I can help."

I look up, surprised he's down-to-earth enough to worry

about what's fair. Although maybe he's just worried I'll screw it up on my own.

I nod. "I'll text you when it's done, and you can video-chat me if you get the chance."

"Cool. Thanks." I stop because we've reached my calc class. Jett looks around, as if he's just realized he's arrived somewhere unfamiliar.

"Mrs. McKinnon's class?" I ask.

Jett nods.

"Down this hall, make a left, and it will be the third door on the right."

"Thanks, Ryleigh."

Jett looks at me a moment too long.

"See you," I say, dropping my gaze. Damn. This was exactly like staring a skater down in a game and I just let him win. I refuse to give him the satisfaction of thinking I'm like those girls who melt when he zeroes his attention in on them. The only thing he makes me is annoyed.

Jett chuckles, but I don't spend another glance on him as I turn in to the torment of calculus.

I sit in Imani's seat at lunch. I'm breaking the unwritten rule of all school seating—that you don't move spots once you have one—but I really don't want to be squeezed in next to Jett another day.

When Imani shows up, she gives me a pointed glare and

then takes my seat. I press my lips together and pretend I haven't noticed. Lewis slips in beside Imani as if nothing is different from usual. Just when I'm feeling especially smug, Jett slides in beside me, squeezing himself onto the end so that I'm forced to push into Matt, who pulls his head back like I'm the problem for making us switch sides.

Jett plops a small protein shake and some grilled chicken nuggets in front of me.

"Here," he says. "You don't eat enough protein."

Imani and Matt exchange glances.

"Thanks," I say, "but I'm on top of my training diet."

"You like chocolate," he says.

I contemplate the organic shake. I do like chocolate. Which he knows because it's the Achilles' heel in my training diet. I always end lunch with some.

"Someone who works out as much as you do can't get enough protein," he adds.

"That's so sweet," Imani says.

"Well, I owe her," Jett says, "since I'm flaking on our first chem lab."

Our table bursts into chatter then as everyone shares the latest news from morning classes.

"Can you let me out a minute?" I ask Jett. "I forgot my water bottle."

Jett slides out, and I go to the vending machine. As I walk back to our table, Cooper Mayhew crosses my path and stops me.

"Hey, Ryleigh, do you have a sec?" His rower's shoulders

are even more defined than they were last year. He must have spent all summer on the river. He shakes his curly brown hair from his eyes.

"Sure, what's up?" In my peripheral vision, Imani swivels her head to see what's happening. I turn so she can't see my face.

"I know it's still September, but I wanted to ask you before anyone else did," Cooper says. He clears his throat and drops his voice a bit. "Will you go to homecoming with me?"

I look at him. He's a nice guy, and I don't like hurting anyone's feelings. He's cute, too, especially standing in the middle of the cafeteria putting his heart on the line. I doubt anyone can hear us over the noise of lunch, but our awkwardness is probably giving enough away to make us this afternoon's gossip. Still, I'm not breaking my no-dating rule for Cooper Mayhew or anyone else.

"Thanks, Cooper, but I have hockey that weekend."

Cooper nods. "Right, I kind of figured, but if it turns out that you can . . ." He lets the rest of the sentence fall off.

"Thanks," I say.

"I heard you have a no-dating policy this season," he adds, almost hopefully. I get it. Nobody enjoys being rejected.

I nod vigorously to save him some pride. He smiles and nods back. "Good luck with getting that scholarship."

"Thanks, Cooper, I appreciate it."

"No problem. And let me know if you change your mind." He smiles his goodbye.

When I turn around, Imani, Matt, and Jett are staring at

me. I weave my way back to our table, and Jett gets up to let me into my seat.

"Did you just shoot down Cooper Mayhew?" Matt asks. His mouth hangs open as if he's not sure whether to be impressed or appalled.

"I didn't shoot him down," I say.

"You know she has a no-dating policy," Imani says.

Jett raises his eyebrows. "A no-dating policy?"

Matt laughs. "Yeah, Ryleigh has sworn off guys until she gets her scholarship."

"Seriously?" Jett asks. His tone lets me know that this is the weirdest hockey thing he's ever heard. And hockey is filled with weirdos, especially the goalies.

"Seriously," I say. "There is no guy worth losing a scholarship over."

"She's dead serious about it," Imani says. "She was like this last year, too. She wouldn't even go to prom, and two good choices asked her."

"Is Ronnie Walkowski really a good choice?" Matt asks.

Imani tosses a French fry at him, and he catches it in his mouth and eats it.

"He's fine," she says.

Jett is still contemplating me.

"What?" I ask. "I can't afford distractions." Not after last year.

He shakes his head. "Nothing. I admire your dedication. I still think we should hit stick time."

“Your schedule is going to be tighter than mine,” I say.

Jett smiles. “I can always find ice time. It’s one of my superpowers.”

“I’m sure it is, but I’m good. Thanks anyway.”

“Tough customer,” Jett says, and takes a bite of his chicken-and-spinach wrap. He chews his mouthful and then says, “So, no dating anyone? Not even hockey players? You could help each other.”

Is he hinting at something?

“Especially not hockey players. I have enough of my own challenges, I don’t need to take on anyone else’s.”

Jett purses his lips and nods like that makes sense.

“See, she’s the toughest,” Imani says, just as Peyton Malloy walks up. She stands behind Imani and glances around our table until her gaze settles back on me.

“How was your summer, Ryleigh?” She smiles, but it’s clear she’s here to check out Jett. Not because she wants him, she just wants to be wanted by him. While I have a no-dating rule, Peyton has a dating rule that excludes any guy who isn’t at least a junior in college. Meanwhile, the only guys who are juniors in college who want to date high schoolers are creeps. But Peyton thinks she’s way more sophisticated than the rest of us.

“It was great. How about yours?” I pretend I don’t get that she wants me to introduce her to Jett. But Peyton and I have known each other long enough that we both understand what’s really going on here.

“Stellar. I was in Cali for a couple of cheer camps and then spent three weeks in the South of France with my cousin who goes to Pepperdine."

Imani taps my shin under the table with her toe. She finds Peyton more annoying than I do. We nod in unison.

"French guys, you know?" Peyton says, and smiles.

I laugh before I can stop myself. Did she just say that because she knows Jett's first language is French, or was it totally coincidental? Either is possible with Peyton. I should probably get it over with before this gets any more awkward.

I compose my face as best I can.

"This is Jett," I say as I tick my thumb toward him.

Peyton looks at him as if she's just noticed him. She presses her lips into a pout, which makes me want to hurl even as I admit in my head that she's ridiculously pretty.

Jett half smiles at her. I swear if he says something cringe like "Enchanté," I'm moving lunch tables even if it means sitting with a bunch of ninth-grade boys.

"This is Peyton," I tell him.

Jett bobs his head and says, "What's up?"

Peyton gives him a sultry glance. She watches too many teen dramas. "Catch you later," she says as she glances around the table once more. She promenades off with her little cheer bounce.

Jett watches her walk away. Matt fills him in on Peyton's status as an unreachable star for any guy who isn't an upperclassman in college with his own sports car, while Imani peppers in her own commentary on our school's cheer captain femme fatale. I zone out on their chatter. It's been a long time since the antics of Peyton meant anything to me one way or the other. Instead, I spend the rest of lunch worrying about how I'm going to keep my grades up in chemistry with my soon-to-be constantly absent lab partner who already has a D1 scholarship, as he munches away on his perfectly balanced athlete's lunch without a care in the world.

Chapter 6

New Beginnings

A WEEK LATER IN CHEMISTRY, I'M THE ONLY ONE WITHOUT A LAB partner. Mr. G. notices immediately. As soon as he's given us our instructions and we've gotten our supplies, he shuffles over to me.

"Ms. Vento, where is your lab partner?" He exaggerates the *z* sound in "Ms." He looks just like that Muppet scientist guy. Not the skinny one with the goofy hair named Beaker, but the bald one with the glasses.

I don't know why, just because Jett and I are lab partners, he presumes I'd have Jett's daily schedule memorized, but in this case I kind of do.

"He had to take today off for a hockey trip, Mr. Polachuk."

Mr. G. snorts. "Oh, that's right. You both play hockey." We might as well have rabies in Mr. G.'s eyes. "I don't know how you're going to complete the lab, then. There are some parts that require two people."

"I'll have to do my best, I guess." Why is it fair to punish me because my lab partner didn't show up today and we play the same sport? It's not like I began playing hockey in fourth grade just to become Jett Robitaille's lab teammate in my senior chemistry class and ruin Mr. G.'s life. All the rumors I've heard about this guy are now fully confirmed.

"I'll help you, Ryleigh," Danny Ayers says from several tables away. "As soon as I'm done here."

Mr. G. sweeps his gaze from Danny to me, as if we are somehow cheating the system.

"Thanks, Danny."

Danny nods and goes back to measuring out the sodium hydroxide in our experiment. Mr. G. sniffs and moves on to torture the two girls next to me, who are giggling over some foaming mess they've made. He's pretty bent about it, and I send a silent thanks to the universe that they're in this class.

When I get home, I text Jett to let him know the lab is done except for our report. I don't hear back from him, but I'm not surprised since they have a game tonight in Maine. They're probably deep in the land of moose and blueberries by now. Once they reach Lewiston, they'll be busy with warm-ups and equipment care and coaching instructions. It's one of my favorite parts of travel hockey, when you walk around a foreign rink with all the excitement of the game to come still in the air. It makes me feel special, like I'm part of something a lot bigger than myself.

I'm bouncing a rubber ball off the wall in the basement to work on my reflexes when my mom asks me to pick up my fifteen-year-old sister, Harper, from soccer practice.

I mock groan. "I can't wait until next year when she can drive."

"Same," my mom says, but she's smiling.

I make a face at her. "You were a basket case when I was learning to drive."

She laughs. Her thin cheeks are still drawn from everything she went through last year with her cancer. "That was different. The oldest always breaks their parents in for the younger ones. You know that."

"Mmmm," I say. I did have to grow up fast when my mom got diagnosed. Harper and our twelve-year-old sister, London, were pretty much helpless through the whole ordeal.

"I could never have managed this past year without you." My mom comes over and gives me a hug. She's been slowly gaining weight since she was declared cancer-free, but she still feels like a paper doll to me. I miss her sturdy hugs.

"Are you ready for your scrimmage tomorrow?" she asks, pulling away and studying me.

I nod. "Coach is playing each of us half the game no matter what."

She nods back. "And how's school?"

"It's fine."

"You can tell me when things aren't fine," she says.

"I know," I say. But the reality is, I will never again tell my mom something that would worry her. She needs to put all her focus into regaining her strength and staying healthy, not stressing over my worries. Like Jett Robitaille being my chem partner or my dwindling prospects for playing D1. Or her cancer returning. Or losing someone I can't lose. If last year taught me anything, it's to be afraid of what life can do to you.

"I'm off," I say.

"Be careful," she says. "You have—"

"Precious cargo," I say at the same time she does, although I say it in a singsong voice to make fun of her.

She laughs, her hazel eyes sizing me up, and I'm filled with a warmth at the absolute miracle of her standing here for me to tease. I run past her and grab my keys from the bronze cat key holder near the garage door and take off before she sees the tears in my eyes.

My mom and London come to my scrimmage. I wish they hadn't. Somehow it feels like more pressure, since my mom knows how much her illness impacted me last season. It was hard to concentrate with her going through treatment. I didn't have any time off the ice to work on skills because all that time went to helping with chores and taking care of Harper and London or driving my mom to and from treatments when my dad couldn't, and even when I did get to play, my family wasn't in the stands to cheer me on when I needed it most.

Or worse, my mom would come when she should have been tucked in her warm bed fighting the nausea and fatigue.

I'm grateful my mom can be here, but this is just a scrimmage, and I already have too much riding on it. This is the first time Coach Kaitlyn will get to see me in a game situation. I don't need to be reminded of how horrible last year was in every possible way.

When we skate onto the ice, I spot my mom and London on the far side, where I'll take over in net halfway through the scrimmage. My mom's thin frame is wrapped in a blue down puffer jacket, while London is in a hoodie and her favorite yarn gloves. Her brown bangs frame her light amber eyes.

Hailey plays well, and the game is tied at one all when we get to a point in the second period where I can jump in. It's always a little hard for goalies to switch off like this, because if you're playing second and the game is tight, you don't want to be the reason your team loses. It automatically adds a layer of anxiety.

Shots have been fairly even for both teams so far, although the one Hailey gave up really wasn't her fault. It was a cross-ice pass from the left to a player standing on her right with no one from our team covering the back door, as we call the side of the net that's opposite the action. It's hard to switch sides that quickly, and one of our defensemen should have been keeping that player busy for her.

When I get to the net, I push on my blades to get a feel for the firmness of the ice. Then I tap both sides of the net with my stick for good luck and sweep a half circle of excess ice from in front of me with the wide blade of my stick. Every time my mom wants me to vacuum, she tells me to pretend I'm cleaning my net. The loose ice doesn't really make a difference, but it's still something that goalies do, like a ritual we're all compelled to perform. Sometimes I wonder who the first goalie was to start it, or if it's just something instinctive that we would do even if we'd never seen another goalie do it, like the way some animals just know what to do to survive.

Adrenaline is pounding to every part of my body when the referee drops the puck. I'm already crouched in the ready position, my glove hand up, my stick down to block an incoming shot, my knees bent, my eyes focused on the hard little black disc that feels like a rock when it hits you. Almost immediately, there's a shot, but I'm able to block it and the puck flies out toward the boards and gets cleared to center ice. This is a good start.

We play well. The other team gets a fair number of shots, but they're all low. Playing down low is my strongest goalie skill. My size doesn't matter much there, unless I have to slide to the back-door side of the net. It's also my favorite position to play, probably because I have a lot of confidence doing it.

I work up a good sweat. More than once when the action stops, I push my helmet up to get a drink from the water bottle we keep on top of the net and wipe the sweat from my face with my sleeve.

About midway through the third period, I get screened when a big forward from the other team stands in front of me. I try to push her out of the crease, the blue paint in front of the net, but she's strong and digs her blade into the ice to keep me from shoving her out. Before I can look around her for the puck, it comes whirring past my helmet.

Their bench erupts into cheers, along with their fans. A couple of my teammates swing by the net and tap my pads with their sticks.

"That wasn't your fault," one says.

"It's okay," another says. "We'll get it back."

I really hope we do score to make it even again, but our shots haven't been quality ones for most of this period.

What's worse is that the other team picks up on the idea that, while I'm tough to beat down low, the same isn't true if they shoot the puck high. In hockey, the high part of the net is called top shelf, or top cheese, which I have no explanation for except that hockey bros are weird.

Every shot I see the rest of the scrimmage is high. Some fly over the net out of harm's way, but three make it past me, over my shoulder. No matter how quick I am with my side-to-sides, no matter how hard I lunge to put my glove or stick where they need to be, no matter how disciplined I am at staying up, I can't seem to get there. One high puck hits the crossbar and bounces down, setting off the buzzer to ring in my ears as if I just got punched in the face. Sometimes pucks bounce out, but that's not my luck today. And excuses don't change anything in hockey.

With every shot I miss, I can feel the tension rising in my mom and London. I don't need to be in the stands to know that London is critiquing my play as if she's a goalie coach. I've heard enough snippets of her commentary on videos my mom has taken. "She needs to come out farther," she'll say, or "Her glove isn't broken in enough." She's more into piano than sports unless it's to critique her oldest sister. My team gets anxious, too. They leap like antelopes to block shots rather than risk them getting past me. Coach Kaitlyn watches intently as soon as the other team comes into our zone, and it's hard to concentrate.

"Focus on your angles, not on what everyone is thinking," I tell myself, but it's kind of like convincing yourself to go to sleep when your mind is racing and your alarm clock is about to go off in an hour anyway on a day that you have two tests at school. Form is more important than the scoreboard, though, especially today. Today's goals won't be in my official statistics. So every time they come at me, I skate out, angling myself against the incoming shooter to take away her view of the net. The trick is not to get so far out that you can't get back fast enough if they sidestep you. But my angles are sloppy today. In the end, not only do we lose by three goals, but I know I've underperformed everyone's expectations, including my own.

When the final buzzer sounds, my teammates rally around me because there's a strong culture of sportsmanship in hockey. But I know from the effort they put into telling me I had a good game that they think it's going to be a long year. Being a goalie is a lot of responsibility. Even though you aren't the captain, your team gains confidence from knowing that you've got their backs when they let a shot through. You're the anchor. And I just let our boat get dragged through a storm.

I glance at the stands. My mom gives me a bright smile and two thumbs-up. That much enthusiasm means that I sucked even more than I already think I did.

When I get to the locker room, everyone is chattering about the game.

"That Number Five has a wicked shot," a girl named Emma says.

"Where did she get that backhand?" one of our forwards, Shannon, says.

"How about when Fifty-Seven ran the ref over?" Hailey says, and they all laugh.

A girl named Alana slumps down on the bench, still panting from the last shift. "I was ready to deck that girl they were all calling Slim," she says, and the room bursts into all their grievances about when they got elbowed or interfered with and the refs missed the call.

I slip to the floor and unlace my leg pads from my skates, then I unhook the buckles that strap my pads in the back and leave them on the floor. I stand up and yank my jersey off and undo all the Velcro straps until I pop free of my chest pads. I pull my phone from my bag as I sit on the bench. There's a missed call from Jett. And a text from my mom telling me I had a great first game back, and that they'll see me at home later. Everything feels heavy, from the weight of letting my mom down, even though she'd never admit it, to the weight of carrying honors chemistry with a partner who is never going to be available when I am, to my team doing their best to shrug off my bad game.

We're still in our half-undressed state, most of us in sports bras and the shorts or leggings we wear under our hockey pants, when the coaches come in to talk to us. They go over the pros and the cons of the scrimmage, and I can tell Coach Kaitlyn has some things to say to me privately by the way she tells Hailey she had a good game but doesn't mention me.

Sure enough, on my way out, she snags me in the hall and pulls me aside.

"That wasn't the start for you that I was hoping for. We're going to work on your angles and those high-glove side shots in practice from now on. I've never been a goalie, so I can't pretend to be an expert on what you should do, but we'll pull in our goalie coaches to figure it out."

I nod. "Thanks, Coach." At this rate, there is no way I am going D1. I may end up on the bench most of the season like last year. But at least she isn't belittling me the way Coach Blackmon would have. He would have loved seeing me fail today.

"All right," she says, and pats my shoulder. "We have a lot of work ahead of us. Go home and get some rest. I'll see you on Monday night."

Just then, someone calls to her and she turns away. I escape down the hall and out to the parking lot. I check the voicemail Jett left as I reach my Rogue.

"Hey, Ryleigh, this is Jett. Just trying to catch you about the chem lab. We're heading to lunch soon. I'll try you later."

“See you on Monday, Ryleigh,” Alana calls as she hops in her car a few spots away, her straight dark hair moving with the breeze.

I wave to her and toss my gear into my car. Then I get in and drive to the nearest park. I find an empty parking area, and I sit there and cry.

Chapter 7

It's Okay to Ask for Help

AFTER I GET HOME AND SHOWER, I CALL JETT BACK. IT GOES TO voicemail.

I say the same thing he said, except I give him an out to not call back. "Hey, this is Ryleigh, just checking in for our chem lab. It's no big deal if you're too busy. I can finish it later tonight or tomorrow. Good luck with your game."

I know they play at seven because I checked his schedule yesterday. Not because I care, just because I was curious, one hockey player to another. Besides, I needed to know when he might be free to work on our lab.

I'd like to sit in my room and sulk, but if I don't push my sisters to do chores, then they won't. My mom's not one to ask for help unless she absolutely has no other choice, so last year when I saw her struggling, I stepped up, since I'm the most disciplined. My sisters didn't like me "bossing them around," but more than once when they complained, my dad gave them the dip and stare—the way dads lower their face and raise their eyes to ask if you're for real right now.

Now that my mom has gotten the all clear, Harper and London think everything should go back to the way it was, with our mom basically spoiling us every minute. They just don't understand how delicate she still is. I can give London a pass because she's only in grade school. But Harper should know better.

"Come on, Harps," I say, and knock on her door. "It's laundry time."

"Arghhh!" she groans. "I'm watching the game." She's sprawled across her beanbag chair with her head upside down and holding her phone in front of her. I'm surprised she doesn't need physical therapy, the way she's twisted up. Her face is broad, while mine is round, but it works for her. She's pretty in a commanding way.

"How many games have you seen today?" She would stream soccer matches all day if she could. I think she likes watching it a lot more than playing it. I'd rather play hockey, in any form, than see it on a screen.

She deadpans her expression and glares at me, but she clicks her screen off.

"Fine!" she says, her brown ponytail swinging as she sits up. When she stands, she's two inches taller than me. I don't think you need to be tall for soccer. I guess I should have liked that sport instead.

"Fine," I say.

We gather up the dirty clothes and towels and take them to the laundry room, next to the kitchen, to sort everything. Hots, regulars, whites. Mom gets stressed if we don't do it correctly.

"Ryleigh," Harper says as we sort, "Mom said your scrimmage was rough." She has braces, so her *s* sounds are a tiny bit muffled.

I snort. "That's an understatement."

She studies me in her peripheral vision, as if I can't tell she's doing it.

"If you don't go D1," she says, "you could still go to a really good D3 program."

I take a deep breath. Even my family has given up on me. I wonder if my mom asked Harper to put the idea of settling into my head. I'm not usually super driven. But hockey is different. I've wanted this since I started playing.

"I looked at some," she says, kind of quietly, as if she's a little afraid of me. "Tufts has a good program."

"They also have a junior and two sophomores. They aren't looking for next year." I spit the words out without thinking.

Harper pulls her lips in.

I shrug. "I look at all my options. I'm not a racehorse with blinders on."

She nods, satisfied that she has something good to report back to Mom.

After getting the laundry started, I go to my room and work on the lab report. I finish everything except the last section, and then I take a break. I roll my shoulders and open my browser and type in "Jett Robitaille."

My chem nem stares back at me in multiple pictures. Most of them are team headshots, but a few are from sports reports like *Junior Hockey Magazine* and *Le Journal de Montréal.* Cornell has his signing announcement on their website, complete with a little video.

His former coaches say things about him like "natural skater," "natural leader," and "extremely hard worker."

"I bet," I say at that last one.

The articles on him say he's sure to be in the US Hockey League next year, which is the top league in the United States, for additional development before going to Cornell. One article says he's expected to be drafted early in the second round in the NHL draft this spring, when he becomes eligible. He's also been selected to be on Team Canada in the World Junior Championship this December. It's mostly over our winter break, so at least he won't miss a lot of school for that. Then I look at his stats from last year. He really is a hotshot.

I spend the rest of the day stewing. I'm not a natural skater. Or a natural leader. But I'm pretty sure I work harder than Mr. Miracle-on-Ice.

After dinner, I decide to watch Jett's game. My parents subscribe to a streaming app that covers most of the elite games so they can watch me play when I travel and they can't make the games.

It doesn't take long to pick Jett out, though the camera quality isn't exactly NHL-worthy. I recognize the easy way he glides on his blades. I'll give him this: He hustles on the ice. I wish he'd hustle like that for chemistry.

There's a soft knock on my open door. My dad stands there smiling.

"Hey, Dad."

He comes in and sits on the bed beside me. When he slumps, you can see his middle-age spread starting. "What are you watching?"

I turn my screen so he can see it.

"What game is this?"

"Remember I said that my chemistry partner plays for the Jr. Hat Tricks?"

He nods. "Oh, right, the kid who isn't going to be able to pull his weight."

"That's the one."

"What's his number?" My dad's muddy blue eyes scan the screen.

"Eighty-Seven," I say, and point to him.

As if on cue, Jett shoots a rocket at the opposing net and scores.

"Wow," my dad says. His hair is receding, but he's still got enough of it to remind me of his pictures when he was my age.

I sigh. "He's pretty good."

My dad chuckles. "You don't seem to have softened toward him at all."

I shrug.

"I know you're frustrated, Rye, and I know how much you

want to get a D1 slot, but don't forget why you love playing hockey in the first place."

"Because of the rush," I say. Nothing makes your heart pound like facing down an exceptional shooter like Jett.

My dad smiles. "I thought you were going to say teamwork. I guess my great-parenting moment will have to wait for another day."

I laugh. "I like being part of a team, too."

"Ah, see, you did know where I was going with that." He elbows me. "Ryleigh, hockey has taught you some great lessons about perseverance, and hard work, and dedication. But don't forget that it's also taught you how to work with others. You haven't always liked some of your teammates. But you've always been a good teammate."

My dad is talking about getting along with Jett for chemistry. He has no idea that Jett offered to help me with hockey. But it's all I've been thinking about since my disaster of a scrimmage this morning. Maybe this is a sign that I should choke down my pride and take Jett up on his offer.

"Thanks, Dad."

He watches me a moment. "And, you know, it's okay, too, to ask for help if you need it."

I tilt my head at him. Can he read minds?

My dad clears his throat. "I just think that you take a lot of responsibility on yourself, and while I'm very proud of you, I want you to know that we all need help sometimes."

This is my dad. There's no way he knows that Jett has offered to help me. But he's always had a sixth sense of when

I'm sad or frustrated or in trouble. Once he called me at the exact right moment when a creepy guy followed me out of a Target near the rink after a late practice. As soon as the guy heard me say "Dad," he veered off and went to his car and drove away. My dad said he called to see if I wanted to watch the latest *Guardians of the Galaxy* movie with him, but the hint that it was taking me too long to get home hung on the line between us.

I nod, and then he pets my head as if I'm a cat who might claw him, but it's just the awkwardness of dads and teen girls, not because he thinks I'm scary. "Well, I'll let you watch the game," he says.

After he goes, I turn my attention back to the screen just as Jett sends another rocket to the net, but this one gets deflected up and away.

I may not like the idea of working with Jett Robitaille, but I like the idea of losing out on a D1 scholarship even less. My dad is right. I've been doing this on my own and it isn't working. Maybe it's time I shelve my pride and ask the Mighty Jett to hit the ice with me.

Chapter 8

Let's Make a Deal

JETT CALLS ME IN THE MORNING AS THEY'RE PACKING UP THE BUS. "I should be home by four o'clock," he says. "Do you want to get together then?"

If I didn't want to take him up on his offer to help, I'd just tell him not to worry about it, that I'd finish the lab. But I feel like seeing him in person, without the constant throng of people who hover around him at school, is more likely to seal the deal.

"Sure," I say. "Where should we meet?"

"Somewhere without people," he says. He lowers his voice and adds, "I'm peopled out."

I laugh, because that sounds like something I'd say. "There's an Ecuadorian coffee shop near my house that has amazing hot chocolate. I'll send you the link. Just let me know when you think you can get there."

"Perfect," Jett says. In the background, I hear someone calling for them to board the bus. "I'll see you later, Rye."

Rye? Since when are we on nickname terms?

"Okay, bye." I hang up and search for the coffee shop website and send it to Jett. He marks it with a thumbs-up emoji.

I pull into a parking space across the street from the café and check my infotainment center. It's 4:07. I peer through the passenger window all the way through the plate glass window of the café. There's no sign of Jett.

I scroll through hockey reels in one of my apps. The algorithm knows me too well. It feeds me videos of goalies making amazing saves, with an occasional shenanigan, like a goalie trying to trip Connor Bedard with his stick. Someone taps on my window, and I jump. When I glance up, Jett is smirking at me.

I look away and grab my backpack and open the door as Jett steps back to let me out.

"Were you going to keep me waiting all day?" he says. He's wearing a Vancouver Canucks T-shirt, canvas joggers, and a pair of mid boots with Kamik stamped on them. If he makes it to the NHL, he'll definitely be asked to do ads for some high-end designer. I bet he has a social media feed that is one picture of himself after another, all of them hearted by teenage girls across North America.

"I could see you weren't in the shop yet," I say. He is so annoying. "How was I supposed to know you'd be lurking around on the street?"

Jett laughs. "Want me to carry your backpack?"

I narrow my eyes at him. "No, thanks. I can manage it."

"True," he says, "it has to be lighter than that giant hockey bag that's twice your size."

Are we here to critique my petiteness or do chemistry? I step past him and head for the crosswalk. Jett follows.

We stand on the corner and wait for the light to change. "Are you mad at me because you had to do the lab by yourself?" he asks.

I open my mouth to say something, but I don't even know what that is. Am I even mad at him, really? Or just mad at myself? He's never going to agree to help me if I don't shake off how annoyed I am.

I smile. "No, I'm not upset with you. Mr. G. wanted us to fail this one, since it required two people to do some of the mixing, but Danny Ayers offered to help, so it wasn't a problem."

Jett's smile fades. "Ah, sorry about that."

I shake my head as we cross the street. "It's fine. Danny saved the day." That's a sentence I never thought would come out of my mouth.

Jett nods, still without a smile. He should be grateful to Danny.

"I just want to do well in this class. I'm thinking about going into scientific research, so chemistry is important."

"Scientific research? How come?" he asks.

I look at him and shrug. There is no way Jett could understand why it would be important to me.

We go into the coffee shop and place our orders. I get hot chocolate, Jett chooses the hot chocolate and empanadas de viento.

"Are you sure that's all you want?" Jett asks. "Those little white things look so good. What are they?"

"Meringue kisses," I say.

Jett smiles. "Sounds delicious." He turns his dimples to the lady behind the counter. "Can I add a few of those, too?"

Then he shifts back to me. "How'd you find this place?"

"Imani and I used to come here a lot."

Jett raises his eyebrows. "And you don't anymore?"

"She's busy with Lewis and I'm busy with hockey."

Jett's head bobs slowly as if he's not sure that he should agree with this.

When we go to pay, Jett brushes my arm back as he pulls his wallet from his pocket. "It's the least I can do."

He's right about that, but I need to keep him on my side, so I just say thanks.

The lady rings us up. Jett has also grabbed an orange from a nearby basket. "Did you get this?" he asks the lady.

"Oh, no, I missed it. Thank you," she says, and adds it to the total.

The shop smells of coffee and chocolate and sugar, with its pretty cases filled with tres leches cakes and slow-roasted figs in syrup that are called dulce de higos. Bright green tropical plants sprout from containers scattered around the café, and the walls are painted a happy coral color with yellow accents.

We grab a table by the window. I take out our lab notebook and show Jett everything I've done so far. We go over the process, and then we talk about the results. I write in the observations we come up with while Jett munches on his empanadas.

When I've written down everything we want to say, I close the notebook.

Jett pushes his dish over to me. "Do you want one?"

I pull an empanada apart and take half. "Thanks." The gooey mozzarella oozes from inside. It's so good, the fried dough dusted with sugar.

"Listen," I say as Jett licks hot chocolate from his lips. "I was thinking about what you said, you know, about helping me with stick time, and I was thinking maybe we could do that when you have the chance."

Jett's gaze locks onto mine. He starts to smile, but then his whole face freezes as if he's rethinking his offer.

"I mean, if you have the time. I know you're super busy." A rush of awkwardness rolls over me. Why did I ask him? I should not have asked him.

Jett suppresses a smile and wipes his knuckle over his lips.

"I was thinking about that offer," he says. And then he doesn't say anything else.

I stare at him a moment, but he still doesn't say anything.

"Never mind," I say as my face burns. "It's really nothing." Nothing but my entire shot at a D1 scholarship. But this guy is clearly jerking me around now.

Jett laughs. "Look, I'd be happy to help you. It's just that something's come up that I could use some help with, too. Maybe we could do a quid pro quo."

"A what?"

"You know, an even exchange."

Oh, here we go. What a salesman! Now he's going to say he'll help me if I do all the chemistry labs myself or find someone else to help me. Every time I start to think that, just maybe, I could get along with this guy, he ticks me off all over again.

"I'm not begging Danny to do all the labs with me," I say. "Just forget I mentioned it." I slip the notebook from the table and drop it into my backpack.

Jett puts his hand on my wrist. "I'm not trying to flake out on doing the labs, Rye."

My head is still tilted toward my backpack, but I lift it to look at him.

"Okay," I say, and pull my wrist from his grasp, "what would I need to do to get your help?"

"How well do you know Peyton Malloy?"

I drop my shoulders. "As well as anyone knows Peyton. What about her?"

"I want to ask her out, but she only dates college guys." Jett studies me.

"That's correct."

"So," Jett says, dragging the word out a bit, "I was thinking that I need something to entice her."

It's hard to picture Jett Robitaille needing additional leverage to win a girl over, but he's right about Peyton. Not because she wouldn't think he was hot enough, she's just determined to keep her reputation at school as someone who is way out of the league of the rest of us. She wouldn't sacrifice that for anyone. Not even Mr. Miracle.

"And how am I supposed to help? She and I aren't friends. She wouldn't listen to me even if I raved about you."

Jett's dark chocolate eyes light up. "But she might get jealous if she thinks you're dating me."

I snort. "What? That's the most ridiculous thing I've ever heard anyone say."

Jett shakes his head to disagree with me. "You know if someone is taken, it always makes them seem more desirable. So I was thinking that you could pretend to be my girlfriend."

I stare at him. He can't be serious.

"What do you think?" he asks.

"I think you must have gotten hit in the head this weekend. Are you okay? Should I drive you to the ER?"

Jett laughs, flashing his dimples with just the right amount of confidence and modesty to make him almost irresistible.

"I heard you two have a little rivalry."

I shake my head. "Peyton has a rivalry. I have not the slightest interest in either her or her misconceptions."

"So then you shouldn't mind helping me." He looks almost puppy doggish.

I take a deep breath. If anyone can help Jett to get Peyton's attention, it's me. She hasn't liked me since fourth grade when the boys thought I was cooler for choosing hockey over cheer.

"Why would you even want to go out with her?" I ask.

Jett tilts his head and presses his lips together.

"Okay, yes, she's the hottest girl in school. But looks aren't everything."

"Come on," Jett says, "help a guy out."

"I do not have time to pretend to be your girlfriend." I look outside, and already the leaves on the trees are turning all shades of yellow and red. Every month between now and the early spring, my window for getting a D1 slot is going to close more and more until it's completely shut.

"I promise, I'll make it worth your while. And you don't have to do much. Most of the time we spend together will be on the ice or in school."

I turn my gaze back to him. This is like something out of one of those teen rom-com movies that Imani loves so much. It's absolutely bonkers. But I've seen him play. Jett has the skill to help me. And the truth is, he may be the only real chance I have left.

"It's never going to work," I say.

"You don't have to make any guarantees," he says. "Just let her think you and I are an item. How hard is that?"

I take a deep breath and hold it for just a second before I

let it out. "All the time we spend together will be on the ice or in school."

"So that's a yes?" Jett's smile is brighter than the sunset that's glowing on the store windows across the street.

I harden my face. "Fine," I say. "But you'd better make this worth my while."

Chapter 9

New Beginnings

WHEN I GET HOME, I LOOK JETT UP ON SOCIALS. HE ISN'T ON many, but I do find him. Of course. I click on his profile, but it's not what I expected.

Instead of one picture after another of him acting like a model, there are hardly any posts at all. There's one of a dark-haired middle-aged lady standing at a kitchen sink, her face lit up with laughter. The caption is in French and reads: *Happy birthday to the best hockey mom in the world! I wouldn't be where I am without your constant love and support!* I study the picture. The resemblance is unmistakable, from the dimples to the intensity of her dark eyes.

There's also a picture of his signing with Cornell, and a few team pictures, but nothing else. My new "boyfriend" is way more private than I expected.

Around ten o'clock, Jett texts me.

What are you doing tomorrow at five?

I'm suspicious but curious.

Having dinner, I reply.

It's almost as if I can hear him let out a breath.

No, tendy, AM.

"Tendy" is short for "goaltender." Oh. Sleeping.

Wrong. Be at the rink where we met.

I stare at my phone. Is he serious right now?

Seriously.

Okay, now he's just reading my mind.

I got us ice time before school, so don't be late, he adds.

There is no "us." I go to text him back, but now his text thread says, *Jett has notifications silenced.*

He can't possibly be asleep yet, so I text him anyway.

Ice time is expensive. Maybe he's rich, but I'm not. I have some money saved up, but sharing ice fees even twice would wipe out a good chunk of it.

I wait for a reply, but there's nothing. Not even three little dots jumping up and down like the little mind game they are.

I drop my phone on the bed, and it dings as if on cue.

It's on me.

That's too much, I text. He really is not all put together upstairs.

It's not costing me money, he replies. Just be there. And let me sleep. It's way past late.

It's not even ten-fifteen. He really is disciplined. But, if it's not costing him money, what is it costing him? Then again, why should I care? "Fine," I say out loud since I'm not supposed to text him. I set my alarm for four-thirty. That will give me just enough time to brush my teeth and arrive with eight minutes to get dressed. Assuming we can really get on the ice. I get ready for bed, and then I pop downstairs to tell my mom my new plans for tomorrow. She's in the kitchen making lunches for my sisters and me.

My mom furrows her brow as if she's as suspicious of the whole thing as I am.

"Are you sure he's safe? I don't like you being at the rink alone with a boy you hardly know at that hour. It will be completely empty."

"He's not dangerous, just annoying. Who knows, he may be pranking me, and I'll get there and the rink will be all locked up."

My mom frowns. "Text me that you're okay. I will be there faster than Superman if he even seems the slightest bit shady. Don't be afraid to call 911."

I laugh and swing my pinky up and she shakes it with hers.

"I need to have Dad get you some Mace," she adds.

"Sure," I say, "if it makes you feel better." For just a moment, I imagine squirting Jett with Mace. I smile, but then I shake my head. I should feel terrible about thinking that. He's not that bad, really. But it's also a little bit funny?

“Well, I’m off to bed since I’m getting up before the birds,” I say, and head upstairs. Before I crawl into bed, I set my clothes and backpack out for tomorrow. If Jett somehow got an hour of ice time, that leaves me less than an hour and a half to get home, shower, and get Harper and myself to school and in our seats by our 7:25 start time. I try to go to sleep right away, but my mind isn’t used to sleeping at 10:37 p.m., and instead I lie there with my eyes closed contemplating all the ways that tomorrow’s ice time could go wrong, from Jett breaking my hand with a hard shot to me humiliating myself by missing every single puck he sends in my direction.

I don’t know when I fall asleep, but when my alarm goes off, it’s a good thing I set three alarms in a row, because I must have shut off the first one without knowing what I was doing. By the time I’m awake enough to drag myself out of bed, it’s 4:35 a.m. I comb my hair into a ponytail. I slip on a sports bra, my favorite long-sleeve flannel shirt, and sweatpants. Then I brush my teeth and head out.

It’s still dark when I unlock my car and crawl into it. I’m not a morning person, and I’ve never liked early practices or games. Plus, it’s getting cold at night as September winds down its last few days. I yawn and shiver as my car blows cold air from the vents until it warms up.

When I pull into the rink parking lot, there are two cars parked out front, so I take the third spot beyond the handicapped spaces. They’re sports cars, but one is sleek and modern and the other is some quirky antique Impreza that must be left over from the nineties. I shake my head. Of course Jett would have a model-pretty car to match his looks. I glance at the license plates, and they're both Canadian. Lights shine from inside the building. I guess this isn't a prank, which is good, because I'd really want to hurt Jett if I'd gotten up this early for nothing.

I push the button to open my back hatch, and by the time I've gotten out of the car, Jett is running over, all dressed except for his helmet and skates.

"What are you doing?" I ask him.

He pulls up beside me and reaches to grab my bag.

I push his arm away. "I can carry my own bag."

Jett steps back. "Right, sorry, it just seems so enormous compared to you."

The weight of it can knock me over if I don't get it balanced right, but I'm not telling him that. Instead, I slip a tight grip around the straps and use all my weight to sling it up and onto my shoulder, one foot back to balance me when all that weight hits. Then I lift my leg pads and drape them over my other shoulder. I pull my stick from the side of the cargo area and tap the button to close the hatch. I already pushed the lock button after I opened the back hatch when I got out, so the car will lock without me having to fish around in my pocket for my keys. I have a system for a reason.

"We're burning daylight," Jett says. "You need to hurry." He sounds like my dad.

"How did you manage this?" I ask. "Are you sure it's not costing you money?"

Jett laughs. "I'll answer your questions one at a time for each puck you stop." He turns and runs to the entrance.

I follow him into the rink, and he points at the closest locker room to the ice sheet we'll be on so that I can change.

When I step into the rink, the door to the ice is open, and Jett is out there already with a huge goalie in a black practice jersey from a Princeton elite summer camp. I skate over to them.

"Ryleigh, this is Dominic," Jett says. "He plays on the Hat Tricks with me."

I nod at the guy. I barely come up to his armpit.

"Nice to meet you," Dominic says. "Jett says you could use some help." He smiles and taps my leg pad with his stick.

I side-eye Jett. Did he really pull this off? I look around the rink, wondering if it's even okay for us to be here. What if he broke in or something? And how did he get this guy to come? I mean, hockey players never say no to ice, but still, it's zero dark thirty out, as my former-military dad would say.

"Let's go, let's go!" Jett says, full of energy.

Dominic motions for me to take the net. He seems closer to twenty than seventeen. He's probably going to age out of junior hockey this year.

"Let her warm up," Dominic warns my chem nem. Jett waves his gloved hand at us as he scoops a puck onto his stick and takes off for a couple laps around the rink while Dominic shoots on me. All his shots are intentionally lukewarm, and I manage each of them despite having a hard time looking away from the sight of Jett skating. He really is a work of art, his body angled into the ice as he seems to float above it, the puck disappearing and reappearing on his stick as he moves it forward and backward with the speed of a magician.

"Are you ready?" Dominic asks after a few minutes.

I nod, and he hollers to Jett to come in as if he's on a breakaway. Jett skates in fast. He locks his gaze on mine to keep me from guessing where he'll shoot, but I already know he'll strike low because he's not going to want to go hard on me all at once. The only question is which side, but I think the near side.

"Angle out more," Dominic says, so I do just as Jett rips a rocket past my ear.

I look at Dominic. "Sorry, I guess I'm still a little sleepy."

Dominic laughs, not fooled at all by my wounded-pride excuse.

"It's okay," he says. "Jett's heartless on the ice. You thought he was going to shoot low, didn't you?"

I nod.

"He told me you're fire down low."

I shrug. "More like a small group of birthday candles."

Jett, in the meantime, is whooping and sliding around on one knee as if he's a fifth grader imitating an NHL star. I let out a heavy breath.

Jett drops his antics and pulls up in front of us. "She's got way too much net exposed," he says to Dominic.

Dominic nods and turns to me. "You're going to have to be really aggressive in your positioning and angles to compensate for your mini-ness."

"My mini-ness?"

He glides over and stares down at me.

I look away.

"See," Jett says, "I told you she's stubborn enough to make this a fun challenge."

"Is that what I am to you? A challenge?"

Jett purses his lips and nods.

"If we're just here to make fun of me, then let's forget the whole thing." I start to skate toward the door.

"Wait, wait, wait," Jett says, and circles in front of me. "All I told Dom was that you'd be a worthy challenge because he didn't want to get sucked into helping someone who is just going to waste his time."

"You're not going to waste my time, are you, Ryleigh?" Dominic asks. His goalie gaze zeroes in on me as if I'm a puck that could go anywhere.

I sigh and skate back to the net. "No, but I already know I need to be more agile and improve my angles. I've been trying."

They look at each other and smile as if they're co-conspirators.

"All right, here's what I want you to do," Dominic says, and they spend the rest of our ice time putting me through my paces with one high shot after another while Dominic critiques my every little movement and sometimes takes the shots to show me what he means. I'm glad when he takes net and all I have to do is watch because guarding the net from Jett is exhausting.

Every so often, Jett will shoot low just to keep me sharp, but I can stop some of those. I'm going to be black and blue in a few places tomorrow. The hour is filled with the clack of Jett's stick hitting pucks and the soft swoosh of pucks whirring past my head and the clang of the puck hitting the crossbar and, every once in a while, the light thwack of a puck hitting my glove. But even then, it's usually bouncing off and not landing as a clean scoop to stay there. It's frustrating. Really frustrating. I've never given up this many shots in a practice. But I've never practiced with anyone of Jett's caliber.

Even more frustrating is that Jett sticks to his one-answer-per-save rule. All I know by the end of the session is that he asked for a favor to get us ice time, and he needs to repay it. And that his backhand cross-roof shot is his favorite. I didn't ask that as a serious question. But I did technically say "Is that your favorite shot?" when he beat me for the fourth time in a row with it. He answered that one the next time I stopped one of his shots.

By six a.m., I'm a sweaty, panting mess, but I've finally managed to stop a couple of Jett's high shots. They aren't his hardest shots, even when they're rockets. I can tell he's holding back because I've seen what he can do in a game. And he has the control to make sure my head is never in danger, even if I make a mistake.

When the buzzer sounds to let us know time's up, we huddle at the net, passing a plastic Gatorade bottle around to squirt water in our mouths and on our faces. Jett has his helmet off, but Dominic and I have ours lifted so that our cages rest on our foreheads like sunglasses. Dominic hasn't broken a sweat, but Jett and I are drenched.

“Your face is so red,” Jett says.

I narrow my eyes, but I can’t think of a single retort. He still looks magazine ready, even soaked with sweat.

“I have to go run the Zamboni,” he says. “Rye, I’ll catch you at school?” He squirts my face with some water from the bottle.

Dominic shakes his head. “You children run along. I don’t have to be at my part-time job until eleven. I’ll clean the ice.”

“Thanks, Dom,” Jett says. “And don’t forget to lock up.”

Dom nods and goes to the Zamboni gate while Jett and I move the nets so that he can make his first pass. Once he’s done that, we slide the nets over to the wall and head off.

“So,” Jett says as I waddle into the lobby beside his stride, “did I make this worth your while?”

I glance at him as I push the locker room door open. “Possibly,” I say. If Jett Robitaille can’t make me a D1 player, then nobody can.

Jett smiles his impossible smile. “That’s a great start, my girlfriend.”

I shake my head and disappear into the locker room.

Chapter 10

Girlfriend, My Girlfriend

THE NEXT TIME I SEE JETT IS WHEN HE SLIDES INTO HIS SEAT BE-side me for chemistry. He smiles like we share a happy secret. He is way too invested in this Peyton quest.

I turn my attention to Mr. G. as he launches into his best Muppet impersonation. Jett inclines his head and leans forward just a touch so that he's sure I can see him in my peripheral vision.

"Did you need something?" I whisper without looking at him.

His soft chuckle brushes my ear, and he turns to face Mr. G.

"Is everything all right, Mr. Robitaille?" Mr. G. asks. "You seem particularly happy today for someone who missed the first lab assignment."

Jett clears his throat. "Everything's fine, Mr. G—Polachuk, thanks for asking."

I stare at him. He didn't mean to almost call Mr. G. by his nickname, but a snicker ripples through the class.

Mr. G. narrows his eyes at Jett but continues the lesson. When he gets to the part where he wants to ask a question, though, he lasers in on me. Just like in hockey, Jett may have taken the penalty, but I'm the one who has to kill it off.

"Mizz Vento," Mr. G. says, his mouth exaggerating the *o* at the end of my name. "What would be the correct element to use in this situation to get the desired result?" He tilts his head. "I realize this isn't field hockey, but perhaps you will be able to conjure an answer." His emphasis on "field" makes everyone turn toward me. People raise their eyebrows as if they are asking if I'm going to let this slide. But I have enough battles to fight in life without making things worse with Mr. G., who already has it in for me just for being an athlete. Plus, he must know we call him Mr. G. behind his back, so now Jett has another strike against us.

I swallow. I don't like being the center of attention. Especially when a teacher is trying to embarrass me to feed his own ego. But if I do decide to go into some kind of battle against toxins for a major, I need to do well in this class. I take a quick breath and open my mouth.

"Ms. Vento doesn't play field hockey," Jett says before I can answer.

My eyes widen and my head swivels to look at him. The whole class is watching.

"Ms. Vento plays ice hockey." Jett leans back in his chair, arms crossed, shoulders wide. His deltoids and biceps seem as hard as a suit of armor. His shiny dark hair falls on either side of his forehead as if he's ready for a *GQ* close-up.

"In fact, she sets the ice on fire," he adds. The smile he turns on me is full of admiration. Which I don't deserve, considering how few of his shots I can stop. But he's only sticking up for me to make people think he likes me.

It works. The class makes a collective *oooh* sound and a couple boys whoop. Danny Ayers laughs as he nudges his seatmate. I bite my lip and wish I could slip under the desk and disappear like a piece of paper falling into a gorge.

Mr. G. slaps a ruler against the whiteboard and everyone stops. "Thank you, Mr. Robitaille, for that clarification. Let's hope that you can be as precise on your assignments." He sends every student a dagger gaze before settling his glare back on me. He raises his eyebrows to tell me to answer.

"Hydrogen?" I suggest. I think that's right.

Mr. G. continues the glare until I doubt myself. This happens in net sometimes when I'm not sure I can beat a breakaway. My heart pounds and my brain whizzes through the elements it could possibly be. But then he nods and continues the lesson. I exhale.

What is wrong with you? I write on my notebook paper and then angle it so that Jett can read it.

He reaches over and writes his answer. *Just sticking up for my girlfriend ;)*

I grip my pencil harder. I'm never going to survive this. Him.

I'm never going to survive him. *Keep your eye on the prize, Ryleigh*, I tell myself.

When the bell rings, I collect my stuff and slip out of my seat without looking at my chem nem. I have one glorious period without him and then he'll be back to torture me for lunch. I walk out of class and a hand grabs mine. I haven't held hands with a boy since ninth grade when I dated Kevin Myers, who moved away that summer. Jett's hand feels different, strong and warm. I pull away, but Jett has a firm grip and tugs me closer.

"What are you doing?" I whisper with enough ferocity that anyone with any sense would let go.

Jett scoffs. "Walking my girlfriend to her next class, obviously."

My mouth drops open and Jett's face lights up.

"Come on, we don't want to be late for class," he adds.

I've never met anyone who took life less seriously. Why did I trust him? One thing I learned from my mom being sick is that the world can flip you at any moment. The more control you can keep, the better. Sure, he's a great hockey player. And yes, I know this morning's ice time helped me. But he's just too much. He's too unreliable. In a world that's already completely unreliable. This whole agreement with Jett is to help me keep control, not lose it. But he's as predictable as a tornado.

Around us, people whisper and stare at our linked hands. I can't let this gossip reach Harper. I tug my hand out of Jett's, but he pulls it back in.

There are a lot of degrees of separation between the tenth

and twelfth graders. Their classes are on another floor, so they only come to ours if they are in advanced classes, and only those kids eat at the same time as us. Harper doesn't have any accelerated subjects, and we have different lunchtimes. I take a breath and tell myself it will be okay.

When we get to my locker, I finally glance at Jett. "May I have my hand back now?"

"Oh, right, I guess you need that, don't you?" He is never, ever serious. I wipe my palm against my jeans even though it's not sweaty, just warm.

"Do you really think all this is necessary?"

Jett shrugs. "The game plan only works if word gets out. Your school is such a bunch of gossip girls." He says this quietly, just between us. Somehow, he even makes a complaint feel intimate. He leans his back against the lockers next to mine and takes in the hallway scene.

"Isn't every high school?"

Jett laughs. "No way, Canadians are too nice."

I sputter a short laugh. "Yeah, right. Remind me to tell you about the Toronto team we played last year, and the girl who tried to rip my helmet off in a scrum. Besides, this is your high school now, too."

I change my notebooks out while Jett studies Imani's poster, a smile on his face. Then he walks me to calculus; he even carries my backpack.

"See you at lunch," he says with a wave when I take my things from him.

"Can't wait!" I say, not even trying to hide my sarcasm. Jett laughs again.

I try to focus on calculus, but most of the period I spend replaying every exasperating thing Jett has done this morning. But then I feel guilty when I think about him getting ice time just for me. He must really have the hots for Peyton.

By the time we get to lunch period, the news has spread through school faster than an A-list celebrity dating scandal. Jett is waiting for me outside the cafeteria and scoops up my hand as we enter.

I fake smile. "Must we hold hands?"

"Peyton is already here, so yes," he replies. "What, don't you like it?"

As soon as he asks, I'm sorry I said anything. It can't ever be a good idea to encourage Jett Robitaille to tease me. But I don't like it. It makes me way more self-conscious than it should.

When we get to our lunch table, Jett releases my hand. If Imani's eyes were any bigger, her eyeballs might fall out of her head. I wanted to tell her what we were up to, but Jett insisted that not even Imani could know. "She'll want to tell Lewis, and before you know it, it's either a secret that's burdening her or it's all over the place," he'd said.

He's right about that. If I told Imani the truth, she'd feel bad about keeping it from her boyfriend. Or she'd accidentally tell him. It's just too risky. I'd be so far beyond embarrassed if people knew I was Jett's pretend love interest so he could chase someone else in exchange for some badly needed hockey skills. Especially the girl everyone thinks is my rival. It would make me look completely pathetic.

Which I am since I need his help, and I've lowered myself to this ridiculous charade. But no one knows that, and I have to keep it that way.

Jett motions for me to slide into what's become my usual place, one over from the end. I don't like being trapped, but he squeezes me in, and we go about our usual routine. Everyone at the table stares at us.

"How's the musical coming along?" I ask one girl to get the conversation started and away from us.

"Oh," she says, her blond ponytail bouncing with her head, "it's going to be great! You have to come if you can."

"I promise I will if I'm not away."

She smiles and the conversation nose-dives faster than a paper airplane.

Jett sets a small chocolate protein shake in front of me. Lewis elbows Imani as Matt flashes a look at them. You'd think Jett had just produced a ring box like people do when they propose.

"Thanks," I say.

Jett nudges into me to say, "You're welcome." The way the layers of his hair fade down to his neck is almost artwork. I pull away as much as the limited space allows. I don't know why he's so touchy-feely. It's too much. Just like him. Imani kicks me softly under the table. I shrug at her. She's the one always pestering me to date. She should be happy.

When I get up to get water, because, as usual, I've forgotten my water bottle, Imani is behind me faster than a crowd reacts to a goal.

She grabs my elbow as we reach the vending machines. "Are you kidding me?"

"Nope," I say, and swing my head from side to side.

Her brow furrows. "He seems way happier about this than you do."

I put my school card into the machine and punch the numbers for a water. "It's just a lot to handle, that's all. I can't afford to get distracted." Or too entangled with a guy who thinks Peyton Malloy is worth chasing. "But you're right. I should have some fun." Such a lie. I am such a big, horrible liar. I motion for her to turn around and fix her ponytail. She hates when it isn't perfect.

Imani smiles, her pretty face glowing. "I told you it would be hard to resist all that." She glances over at Jett. His gaze is settled on us as if he wishes he could hear what we're saying.

I return her smile to make her happy. "Yep, he's just too much to resist." She must not hear the sarcasm seeping out of me because she keeps smiling. You'd think she was my mom congratulating me for winning the science fair.

"I'm so proud of you, my little padawan!" She places her hand on my shoulder as if she's knighting me.

I chuckle. "Whatever. Don't get too attached to the idea. It's just temporary." It's best to set her expectations low. It shouldn't take long to make Peyton jealous once she thinks Jett is into me. Not that I think Peyton will date Jett since he isn't in college, but once I've done my part, Jett and I are even. I just need to drag this out long enough to improve my hockey skills and earn a scholarship. My biggest fear is that Jett might give up when he doesn't immediately win Peyton over. I need to make this last as long as I can. Between Dominic's goalie knowledge and Jett's wicked shot, I can't help but get better.

"Why is it just temporary?" Imani's eyebrows are knit.

I take a swig of water. "I just mean that he's off to two more years of junior hockey while I head to college. It's nothing serious. I wouldn't be surprised if he starts dating someone new in a month or two."

Imani studies me. She knows me too well. I need to end this interrogation before she realizes my entire relationship is a quid pro quo, as Jett calls it.

"Come on," I say, and fake a smile, "my new boyfriend looks adorably lonely over there." He does look adorable. But he's only doing this to make the shallowest girl in our school jealous. Which is so cliché it makes me lose my appetite.

I push Imani back toward our table and try not to gag as we go.

Chapter 11

Middle School Grudges Die Hard

IT ONLY TAKES A WEEK FOR PEYTON MALLOY TO ZERO IN ON MY new relationship status and make her first assault. She stops Jett as he crosses the cafeteria to get to our table. They look really good together, which puts me in a sourer mood than it should. She's the perfect height for him. Her blond hair, green eyes, and perfectly proportioned nose round out her all-American-beauty résumé. She is exceptionally pretty. And she's not brainless. Outside of her need to impress everyone with her college-boys-only vibe, she's kind of perfect for Jett. Everyone is probably surprised he chose me over her. Which in fact would be an accurate feeling since he *has* chosen her over me. Not that I want him to choose me. Or for anyone to talk about this so much that it gets back to Harper and, from there, our parents. I shake my head. This is too complicated.

I only know that I'd rather move to Antarctica than have anyone ever find this out.

Matt chucks his chin at Imani, and she and Lewis turn their heads to catch the Jett and Peyton Show. My chem nem and my middle school nemesis, together. All that's missing is a golden halo of light—until the sun breaks through some clouds and streams through the window, backlighting them. Seriously, even Mother Nature is mocking me.

Jett glances at our table and waves to me. Peyton's gaze follows his, so I wave back. I have never felt more ridiculous in my entire life. Not even when I accidentally Rollerbladed into our mailbox playing inline hockey in the driveway with my boy cousins when I was twelve. They still love to bring that story up at every family get-together.

Imani nudges me with her foot.

What? I mouth, and shrug.

She tilts her head and purses her lips to tell me I shouldn't let Peyton take what's mine. In middle school, Peyton took my favorite pair of Converses when she tricked me into a bet I couldn't win. My dad and I were going to a Rangers game at Madison Square Garden that night, and she insisted I wouldn't get to see the goalie I knew was scheduled to play. She egged me on until I agreed to the bet. But Peyton had already heard that he'd been traded that morning. And when the captain of the middle school basketball team liked me, she started a rumor that I said basketball was the worst sport ever invented. Anyone who knows me knows this is baseball, but he took Peyton to the spring dance instead of me. She was welcome to him, as far as I was concerned, but everyone chalked it up as a win for Peyton.

Imani narrows her eyes and starts to get up but then sits back down when she sees Jett turn from Peyton and make his way over.

He slides into his spot and offers me a chocolate protein shake, which I accept.

"What did Peyton want?" Imani asks. This time, it's my turn to kick her under the table.

Jett shrugs innocently, as if he has no idea that the fastest way to get Peyton's attention is through me. "She just asked how I like it here."

Lewis scoffs. "Peyton never talks to anyone without an agenda." Imani pats his tight Afro to thank him for backing her.

Jett looks at me as if he wants me to confirm this, so I raise my eyebrows in agreement.

"Do you guys have games this weekend?" Matt asks. He probably wants to change the subject. He thinks this is real, so he must be worried that it bothers me that Jett let Peyton flirt with him. Or maybe he's scared Imani will cause a scene.

Jett and I nod and compare schedules. We're both home this weekend. He plays Friday and Saturday nights. I play Saturday night and Sunday afternoon. I'd like to watch him play in real life, but there's no way I'd admit that to him.

"We should come to your Sunday game," Matt says to me. Jett stops eating and looks at me. There's no reason for my schedule to suddenly interest him. My friends come to games sometimes, so that part isn't weird. Just the fact that Jett is now nominally a part of our group.

"Are you playing?" Imani asks.

I nod before I realize I'm doing it. Then I close my eyes for a second. My gut is telling me that I shouldn't have let them know in front of Jett. He is sure to make it weird somehow.

"Don't worry about it," I say as I rush to fill the silence. "Coach may change her mind by then. I haven't been doing well in practice lately." This, sadly, is not a lie.

Jett doesn't say anything. I turn to Matt and ask him if he still needs help with *Hamlet*, which he does, so I explain the part we're reading in English class. Matt calls me his walking CliffsNotes.

The next couple of days go along the same. I don't have much time to think, or I should say worry, about what Jett might do next, because there simply isn't time between school, hockey practice, homework, and helping my mom around the house. I barely have time to breathe.

By the time I get home on Wednesday, I'm more tired than I've been since the end of last season. Later, when I crawl into bed to hit my French language app because we have a test on Friday, I get a text from Hotshot, as he's saved in my contacts.

Tendy, I got us ice tomorrow morning.

Normally, I'd be thrilled at this idea, but my shoulders slump at the idea of waking up in the middle of the night. Still, it's not like I can say no.

I go to text him thanks, but he now has his notifications silenced. It's 10:07. How does he even get everything done so he can go to sleep this early? I still have to work on my French and get my clothes ready for tomorrow, and now I need to make sure Harper gets up in time to shower before I rush back home tomorrow morning.

I set my alarm for four-fifteen. This time, I plan to make sure I don't waste a second of ice time since he'll probably bring Dominic. When I get to the rink, there are two cars there, but they've left the first spot beyond the handicapped parking for me.

The lobby is quiet, and I grab the same locker room I had last time. As I throw my gear on, I shiver. By the time we're done, I'll be sweating enough to keep me warm for hours, but for now, I'm chilled and tired. I yawn as I secure my helmet and grab my glove and blocker and stick. When I come out of the locker room, Jett is waiting for me.

"Why aren't you on the ice?" I ask.

"I was just about to pound on the door and ask you the same thing," he says, but his dimples are on full display behind his cage. I shake my head and walk past him.

"You know what my favorite thing about goalies is?" he asks.

"No idea."

He pulls open the door to the rink and I lumber through.

"You guys are just like ducks."

I give him a flat stare. "Yeah, I know. We waddle."

Jett laughs. "Off the ice. But once you're on the ice, you're likes ducks in water. There's nothing you can't do."

He seems genuinely impressed, and it softens my bricked-up heart a little. The door to the ice is open and we step through, and Jett clangs it closed. Jett glides beside me on his magic blades as if he's more apparition than human. Dominic is messing with the net at the far end.

"Did you know," Jett continues as he bounces around me when I drop to stretch, "that Fleury could do a cartwheel in all his gear? I mean, a full cartwheel. In goalie pads!"

I laugh. "I've seen video of it. He was my hero growing up."

"Ouais?"

"Yeah."

"He's French Canadian."

"I know," I say.

"Who's French Canadian?" Dominic asks as he skates up and taps my leg pad with his stick to say hello.

"Fleury," I say, and get up and back into the net.

The two of them banter then about all the great hockey players from French-speaking Canada, like Kris Letang, Jonathan Marchessault, and Patrice Bergeron, while they put me through the second-toughest workout I've ever had in my life. Just like the first time, Jett can beat me on any shot he has except when he goes low. Even those I have a hard time with since it's like being in a shoot-out unless Dominic is playing defense.

"Trying to see past you is like trying to see past two defenders with all that gear," Jett complains when Dominic pushes him too wide to get a shot off, but mostly it's me versus Jett, with Dominic watching like a coach. He drills me on basic stance pointers, like how to elongate my chest while still leaning forward in the ready position so I take up more net. I know this is helping me, but I also know that none of this is an overnight fix. Pucks whiz past my head, graze my shoulders, and find the little bit of light between my elbow and my side as I'm just a half second behind tracking where he's going to put them. With each shot I miss, I let out a soft swear.

When I manage to stop a shot, Dominic cheers, but I zero my gaze at Jett in triumph. "How are you getting this ice time? Exactly," I ask. Finally.

He looks at Dominic. "Should I tell her?"

"You said you'd answer a question for every shot she stopped." Dominic slow blinks repeatedly for comic emphasis.

Jett pulls up to the crease, still panting. He towers over me as he leans on his stick. "My host family owns the rink."

"Are you kidding me? And they're just giving you the time?"

Jett shakes a gloved hand at me. "That's two questions beyond the one you already asked. You've got a lot more work to do to find out those answers."

He and Dominic exchange smiles. We start back up, but the only thing I learn after this is that he's not kidding.

"Dom, can you get the Zamboni?" Jett asks when the buzzer sounds and our magical hour of ice disappears like Cinderella's pumpkin carriage.

Dominic nods. "Yeah, yeah. You tykes get to school. And when I'm done, I'm going to go take a nap before work." He skates off and revs up the beast as Jett and I wait to move the nets for him.

"Thanks," I say.

Jett nods. "You're welcome, Rye."

Normally, I'd tell him not to call me a nickname since we don't really have that kind of relationship. But I'm too frustrated with how slowly I'm improving. If I'm improving at all. I can't even tell yet.

"I'm sorry I'm not picking this up faster," I say. My face is already the color of tomato sauce, but I still blush as Coach Blackmon creeps into my head to tell me I'm a lost cause. I can't look at Jett, so I stare at the net instead. "I haven't played against anyone with your skill."

"Whoa, whoa, whoa, was that a compliment, Mizzzz Vento?"

I snicker at him impersonating Mr. G. "No, obviously not."

Jett laughs. "You're doing great. Honestly, if Dom were your size, he'd struggle as much as you do to beat me. It will come, just be patient."

I stare at him. "Is that a compliment for me or shade for Dom?"

"Both," Jett says. "Can't it be both?"

He radiates joy as the Zamboni makes a pass around the ice and we move the first net up against the boards. It's getting harder to dislike his happy-go-lucky attitude when he's trying so genuinely to help me.

"But your host family isn't giving you this ice time for nothing," I say, still worried about what it's costing him. I don't like the idea of owing him more than I can pay back. Peyton is never going to go for him. Not when she has a cool meter that only registers college guys. We follow Dominic down to the other end. Jett lifts the heavy red net off the pegs that secure it in place, and we push it to the boards.

"Don't worry about it, Goalie Girl. I got this."

He stops and smiles at me. Not his smile that oozes confidence and sparkles with dimples. Just a smile that tells me it's okay. A smile that drops my stomach like a rubber ball falling down steps, thump after thump.

We turn and skate side by side back to the door to go to the locker rooms, gliding along in a moment of harmony. The chill I had before practice is gone. I'm just not sure if the warmth flooding through me now is from all the blood my heart's pumped in the last hour to keep up with two elite boys' hockey players or from the dark roast coffee brewing in Jett Robitaille's smoldering eyes.

Chapter 12

What Are You Doing Here?

WHEN I GET TO THE RINK ON SUNDAY, I'M FEELING SLIGHTLY CONfident. The kind of confident where you think you are entitled, at least a little, but you also don't want to jinx yourself, as if there might be an entire bucket of karma you don't even know about hanging over your head, ready to drench you at the slightest imbalance.

Thursday night's practice went better than I had hoped. Coach Kaitlyn said my angles seem a bit stronger, and she likes my ready stance, which is a little taller than it used to be. I have a long way to go. But I'm beginning to see how much those couple of sessions with Jett and Dom have helped me.

Outside of lunch and chemistry, I haven't talked much to Jett. Between hockey and school, our schedules don't really align. Plus, we haven't had anything we had to talk about over the last few days. We didn't have a lab due this week, and it's not like we're besties. I can't really help him with Peyton directly. The last time Peyton listened to anything I said was in eighth grade when I told her that her blue eye shadow was too heavy. She responded by making it so heavy that she looked like two bluebirds had landed on her face for the next three months, until she was sure I got the message that my opinion was trash to her.

Jett did text this morning to ask me how my bench warming went last night, but I wasn't about to give him the satisfaction of knowing that I saw his Friday-night game online, so I only replied very funny. Besides, I only watched his game to see Dominic in action. And to observe, objectively, the performance artistry of Jett's game. He's one of those rare players who are just a lot of fun to see on the ice.

We get to the rink an hour before games. Then we do warm-up drills in the parking lot. Usually kicking around a soccer ball and some calisthenics, maybe a run around the area if there is somewhere safe to run. Then we get dressed. There's always a lot of time to get dressed, so we float in and out of the locker room, checking out the game ahead of us or running to the rink's pro shop for a skate sharpening or more tape or whatever we need. We retape our sticks. We talk to our friends' parents. Everyone acts calm, but there's always an undercurrent of energy, a pulse of pressure that surrounds each one of us as we mentally prepare to do our best. Most goalies have rituals. Some listen to a certain kind of music, some meditate, some won't talk to anyone. We're all different, and we're all the same. We're weighted down with the pressure of knowing that, more than anyone else on the team, everything we do will be seen and judged by everyone at the rink. Even the Zamboni guy will probably be watching some of it.

I stand outside the locker room in the hallway and give myself a silent pep talk while listening to ridiculous but inspirational Disney hits from my childhood. I try to envision myself stopping the puck in my weakest areas, and I repeat mantras like "Strong girls make strong goalies," something my peewee coach used to tell me. Coach comes down the hall to give her pregame talk. She stops when she reaches me.

"Are you ready, Twenty-Nine?" she says. The same number Fleury always used. It's a very popular goalies' number.

I nod. She locks her gaze on mine as if she's some sort of polygraph machine. Then she nods back. I'm not sure she believes me, but at least she isn't going to tear me down before I even go out there, the way Coach Blackmon used to do. "Try not to lose sight of the puck today," he'd say, as if I would be out there counting the light bulbs in the ceiling instead of watching the game. His bullying stressed me out so much that my asthma was off the charts last year, which didn't do anything to help my game.

I follow Coach Kaitlyn into the locker room. She goes over our game plan. The team we're playing isn't as strong as last night's team. They're a little slower and less aggressive. Which is why I'm playing today instead of last night. Hailey did a great job, and we won. Which means there is more pressure on me to keep it going since this should be an easier game. But every game is different. I glance around to gauge the energy in the room. It's on me to be the anchor, though, whether the rest of the team is bringing it today or not.

I don't look at the crowd when we hit the ice. I can tell from my peripheral vision that the stands are pretty full. Lots of people to watch me fail. *Stop!* I say in my head. The mental part of being a goalie is just as important as the physical part. Hailey and I stretch and then I take warm-up shots first since I'm the one who will be in net today. All my focus is on the shots coming in as my team takes turns in a line on either side of me. Compared with Jett's shots, these now seem almost slow, but it won't feel that way once the game starts. Coach Kaitlyn is focused on the other team to evaluate their goalie and anyone who stands out just by their warm-up shots. Their coaches are doing the same to us.

When I leave the net to let Hailey take a turn, she comes in close as she passes me. "You really brought a punch," she says with a smile.

"What do you mean?"

She stops and nods at the bleachers.

I turn to look at the crowd on the home side. My family, minus Harper, is where they usually sit perched up high enough to have a perfect view of every shot that will come to me. My mom waves to me like I'm still in peewee sports, and I sigh. But I also smile and wave my gloved hand back at her. She's alive. And she's here. Which makes me lucky no matter how I play today.

Hailey goes in net for some practice shots, and Shannon

and Alana skate over to me. "Who's the guy with the sign?" Shannon asks, her face twisted in a teasing smile.

I pull my gaze away from my family and scan the crowd. Jett and Dom are sitting at the bottom of the stands right beside the net area. Jett is holding a sign that says, in bold red letters, "29 HOLDS THE LINE," complete with the picture of a bonfire they must have printed and pasted to the poster board. My team photo is plastered on the top left corner. Please tell me I've died and landed in the wrong place.

My mouth drops open. What the hell is wrong with him?

"Is he your boyfriend?" Alana asks.

"No, absolutely not," I say. "Well, not exactly. Sort of, temporarily." Jett and Dom wave. They're wearing their Jr. Hat Tricks team warm-up jackets, and Jett has on a Habs baseball hat backward. Dom looks like he hasn't shaved since Thursday and is wearing a Sharks beanie.

Alana and Shannon laugh. "I wouldn't deny him," Alana says as she shakes her head at me. "Does he really play for the Jr. Hat Tricks?"

I nod and glance back at my family. *Please, gods of the hockey universe, don't let them see him.* I turn my head and pretend I didn't see my new fans wave. But my heart is racing with my mind as if they're now competing in a slalom to see which can panic faster.

The buzzer sounds to tell us the game is about to start. I skate over to the bench with the rest of the team. We all huddle in to hear Coach. "Remember the game plan," she says. "Their goalie is weak left side, so strike there. Keep an eye on Twenty-Six, I want two people on her at all times. And this team has a lot of size, so make sure Ryleigh isn't getting screened. Emma, I want you clearing that crease like a Zamboni, you got it?"

"Yes, Coach!" Emma yells. Emma is our best defenseman.

"Ryleigh, keep yourself big in the net like you've been doing the last few practices. Okay, let's win this one!" We all lean in to do our last cheer. "Polar Bears on three," Coach says.

"One, two, three, Polar Bears!" we yell, and pull away. Those not playing first shift climb over the boards or go through the door. The rest of us skate into position. My heart is pounding. "Calm down, Ryleigh," I say out loud. "Pretend it's just you, Jett, and Dominic." Oh God, Dominic is going to see me play. I mentally run through every piece of advice he's given me, and automatically I adjust to broaden my shoulders and angle my ankles more. I let out a shaky breath and watch the puck drop.

The game is intense. The teams are evenly matched today, and there's constant back-and-forth. I try to quiet the chatter in the back of my thoughts about Jett and Dominic and my family, but it's there, like bees hovering nearby. I never look at them. I don't dare take my eyes off the action.

At the end of the period, neither team has scored, and I take that as a win for now. At least I haven't let anyone down, although I got lucky more than once. I skate off to the locker room without looking toward the stands and say a silent prayer that my family doesn't notice Jett and his embarrassing sign.

What's he even thinking? It's like everything is a giant joke to him.

In the locker room, we breathe heavily and hydrate as Coach gives us her rundown on what we did well and what we need to improve on.

"Ryleigh, you were inconsistent. You seem distracted. Are you okay?" she asks.

I look her in the eye. "Sorry, Coach, I'll focus more."

She nods and moves on.

When we huddle at the door to get back on the ice, I scan the bleachers. My family has moved to the other team's side, so they have a better view of me this period. They always do this. Unfortunately, Jett and Dom have also moved. No one in my family has seen Jett's billboard yet, apparently, as they're still separated by six or seven bench rows and about fifteen feet. But London and my parents are more likely to notice if Jett and Dom react to my playing in enemy territory than they would be on our team's side. There, the guys could be cheering for any of us.

I take a deep breath and exhale. *Focus, Ryleigh.* The refs give us the okay to get on the ice, and we skate for just a minute and then gather at the bench and do our cheer before we take our positions.

I push the looming disaster that is Jett out of my mind as best I can and swipe my stick around the crease as if there is shaved ice to clean. My adrenaline is pumping because I'm so mad at Jett. I try to focus, but every time I make a save, I glance over to see what's happening in the stands. Our team finally scores, so that takes some of the pressure off me. But Dom keeps sending me hand signals to come out of the crease more, and I think London is picking up on it. She seems to be looking down in their direction a lot. Thankfully, my family is behind the guys, so they can't see the sign when Jett waves it. But my team notices and comes by to make little comments like "How do I get a fan like that?" or "He must be really into you with how corny that sign is." If my face were burning any more, I'd need aloe.

A breakaway comes near the end of the period, but it doesn't seem as fast as one of Jett's normal approaches and I have time to calculate and stop it. It's funny I think this way now, after only a couple of hours of his relentless speed shots. Dom, Jett, and my family all jump up and cheer. You'd think I just won us the Olympics. It's sort of sweet, I suppose, but it's also a disaster. My family is now studying the guys and talking among themselves, a little furiously. It completely distracts me, and I lose focus and fail to correctly track an incoming puck. It whizzes over my shoulder and hits the back of the net. A second later, before I'm even done processing what just happened, the period ends. The only thing worse than ending a period on a screwup is ending the last period of the game on a screwup. I need to let this go and redeem myself in the third period.

Coach stops me as I go into the locker room. "What was that? You need to focus the whole period. It's not over until that buzzer sounds." Her jaw is set, which lets me know how disappointed she is more than her words do. She's right, and I blink away the sting in my eyes.

"I'm sorry, Coach. I won't let it happen again."

"I hope not," she says, and pulls the locker room door open. She nods me through and follows.

I slump onto the bench and listen to the recap and new instructions for the third period. But the whole time, what I'm mostly thinking about is my bad luck. There's no way my family isn't going to go talk to Jett and Dominic to find out who they are and why they're cheering for me. My only hope is if he says he's my chemistry partner and they think he's just shown up out of hockey addiction. I mean, hockey players do that. We watch as much hockey as we play. But that sign! That sign is going to be the death of me. My family is sure to think he's got a crush on me, and then they're going to ask Harper to find out if there are any rumors at school and they're going to hear that Jett is supposedly my boyfriend. My mom would kill me if she knew I'd made this deal. Maybe she should.

But still, what choice did I have? I found a guy who can help me improve enough to get the one thing I've wanted since I started playing this game almost a decade ago. And I'm not harming anyone. Peyton isn't going to go for him, and even if she did, it's not like he's a bad guy or anything. He's just ridiculous. How did I get myself into this mess? I finally find a way to get a D1 scholarship, and it's through a guy who turns out to be a loose cannon that's more likely to shoot me out of the sky than launch me into it.

"It's time to roll," our captain, Nina, says.

I get up with the rest of the team and shuffle out the door.

"You okay, Rye?" Nina asks as I pass by.

I look at her and nod. Whatever disaster Jett is about to manufacture for me with my family is going to have to wait for my attention. Right now, I need to keep us in this game as if my life depends on it.

Chapter 13

The Family Meet Catastrophe

I DON'T GIVE UP ANY MORE GOALS AND WE WIN BY ONE, BUT THIS wasn't the game I wanted to show Coach. I'll be lucky if she even gives me another chance. The good news is that this game isn't going to take a huge toll on my stats, and at this point that's about all I can hope for while I work on getting better before it's too late and every spot is taken.

The teams line up to shake hands, and I skate to the head of the line for our team because goalies get that role even though they're rarely team captains. It's a sign of respect for how much weight we carry. As we go through the line and tell each other and the coaches "Good game," I glance at the bleachers. Jett and Dom have disappeared, but my family is waving and cheering for me. No doubt, though, there's going to be an inquisition when I see them. There's no way they completely missed my new number one fan. I'm surprised he didn't bring a giant red foam finger to wave just to prove it.

When I emerge from the locker room, I'm a sweaty, dehydrated mess. I lumber through the lobby as people go past trying to get to a game that's about to start on another sheet of ice. A new game is already in full swing on the sheet we played on.

I'm almost through the crowd when I see them. My family is huddled by the big glass doors with Jett and Dom. My mom and Jett are deep in conversation, almost as if the rest of them don't exist. I think about turning around and going out a side door somewhere, but Dom sees me. Why does he have to be so freaking tall? He immediately chucks his chin up to tell everyone, "There she is!"

I can't hear him, but I can read his lips. Jett and my mother break their little tête-à-tête and smile at me in a weird kind of twinning way. This is not going to go well.

"Hi," I say when I reach them, and drop my bag with a thud.

"Pretty good game," Dom says, and faux punches my arm. "I know what we should work on next time!"

"Great," I say, too exhausted to be excited about this, even though I should be.

"Ryleigh," my mom says. She stops and glances at my dad, who looks down uncomfortably.

When she sees that my dad has punted and left her on her own, she continues, "You didn't tell us you were dating Jett."

I try to smile, but it gets stuck somewhere between a snarl

and a grimace as I look at Jett. "I wouldn't call it dating, exactly," I say. I've never wanted to kick someone in the shins so hard in my life.

My mom raises her eyebrows at me. "What would you call it?"

I bobble my head around and wish it would fall off and roll away. "Hanging out together? Kind of, maybe?"

My mom laughs. "Well, I'm glad we got to meet Jett and Dominic. They're coming to dinner next Sunday, after they get back from their away games."

"Oh, awesome," I say, and try to pretend I'm excited about this. I doubt anyone is buying it.

"She gets a little dehydrated after a game," my mom says to the guys as if this explains my lack of enthusiasm in claiming Jett as my boyfriend.

Dom laughs. "I know just what you mean, Mrs. Vento. I'm always hangry after a game!"

Everyone laughs as if this is super funny, even London.

"Well, we'll see you at home, Rye," my dad says, and motions for my mom and London to scoot. London gives me a big grin, so I will be getting teased about Jett at dinner. My family and the guys say goodbye and the three of us stand there staring at each other. I have no idea if Dominic knows that Jett and I aren't really dating, and that he's just using me to get to another girl. My already-warm cheeks get a little warmer.

Dom goes into coach mode. "This week we should work

on where your weight is on your C-cuts. That will help on those breakaways and two-on-one shots."

"Okay." No one has ever told me before where I should put my weight for a C-cut, which is when you square up and move forward or backward with a shooter.

"And I need to dangle on you more, get your reflexes really humming," Jett says.

I give him a flat look. He smiles and raises his eyebrows to ask if he's forgiven.

He's not. I just stare at him.

He picks my bag up.

"I can carry—"

"Your own bag," Jett finishes my sentence. "I know, Rye-do-self. You remind me of my cousin's toddler. He's always running around saying 'Aya-do-self.' He can't say Alex yet. You're just like him."

"Am not," I say, only partly joking.

Dominic rubs his hand on my head. "Come on," he says, "let's get you some food."

Jett nudges me and hands me a vitamin water, less confident this time that I might forgive him.

"Hey, Rye, great game," Alana calls as she passes us, and heads out the door. She gives Jett the once-over and smirks.

"You too," I say.

Jett leads us outside. "Where are you parked?" he asks as he looks back to make sure I'm coming.

I point to my car and push the button on my fob to open

the hatch. Jett throws my bag in the back, and I toss my pads and stick on top. We agree to meet at a local sandwich shop.

Jett watches me, as if he's waiting for me to offer him a ride which just makes me determined not to.

"See you there," I say, and hop into my car before either of them can say anything.

I get to the sandwich place a minute or two ahead of them, but I wait until they pull into the parking lot so the three of us can walk in together. They're in the sleek little roadster, but Dom is driving. He barely fits behind the wheel. That can't be his car.

We go inside and get our subs and sit at a table by the window. We talk about the game, and Dom sounds like a coach as he draws plays on the table with his finger. I try to concentrate, but I keep thinking about why Jett even showed up today, and why he brought that ridiculous sign. I don't dare ask him in front of Dom, though.

We finish eating and leave the restaurant. As we get to the cars, Jett looks at Dom. "Give us a minute, will you?"

Dom nods and gets in the driver's seat while Jett walks me to my door.

"I'm sorry about the whole thing with your family. We don't have to come to dinner if you don't want us to."

I look at him. "You do, though. My mom isn't going to take no for an answer."

"She seems really nice," he says.

"Why did you come today?"

"I knew you'd be nervous, and I just wanted you to feel like you had support, that's all."

"Why? It's not like it's helping you win Peyton over."

Jett's gaze roams past me to the horizon. "Not everything is about our deal."

"Why?"

Jett laughs. "What do you mean, why? I want you to get your scholarship."

"Why?"

"Oh my God, you really are just like my cousin's two-year-old." Jett shakes his head. "You're a good person, and I think you deserve it."

"How do you know I'm a good person?" I really am curious about this. It's not like I've been super friendly to him. Or even as nice as I should be. It's not his fault that life just drops his dreams into his lap.

Jett pushes his lips together a moment before he answers, like he's not sure he should indulge me in listing off my good qualities. "Well, for one thing, your friends at school are all devoted to you, so that tells me you're a good person. I always see you helping people, whether it's worrying about getting your sister to school on time, or fixing Imani's makeup, or helping Matt in English class. You've pulled a lot of my weight in chemistry. And Matt and Imani told me how much you stepped up for your family when your mom was sick last year." He shrugs. "It just shows."

I'm not sure what to say to this. He does make me sound

reasonably nice. I even almost like me. But that doesn't explain why he just turned this fiasco into a Broadway show.

"Why would you tell my parents we're dating?"

He grimaces. "Your mom kind of asked when she saw my sign and I guess I panicked."

Jett Robitaille panicking is not something I can picture. But I can imagine what my mom said. Probably something like "That's a lovely sign you made my daughter. You two must be quite close." This would have been accompanied by a knowing smile. He probably felt like he was on trial.

"That sign was unnecessarily ludicrous."

Jett laughs in his easy way. "I love it when people make me signs. Maybe because I've played so much away from my family. I'm not above soaking up some random validation."

I smile, but I get that feeling of missing your family in the stands. He fiddles with his phone and mine lights up. He cranes his neck to see me check it.

"Hotshot? You have me saved in your phone as 'Hotshot'?"

I let out a frustrated breath. I am never living this one down. "It's facetious," I say. I open the text he sent and it's a selfie of him and Dom with that embarrassing sign.

Jett smirks and nods. He does not believe me. It's a good thing I didn't save him as Mr. Miracle.

"Does Dom think you and I are dating?"

Jett glances at Dom, who is scrolling on his phone while he waits in his car.

"Well, I haven't said one thing or another to him. It didn't really come up in conversation." He looks at the sky as if he's thinking. "He probably assumes we are, though."

"Well, we'll be breaking up soon anyway. I guess it doesn't matter what he thinks."

"So you think Peyton is starting to like me?" His eyes study me, and only Peyton's name reminds me that I'm just a stand-in. My cheeks prickle.

"Well, I just mean that if this doesn't work, then nothing will. You should know soon enough. If Peyton wants you, she'll make a move. She's not shy about getting what she wants."

Jett nods as he digests this.

"I just don't like dragging my family into this. They're going to want to encourage me to enjoy my senior year and not focus so much on the future." Especially if it's a future I can't make happen.

"Look, Rye, I get it, you've been through a lot."

I laugh. There is no way Jett Robitaille has any idea what I've been through. He's the happiest happy-go-lucky person I have ever met.

Jett just looks at me, his face not judging me.

"So, are we good?" he asks after a few moments. "I promise to keep it light with your parents."

Somehow, it's hard to stay mad at him. Especially when he's helping me like he is. "Yeah, sure, we're good."

Jett smiles. "I'll text you later," he says, and slaps my arm before he jogs off and hops in the car with Dom. Dom waves as he pulls out of the parking space. I watch them drive away before I get in my car. I want to drag this out because they are helping me get better. I still have so much to learn from them. But something deep in my gut is telling me that staying in this deal too long may cost me more than even a D1 scholarship is worth.

Chapter 14

This Just Keeps Getting Weirder

JETT AND DOM SHOW UP AS PROMISED THE NEXT SUNDAY EVENING as soon as they get back from their away games. They pull into the driveway in the Impreza with Jett driving, which London announces with the same reverence that newscasters use to discuss the presidential motorcade.

"Hallelujah," Harper says from the sofa, where she's watching football with my dad. "I'm starving."

"I'll go throw the meat on," my dad says. He's a firm believer that if he can get the grill hot enough to cook something, then it's barbecue season even if there's snow on the ground. It's only in the forties today, nowhere near my dad's cutoff point for outdoor cooking. "Perfect grilling weather," my dad had told us at lunchtime when my mom worried about what to make.

I answer the door. The guys are dressed in suits and ties, the uniform they left the rink wearing. Jett looks like a model in a suit that fits him perfectly, and Dom looks like a Secret Service agent sent to guard Jett in a suit that looks like it came off the rack. Harper does a double take as she glances around, and she even gets up to say hello. My mom comes to greet them.

"We brought you some maple syrup," Jett says, and hands her a bottle.

"Oh, how lovely!" my mom says. "Please, come in and make yourselves at home. Dinner will be ready shortly."

They sit down and watch football with Harps and London while I get them waters. When I come back, they're talking about the Jr. Hat Tricks games from this weekend.

"You watched them?" Jett asks.

"Ryleigh had them on, so we all ended up watching," London says, delivering this information with way more enthusiasm than necessary as her amber eyes make her look like a doe. "Her games were at different times."

"I was watching Dom," I say without looking at anyone.

Dom smiles smugly.

"We have the subscription anyway," I add.

"I was good, right?" Dom asks.

I nod. "You were great."

Jett's eyes narrow at me, but he has a slight smile on his face.

Fifteen minutes later, he's outside schmoozing my dad while Dom has London and Harper filling him in on football and the Connecticut split between the Patriots, Jets, and Giants.

London is Robin to my dad's Batman, so she's even explaining what the call signs are. I don't know how I ended up playing hockey when my dad is such a football fan. I went to the rink with a friend once when her brother was playing, and that was it. I bugged my dad until he found a developmental club I could join. I tried playing out, but I wasn't very aggressive. Even though I swore I'd never play goalie, there was a girl goalie coaching at one of the summer camps I went to, and she was so cool. Just like that, I was all in.

I rub my hands on my jeans and crane my neck to check what's happening on the back deck. Jett and my dad are laughing like Jett's one of Dad's old college buddies. I should go break that up. Most likely, my dad is entertaining Jett with stories about my early days playing hockey.

"Rye," Jett says when I open the door and the smoke from the grill wafts past me, "did you really poke check a kid and send him into the boards?"

I frown at my dad. "He kept trying to slap shot me in the head. I was just trying to knock the puck away. How was I supposed to know the kid couldn't handle a stick between his legs?"

Jett laughs. "I wish I could have seen you toss him!"

"I have the video somewhere," my dad says, but his laugh stops abruptly when he catches the glare I zero in on him. "It was very cute," he adds, looking down. "Anyway, I stopped worrying about her playing hockey that day." He flips the chicken over as it sizzles, the smell of balsamic glaze and fresh herbs rising from the grill.

"She's definitely capable of taking care of herself, Mr. Vento," Jett says.

"The rest of his team was normal," I say. "That kid was just trying to show up a girl. I got it a lot when I played with boys' teams. There was almost always one or two kids on the other team who wanted to teach me that I didn't belong. Although my teammates were usually fine about it. I guess their dads made them be."

"Puck," my dad says, "tell your mom this is ready, please."

I glance at Jett. He has not missed Dad's nickname for me.

I nod and go inside. Jett is at my heels.

"Puck?"

I stop. "Yes. He thinks it's very funny because pucks are hard, fast, durable, and go where they want. Plus, the whole Shakespeare thing." I wave my hand dismissively.

Jett laughs. "That's awesome."

"I'm glad you are enjoying yourself." I turn to my mom. "Dad's ready with the meat."

"Oh, help me get everything on the table," she says as she finishes plating some honeydew and prosciutto.

"I'll help," Jett says, so we wash our hands, and I show him what to take into the dining room. Then I call my sisters and Dom to the table while Jett and I finish helping my mom.

My dad has made steak and chicken because he was worried about what Dom and Jett might want, so there's more meat on the table than our family usually eats in two weeks. My mom has made Parmesan-crusted smashed potatoes, green beans, and some carrots that she's glazed with Jett's maple syrup. And just in case there isn't enough food, my mom has also made mac and cheese and salad, in addition to bake-at-home crescent rolls. "Athletic boys need a lot of calories," she'd said when I complained that she was going to too much trouble.

My parents keep the dinner conversation flowing with endless questions about where Jett and Dom are from and their families and hockey and school. Since Jett pronounced himself my boyfriend, it's my parents' mission to find out everything about him and any of his friends.

Dom is from Nova Scotia and is aging out of juniors this year and will go to University of Maine in the fall. Jett tells my family he's committed to Cornell, but he doesn't mention that he's expected to be drafted this year or that he'll be in the World Juniors in December. I think about supplying that information, because it is impressive, but I don't want him to know that I've paid that kind of attention to him. He's hard enough to deal with as it is. I don't need to make him think I care.

"When do you fellows go home for Thanksgiving break?" my dad asks. "I know Canadian Thanksgiving was last week."

"I'm going home that Monday," Dom says.

"My family is coming here," Jett says. "With school, I didn't really have enough time to go to Montreal, and my mom wants to check out where I'm living. This is my third year of a host family, so you'd think she'd be used to it by now."

"Are you having Thanksgiving dinner with your host family?" my mom asks.

Jett shakes his head. "No, they're going to my host mom's

sister's house on Long Island. Do you know any good restaurants we could go to?"

He says this innocently enough, as if it never occurred to him that my parents will now invite his whole family to join us, but of course they do, because they would consider anything else to be completely rude. Hospitality to my parents is like a badge of honor.

Harper immediately makes her eyebrows jump as she looks at me. I bite my lip.

"We wouldn't want to inconvenience you," Jett says. "But thank you."

My parents are not about to accept defeat, so they insist it isn't any inconvenience, even though for all they know Jett's family could be bigger than the Sopranos. My mom finally asks how many people she is adding to the table after Jett relents and accepts the invitation.

"Just my parents and my younger brother, Marcel."

"Any special food requirements?" my mom asks.

Jett shakes his head. He looks at me tentatively. I grab my water glass and take a sip as if I'm uninvolved in the whole thing. At this rate, he might as well move in with us.

After dinner, Jett and Dom don't stay very long. Dom yawned through dessert, and Jett keeps rubbing his eyes. I'm always worn out after a weekend of away hockey, though, so it's understandable.

"I got us ice tomorrow," Jett says as the guys are saying good night.

"That must be expensive," my dad says. "We should be chipping in."

Jett waves his hand. "No, honestly, my host family owns the rink, so they let me have it."

Dom laughs and Jett shoots him a quick glare. I still don't know what it's really costing him. My dad accepts the explanation, though, and the guys take off.

I close the door, and when I turn around, Harper and London are standing in front of me ready to burst.

"I told you!" London says as she wiggles her eyebrows and looks at Harper.

Harper's mouth is hanging open as she looks from London to me.

"Ryleigh," she says. "How? How is any boy all that? I need ice water!"

I exhale. "He's just a boy. Just like any other."

Harps and London exchange glances as I go to help my mom clean up. If there is one thing Jett Robitaille is not, it's a boy just like any other.

The rink is cold. The first week of November is creeping its way into my veins, dark and icy.

Dom isn't here today. He texted Jett this morning to say he thinks he's coming down with a cold and gave Jett a list of instructions on what I should be doing differently. Jett has his phone on top of the boards by one of the benches and keeps going over to check it as he yells the directions to me. He imitates Dom's broad Canadian accent and it's kind of funny. The little bit of mercy Jett showed me from our first sessions is disappearing as we spend more time on the ice. I guess that's a compliment, because it means I'm getting better even if I'm not stopping more shots. He at least thinks I can take it when he turns the heat up. Jett still clowns around, calling his moves like an announcer would, or celebrating every goal as if this is a real game.

"Robitaille shoots it to the corner and battles to dig it back out," he says as he fakes a shot wide just to keep me on my toes. But then he pulls around the net and dangles me like I'm a novice. I think he's going to cross the net and go left, but he centers it right through my five-hole.

"Whoo!" he yells, and swings around and grabs me and hugs me as if we're teammates.

I shake him off and retrieve the puck and toss it back out again. Being alone with him is exactly like him. It's too much. He keeps me on my toes, though, relentlessly sending pucks to the net without a break for the next forty minutes.

Then he pulls up in front of me with an ice shower, which I enjoy, as I'm sweating now.

"You seem pretty frustrated, but you're definitely improving," he says. He's breathing hard.

I puff my cheeks and blow out a big breath.

"Why don't we just skate a little?" he asks. "It's almost quitting time anyway."

I think about saying "No, let's just keep going," but he's right. I am frustrated, and tired. I nod, and we start doing laps.

"Want to race?" Jett asks.

I flatten my expression to tell him no. There's no way I can compete with a tall guy not hampered by goalie pads.

Jett laughs. "All right, Puck," he says. "We can take it slow."

"Don't call me that."

Jett nudges me and smiles as he skates by my side. "Hold on," he says, and goes over to his phone. He starts playing music.

"What is this? French pop?"

"Oui, mademoiselle," he says. Jett falls in beside me again and we take a lap around the ice.

This, the two of us skating alone, just side by side, feels nice. We skate in perfect rhythm. Our right feet hit the ice at the same moment. Our shoulders dip and sway as if we are one person. It's too nice.

"How's it going with Peyton?" I ask.

Jett glances over and shrugs.

"You're going to need a game plan if you haven't secured her full attention yet."

"Tu penses?" You think? Jett's been dropping French on me since he learned I take it.

I nod. “Something to compete with college guys. Does she know you’re probably getting drafted this spring?”

“I doubt it. Why would she? I’m surprised you know.”

“I saw it somewhere,” I say, not able to look at him. He must think I cyberstalk him. Like I’m not pathetic enough as it is.

“There’s a TV crew coming to film me on Wednesday at school for a show on prospects. Do you think that would impress her?”

“You got the school to agree to that?”

Jett nods. “They like the positive image it shows. As long as the crew follows the school’s publicity permission rules and doesn’t disrupt classes, they said it’s okay.”

“That would be perfect. Peyton loves attention.”

“And you don’t. I’m sorry about that. I’ve been working up my nerve to tell you.”

“Why? It’s not like I’m involved.”

Jett tilts his head at me. “You kind of are, since you’re my girlfriend and they’ll be at lunch with us.”

I raise my gaze to his. “I think I’m going to be feeling sick on Wednesday.”

“See, this is why I didn’t want to tell you. Well, I was more scared you’d be mad than I was worried you wouldn’t show up. Listen, Rye, I know this isn’t something you’d seek out, but it’s probably good timing. NHL teams aren’t going to watch this, but colleges will.”

“You’re already committed.”

Jett stops, so I do, too. "Seriously?"

I shrug to ask *What?*

"This could be a great opportunity to plug you, get your name out there with coaches." He's turned in toward me, so close that his skates are on either side of my right skate, and it feels like we've known each other a long time instead of a couple of months. It feels like we've always been a team.

"No," I say, "I don't want to glom on to your celebrity to get my shot. I want to get this on my own merit. But thanks." I dodge and start skating again and he slides into place beside me.

"I'm just saying that piquing curiosity in any coaches watching isn't a bad thing," Jett says. We've slowed our pace, both of us gliding.

"I'm not even your real girlfriend. What are people going to think when we're not together in a few weeks?"

Jett doesn't answer right away. "You should use my celebrity as much as you can. I want you to."

He's trying to be nice. But he doesn't understand how hard I've had to work to get where I am, or all the challenges I've had to overcome. Everything for him has been smooth sailing. I don't want something I haven't earned. "Nobody needs to know I play, too. The less I'm on camera, the better. I don't really care if they think I'm your girlfriend. That'll be forgotten faster than you can shoot a puck once we stage a breakup."

Jett is slow to answer.

"All right, Puck, whatever you want." We skate to the net

to move it so he can run the Zamboni. He doesn't seem very pleased, but I don't need him to think it's the right choice. I just need him to go along.

"For sure?" I ask.

Jett looks at me and nods. The buzzer blasts its ridiculously loud horn and seals the deal.

Chapter 15

Lights, Camera, Action

THE FIRST TIME I SEE THE CAMERA CREW WITH JETT IS WHEN we're converging on chemistry from opposite sides of the hall. My classmates have been buzzing with excitement over the crew's presence all morning, though. The Secret Service has nothing on this high school. Every movement has been clocked, with Jett and the camera crew assigned call signs. If I have to hear one more time that the Canada lynx is on the move with the snow geese flying in formation right behind, I may need to go to the nurse for anti-nausea meds.

Jett and I reach the door to class at the same time. He smiles at me and then turns to his entourage. "I'm sorry," he says, "but my chemistry teacher is the one who wouldn't give you permission to film."

"Oh, right," the guy who seems to be in charge says.

"We'll take a break while you're in class." He looks at me. "Who's this?"

Jett shifts his backpack. "This is my girlfriend, Ryleigh Vento."

It sounds weird to hear him introduce me to someone like that. It's not that the crew wouldn't have heard about him having a girlfriend from someone, but this lie keeps growing. I don't know when this show will air, but Jett and I will be frozen in this time to everyone watching it as if this is real. My stomach feels like someone dropped an entire packet of Red Hots into it. The crew members introduce themselves to me. The guy in charge is named Ron. I nod hello, and Jett and I go take our seats at our lab table. I look back. There's a cameraman in the hall who seems to have his shoulder camera trained on just Jett and me. I whip my gaze back to the front of the class and keep it there for the rest of the period. Mr. G. must have noticed the commotion before class because he keeps interrupting his usual pacing to stare at Jett and me for just a moment before he begins again. Just enough that everyone gives us the you-are-in-more-trouble-than-usual glance before they look away, confident they've done their duty to warn us that we are getting further on Mr. G.'s bad side. As if he has a good side.

After class, the crew is waiting to follow us. Jett doesn't take my hand the way he usually does, but he sticks close to me and leans against the lockers beside mine the way he always does as I change out my books. When he walks like that, as if we are almost one person in motion, it makes me think of skating with him, only the two of us.

"Just act normally," Ron says. "Talk about whatever you usually talk about."

Jett laughs. "Usually, she's laying a lecture on me by now."

I glance at him. "I am not."

Jett looks down, the smile on his face growing. It makes my stomach flutter. The cameraman moves around us slowly.

"Wait, what's that?" Ron says as his gaze lands on the poster Imani made me.

"Nothing," I say, and close my locker way too hard. It bounces open and I close it again.

"Do you play hockey?" Ron asks, his eyes narrowed as he searches for the story of Jett and me.

I look at Jett in a panic.

"A little," I say at the same time that Jett says, "She's a really great goalie, on a Triple-A team here in Danbury."

"Really?" Ron says. So much for my plan to stay anonymous. "So you're going to play in college? Where are you committed?"

My mouth hangs open, and I can't think of anything to say that won't make me sound like a complete loser.

"She's still evaluating her options," Jett says.

I snap my mouth shut and nod. My eyes water.

"We need to get to class," Jett says. He slips his arm around my shoulders and leads me away, squeezing me close as the camera crew follows us to my calc class. When Jett drops me at the door before he goes to English, he runs his hand along my arm until his hand meets my fingers, and he gives them a squeeze. "I'll see you at lunch, okay?" He says this quietly, as if we are completely alone. As if no one else matters.

I nod and disappear into calc without ever looking at Jett or the camera circling him.

Cheers erupt when Jett and I stride into the cafeteria surrounded by a camera crew, and kids pound the tables and stomp. I just hope this is the apex of my life's embarrassing moments because I don't think I could take much worse. Then it occurs to me that this is going to be seen on national television, even if it is just the hockey network, and I realize the humiliation is just starting. Especially since Jett and I will be over by then.

Jett waves his hand from side to side to ask everyone to knock it off. As we glide by Peyton's table, her gaze is locked on us. This might be enough to lower her standards to a mere high school guy. I should feel happier about that than I do. Still, I smile at Jett as if I'm happy so Peyton will have the extra incentive of kicking me where she thinks it hurts when she steals my star-athlete fake boyfriend. At least I have the self-respect of knowing I'm doing all I can to keep my end of the deal.

There's no way any of us can act or eat normally with a film crew documenting our silly lunch talk, which sounds more inane than usual to me. But we're teenagers. We're supposed to be goofy, not reality TV stars. I've never had to worry about what "the public" thinks of me, but Jett has been carrying this weight since he was probably fourteen. Maybe that's why he takes everything as a joke, because he's had to deal with everyone's opinions of his playing and him as a person for so long.

Jett slides my now-daily chocolate protein shake in front of me wordlessly.

"Thanks," I say, a little softer than I usually do, and he gives me a short smile and nods. We talk about the weekend. My team is headed to Pittsburgh for games, while the Jr. Hat Tricks will be at home. We have a lab, but I don't have to miss chemistry, as I'm not leaving until four o'clock on Friday.

"It's a shame your schedules are so out of sync," Imani says. "I don't know why you can't both have home games on the same weekend."

Jett smiles. "I think we do for a couple of weeks after Thanksgiving."

"Oohhh, we have to come," Imani says, and Matt agrees. Lewis seems less impressed.

"You should focus more on your own boyfriend instead of Ryleigh's," he tells Imani. "I'm cool, too, you know."

This makes us laugh.

"Sorry, Lewis," Matt says, "but you're nowhere near as cool as Jett."

"I'm glad someone said it," Imani says. She smiles and raises her eyebrows as she looks at Lewis to let him know she's sorry she's not sorry.

I think of Jett waving his ridiculous sign at my game and

bite my lip. Maybe I should stick up for Lewis and let them know Jett can be very uncool, but I'd rather move to a polar ice cap than have Matt or Imani know about that sign. Especially since Jett will be "dumping" me soon. I just hope they never find out it was all in pursuit of Peyton. Imani might kill Jett. Or me. Or both of us.

"Okay, it's a plan," Matt says. "We'll go to one of Jett's games with Rye and then we'll go to one of Rye's games with Jett."

Jett high-fives him over me. I shake my head.

After lunch, Jett and I say goodbye for the day. We don't have afternoon classes near each other, and he leaves school early to get to the gym for his pre-practice workout. He smiles at Peyton as we walk out, hand in hand. Outside the cafeteria, he pulls me toward him and pecks my cheek. I'd say he's doing it for the camera crew, but he's always this smooth. I don't know how Peyton, of all people, doesn't fall for this.

"I'll text you after dinner," he says. This will be late, because by the time Jett gets back to his host family's place after practice, it's seven before he gets dinner. But he does always text me before we go to sleep, even on days when he doesn't need to tell me that he got us ice. I seem to be the only real friend he has here who isn't on his team. Dom is his travel roommate and there's a kid he played with two years ago named Bradon who he's close to, but everyone else seems to just exist in his orbit for a season. "Hockey is always changing," he said one night. "Every year you have a new team, new coaches, a new host family. It's like throwing stars together in a vortex. Some constellations form, but most of them are just people you know for a little while and then never see again as if they were sucked away by a black hole."

As I watch Jett saunter down the hall to his locker, Peyton and the camera crew on his heels, it makes me sadder than it should that I'll soon be one of those transitory people who orbited Jett Robitaille's world for a brief moment, only to be forgotten.

Chapter 16

Canadian Invasion

I'M NOT SURE MY MOM IS DOING JETT AND HIS FAMILY ANY FAvors by inviting them to spend Thanksgiving with us, but he seems to be pretty happy about it. He asks me multiple times what they should bring and what time to come.

When they show up, the house is already in deep chaos with three of my grandparents, seven aunts and uncles, and eleven cousins, minus my cousin Buttons, whose real name is Wes but who has been called Buttons since his dad, my uncle Steve, had to Heimlich a button out of his airway when he was three. Buttons is doing a semester abroad, and my aunt Megan won't stop talking about how awful it is that he is missing our family holiday. Buttons, meanwhile, has spent the day texting all us cousins a myriad of GIFs letting us know what losers he thinks we are for being here instead of at a sidewalk café in Barcelona. My guess is we are ten minutes out from when Aunt Megan and Uncle Steve fight about whether they should have gone to Spain for Thanksgiving.

"They don't even celebrate Thanksgiving in Spain," Uncle Steve says to Aunt Megan as I open the door for Jett and his family. I smile for our guests, but it's hard not to wince.

"Ryleigh, this is my mom, Ailene," Jett says. We shake hands and she smiles sweetly.

"Merci, for making Jett feel at home," she says in accented English.

I nod but don't know what to say since I really haven't done anything to make Jett feel at home.

"And this is my stepdad, Pierre, and my little brother, Marcel."

Stepdad? Jett has never mentioned that his parents are divorced. In fact, he rarely talks about himself. When he does, you get the sense that he's handing you a piece of himself that he considers to be very precious.

Before I can even say hello properly, the rest of my family descends on them in a cluster, and I end up being pushed out of the circle so far that I barely catch Jett looking around as if he's searching for me. My family, especially my hockey-playing boy cousins, are falling all over themselves—literally, as my cousin Kenji trips over an end table when my cousin James elbows him out of the way—to get to Jett. Some of this is because I've never had a "real" boyfriend and they want to tell him every embarrassing thing I've done since I was two, and some of it is because they want to fanboy all over him. You'd think this year's number one NHL draft pick just walked into our house.

My dad breaks up the mob scene so that Jett's family can enter the house the way normal people do. He scatters my cousins by promising them they can ask Jett about hockey after dinner. Jett raises his eyebrows at me, and I shrug. I probably should have warned him, but it's not like he needs to present a lecture. He just has to answer a hundred questions as if he's at a team fan greet. Besides, this was between him and my mom. I had nothing to do with inviting his family to this circus.

Marcel shadows Jett. He's tall like Jett, and gangly, with the same dark hair and eyes, and he seems to be uncomfortable with all the commotion. Not that I could blame him. My family is a lot to handle. He doesn't look anyone in the eyes as they talk, but he nods agreeably. Jett answers for him sometimes and sometimes makes him do it himself, but not without an encouraging tap on his arm or a nod.

Jett maneuvers over to me. "You have a big family," he says with a half-smiling, half-pained face.

"Sorry, I should have warned you. Thanksgiving is our big holiday. Christmas is less intense, as we spread it out more."

Jett nods. "Marcel was excited to meet you," Jett says as he nudges his brother the way he always nudges me.

His brother's face turns scarlet.

"I'm really happy to meet you, too, Marcel," I say. "Now I have someone to gang up on Jett with."

I smile and Marcel looks me in the eye for a flickering

moment and then smiles back. "She's teasing, right?" he whispers to Jett. He moves a little bit behind his big brother.

"Yes. I think," Jett says. Then he looks at me. "Marcel will always take my side."

"Noted. Maybe I need to meet some of your cousins. If they're like mine, they'll throw you straight to the wolves."

Jett laughs and the momentary look of worry that had come on Marcel's face dissipates. "Come on," Jett says as he takes my hand, "I want you to meet my mom." Without a word, he puts his other hand on his brother's elbow and steers us toward his mom and stepdad, who are now each holding a glass of something—as they should be, according to my mom's host standards—near the French doors in the family room. They're talking to my aunt Satomi. She's always in charge of guest engagement because she works on Wall Street and has traveled a lot, which means she can usually come up with something interesting to talk about.

"Bonjour," his parents say.

"Bonjour," I say.

"Jett dit que tu parles français?" his mom says.

I glance at Jett. It's not like I'm fluent, although he has started talking to me more in French to help me with it. "Un peu," I say, which means *a little.*

His mom smiles at me. "We can speak English if you prefer."

"Excusez-moi, pourquoi aimez-vous tant Jett?" Marcel asks me. Why do I like Jett so much? My face flushes.

Jett pulls his brother into him, wrapping him in a hug from behind. He whispers in French, "She doesn't really like me that much," and then he looks at me. "Sorry, sometimes my brother doesn't understand social norms."

"It's okay," I say as Marcel's face turns as red as mine. "Ce n'est pas un problème." I reach my hand out without touching him to try to show him I'm not offended. Jett smiles at me, gratitude written in his eyes.

"I really like that Jett is so generous with his time," I say. "He's helped me a lot. He balances me. I'm always stressed and he's always calm."

Jett's parents laugh and agree in French that Jett takes life as it comes. "Jett could find sunshine at midnight," his stepdad says.

I glance at Jett. He's looking down, but he's smiling. Before, I thought his being so optimistic was because his life has been super easy. But I guess if his parents are divorced, then maybe that's not the whole truth.

When we sit down at the table—or tables, I should say, because we're spread out at the dining room table, the island, and a makeshift table in the family room—Jett comes over and slips his fingers into mine. "Is it okay if Marcel is seated between us? I think he'd be more comfortable that way."

I nod, and we take our seats. My mom has made sure that Jett's family all sit at the main table. "Is this your first American Thanksgiving?" she asks.

Jett's mom says yes, but then Jett reminds her that they came to his first host family's town, but his mom reminds him that they got there on Friday because their flight was delayed due to a snowstorm, so they settle on this being their first.

Marcel doesn't eat very much. He fidgets with his fork and clasps his napkin in his other hand on his lap, so I ask him questions to try to make him forget to be nervous.

"What do you and Jett do for fun?" I ask.

Marcel smiles and looks down. "We play video games. I'm a better driver than he is."

"He always gets the best cars," Jett says. "I end up with a clunker and he'll be driving a Lamborghini."

Marcel looks at his brother. "You're a good driver, too. Just not as good as me."

"I know. It's okay, you can be the better video game driver." The smile on his face is enough to make even Peyton fall hard.

"Jett is really good at hockey," Marcel says.

"I've seen him play. He's awesome."

Jett leans forward so he can catch my gaze past his brother. "You think I'm awesome?"

The room gets hot as I realize all the adults at the table are listening to our conversation. "At hockey, yes." I stab my mashed potatoes and shove some in my mouth.

We quiet down then, and slowly, the adults start talking again. "What else do you and Jett do together?" I ask Marcel.

"Mmm, he takes me skating on an ice trail in the winter. And in the summer, we go hiking or bike riding, or to the botanical gardens." Marcels glances at me for just a second. "I like quiet places," he says.

I look at his plate, still mostly full when Jett and I are done. "Hey," I say, "do you want to see my room?"

Marcel looks at Jett, who nods, and I tell my mom we're

going upstairs. I grab the plate and utensils and napkin and tell Jett with a glance to bring Marcel's water. When we get upstairs, I show them to my room. I hurry and set the plate down on my desk and then frantically grab my clothes that are scattered all over the place, including a couple of bras, and shove them into my closet. Then I close the door to my room.

"It's nice and quiet in here, isn't it, Marcel?" Jett asks, and his brother nods. "Why don't you finish your dinner," he adds.

Marcel sits down and starts to eat after a few furtive glances at Jett and me. There's nowhere else to sit in my room except a beanbag and the bed, so Jett and I stand there a minute until he sits on the floor. I take the beanbag. Jett looks around. My walls are lined with old CDs I've painted in beach themes, or for songs I like, or hockey teams I follow. There's a signed, framed Fleury jersey my mom won for me in a raffle at a tournament I played in one year. And there's a cork bulletin board filled with pictures of my family, friends, and teammates over the years.

"I like your room," Jett says. "It's like you, but in a cheerful, best kind of way."

I scrunch my eyebrows together. "What does that mean?"

"Jett says you're prickly," Marcel says, his mouth full of cranberry sauce.

"Prickly?"

"I said 'standoffish.' Just un peu."

"You said 'prickly,'" Marcel says. "Remember, I had to ask you what it meant because you used the English for it? You said 'très prickly.'"

This time I raise my eyebrows. "Très prickly? Got it."

"I—I just meant, you know, that you're very, you know, sure about what you like and stuff . . ." Jett's voice trails away as I glare at him. He looks at his brother and widens his eyes to ask him to stop ratting him out.

"You don't seem that prickly," Marcel says.

"Thanks. I'm only prickly when people deserve it." I stare at Jett as I say this.

He looks away as if he doesn't know what I mean.

"Jett's not home much," Marcel says.

"I know, buddy, I'm sorry. But you're coming to World Juniors with Maman and Pierre, and then I'll be home for a couple days." Jett looks up at his brother from the floor with a hopeful gaze.

Marcel nods, but he doesn't smile.

"Winter break will be here before we know it," I say. "It's only three weeks away now."

Marcel's mouth almost pulls up to a smile.

London comes by and pops the door open. She's all dolled up for the holiday in a green velveteen dress, and it melts my heart how much she looks like Mom. She even sounds like her. "Dessert is ready. Choices are apple, pumpkin, or pecan pie."

"Yes, please," Jett says, jumping up. "Come on, Marcel, let's get some pie." He grabs Marcel's empty plate and utensils and glass. As I brush past him, he stops me. "I didn't mean you're prickly," he whispers. "I just meant that you aren't super, you know, outgoing. Just to prepare him. But I really appreciate how thoughtful you're being to him. I wasn't sure what you'd think."

I raise my eyebrows. Then I turn to Marcel. "Come with me, Marcel. My aunt Patti makes the best apple pie you've ever had. Do you like apple pie?"

Marcel nods and follows me out, forgetting to shadow Jett until we get back downstairs. A smile hovers on Jett's face as he watches me help Marcel to some pie and another quiet corner.

After dessert, we go to the basement to watch my cousins play video games with Harper. They've picked the NHL one because they all want to play against Jett.

"What is she doing?" Jett asks when he sees my sister with a bandana covering one eye.

"Otherwise she can beat them too easily."

"Gotcha."

After Harper finally gets defeated, my cousins beg Jett to play with them until he relents. He's a lot better at real hockey than he is at video game hockey.

"I don't have time to do this kind of stuff," he says, leaning back to catch my gaze when my cousins tease him about it. "Do you?"

I shake my head. Harps is watching me. You have to go all in if you want to play in college. She wants to play, but without going all in. There are no guarantees, but if you really want it, it's more of a compulsion than something you simply want.

After a while, Jett laughingly admits defeat, and Kenji asks Marcel to play.

"Do I have to wear a bandana over my eye?" Marcel asks.

I laugh and tell him no, while my cousins ask him if he's any good.

Jett's been such a sport about losing to my cousins that I've almost forgotten the 'prickly' comment when he comes over to where I'm perched on a stool against the wall and sits down next to me.

"That's a nice home gym your dad has."

"Once a Marine, always a Marine," I say, parroting what my dad and his fellow service buddies say.

"So you don't even have to go to a gym, huh?"

"No, my dad and I lift together on nights I don't have practice."

We grow silent and watch the game. Marcel is doing well.

"You're really sweet with your brother," I say after a minute or two.

Jett gazes at the floor. "He was only eight when our dad died," he says, so that no one else hears. The words take my breath for a moment. He says them so factually. I calculate how long he's had to live with them. Six years. Jett was eleven when his dad died. I want to look at him, but I can't. All this time, I thought his life has been easy.

"My mom says kids imprint on their parents, you know, bond with them, when they're about two years old, but after my dad died, it was like Marcel imprinted all over again on me. Maybe because he's on the spectrum?" Jett shrugs. He watches Marcel lovingly. "Anyway, I had to step up and be there for him." He smiles at me.

My eyes are instantly wet. *I had to step up*. That's exactly what I had to do when my mom was diagnosed. I turn away from Jett and sniffle.

He leans his shoulder against mine.

"You okay?"

I turn back and nod, but I can't look at him. "I'm sorry." I've been so judgy about him, and meanwhile he's had it worse than I have. I only *fear* losing my mom. He's had to *live* with losing his dad.

"It's okay," Jett says, as if I said all of that out loud. "You didn't know. I don't like to talk about it. He died of pancreatic cancer."

I glance up, and we look at each other. I don't like to talk about my mom's illness, either.

Jett puts his hand in front of me, palm up, fingers open. I slowly slide my hand into his and he wraps his fingers around mine. And then we sit there and watch Marcel beat Kenji at NHL hockey and cheer him on together.

Chapter 17

One Step Deeper into the Forest

BEFORE THEY LEAVE, JETT ASKS ME WHERE HE SHOULD TAKE HIS family while they're here. I tilt my head at him.

"You realize this is Danbury, Connecticut, right? It's not New York City."

Jett laughs. "There has to be something to do here?"

"Well, we do have the tallest Uncle Sam statue in the world. In the parking lot of the Railway Museum."

"Yikes."

"There's also a statue of a hatmaker, because we used to be known as the Hat City of the World, until it was discovered that the mercury they used to make the hats was poisoning the hatmakers. The industry kind of died out after that."

"Makes sense."

"We do have a professional minor-league hockey team and

a junior hockey team, but neither is playing this weekend. But I'm sure there are free-skate times at some of the local rinks."

"Funny." Jett's smile fades and he crinkles his brow. "Maybe I should take them to New York?"

"The train is only a couple of hours, so if you go early, you can do it in one day. You'll never get last-minute tickets for things like the top of Rockefeller Center, though. And it will be crowded."

Jett does something I've never seen before. He frowns. It's weirdly discomforting, like watching a toddler's unhappy disbelief as they lick their ice cream scoop right off its cone.

Marcel probably doesn't like crowds, though. "If you don't want to deal with too many people, you could go to New Haven. Does your brother like dinosaurs? Yale has a natural history museum. And a couple of art galleries if your parents like that. Most people will be in New York, so it shouldn't be busy."

Jett's face softens.

"There's also an indoor carousel at Lighthouse Point Park. It's very old and pretty and overlooks the water. It's cool."

The smile I'm learning to take for granted lights up Jett's face. "Do you want to come?"

"I don't want to crash your family time," I say. Sometimes I have hockey on Thanksgiving weekend, but not this year.

"You wouldn't be crashing. You'd be guiding."

I purse my lips before I answer. "So what you are saying is that you want a tour guide?"

"Well, it sounds as if you've been there before?"

"Lots of times. It's only about an hour away."

"So, are you in?" Jett lasers his dimples at me.

I sigh. "Okay. But we should take my car. We're not all going to fit in your Impreza."

Jett laughs. "She's a beaut, isn't she?"

"Sure," I say to humor him. I'm relieved, though, that the flashy sports car is Dom's. Jett is already too much. His driving a car like Dom's would be too over the top. Like a peacock wearing a tiara.

We decide to go on Saturday, but Jett is worried that still leaves tomorrow with nothing for his family to do. "Usually when they come to see me, the weekend is filled with games," he says. "I was thinking maybe I could take them to the beach since it's something different?"

"It's winter, Jett."

"We're from Canada. This is barely fall to us."

"Okay, Hard Charger, as my dad likes to say, but when that ocean breeze is freezing you into statues, don't say I didn't warn you."

Jett shakes his head, but he's biting back a smile. "Where should I take them? Isn't Connecticut filled with nice little beach towns?"

"Hmm, I would say Milford. It has a walkable downtown and the beaches are pretty."

He reaches over and taps my arm. "Want to come with?"

I hesitate for just a moment. Why am I hesitating? Of course I shouldn't go with them. "I think your mom would rather spend time with you than with me."

Jett laughs a little. "She wants to get to know you."

"Because she thinks I'm your girlfriend. Which I'm not." Now that I know his family, it feels really awkward to be lying to them. Especially to help him win a girl I don't even like.

Jett nods as if he's mulling this over. "You can still join," he says.

I'm about to decline when Jett's mom glides over and Jett tells her the plan. His mom is so much like him, charming in a totally relaxed way.

"You have to come with us," she says. "Please." She flashes her deep chocolate eyes and dimples at me, and it's like saying no to Jett. Somehow, I just can't seem to manage it when I should.

I spend so much time with Jett's family over the next two days that it starts to feel as if I really am Jett's girlfriend. We go to Milford and wander around the small downtown and then have lunch at a tavern-style restaurant. When we go to sit down, Marcel slides into the chair next to me, so Jett sits across from us. I expect the meal to feel a little uncomfortable, like I'm a fifth wheel, but Jett and his mom keep the conversation flowing. His family doesn't ask me questions like "Why don't you have a commitment yet?" and instead his mom asks me things like "What do you want to have for lunch?" and "What's your favorite part about playing hockey?"

"Mmmm, I think my favorite part is that feeling I get when I head to the handshake line when I've had a great game. It makes me feel like a superhero." As soon as I say this, my cheeks become fire. "Not that this happens a lot."

"Don't be so hard on yourself," Jett says.

"I'm sure it happens a lot," Jett's mom says, "or you wouldn't be playing at the level you are."

"Especially with your size," Jett's stepdad says.

I laugh. "You mean my mini-ness. That's what Jett and Dom call it."

Jett's mom shakes her head to let me know that Jett and Dom are ridiculous, but she smiles.

"You're cool," Marcel says.

"Thanks," I say.

After lunch, we go to Woodmont Beach. We walk along the sidewalk where the road curves around the water. The waves here are gentle, not like the massive, noisy beauties that roll in on the North Carolina shores. The sun is shining, with only a few wispy clouds hanging around the edges of the sky. After a while, Marcel wants to go down on the sand, so we do. The water smells of brine and sea life.

"Let's race," Jett says.

I make a face at him, but Marcel is instantly running as if he'd just been waiting for the challenge. Jett takes off after him. "Come on, Vento," he calls.

Jett's mom laughs at them, and his stepdad is shaking his head. I chase after them.

I don't even know where the finish line is supposed to be, but suddenly they pull up and Marcel has just managed to beat his brother. I come in a distant third. As I stop beside them, we are all breathing hard, even though I know Jett couldn't have been going full tilt. The cold is hard on my lungs, and the familiar burn spreads across them. I lean over and rest my hands on my thighs.

"Are you okay?" Jett asks.

I nod. "I didn't know I needed my inhaler to bring you to the beach."

"Sorry. Is it in your car? I can run and get it."

I wave it off and we congratulate Marcel and his face beams with pride. "Jett's a better skater," he tells me, "but I'm fast on my feet." He giggles.

"Stop bragging in front of my girlfriend," Jett says. He throws his arm around Marcel's shoulder and hugs him. Marcel looks down. Then he looks up and laughs.

"Mom, did you see?" he calls, and takes off running back to his parents.

Jett and I follow in the chilly breeze, the pebbled beach crunchy under our sneakers. I cough, and Jett asks again if I'm okay.

"It will stop in a few minutes," I say, coughing again.

"Thanks for all this," he says.

"It's my quid pro quo," I say. "It makes me feel less guilty about what it's costing you to get rink time for me, whatever that is."

Jett sighs. "You really don't want to know."

I stop. "It's not money, is it? Seriously, Jett, you shouldn't be buying me ice time."

"Relax, Puck. I shouldn't tell you this because I should make you work for the answer, but since you're so worried, I will."

I watch him expectantly, but he gives his revelation a dramatic pause.

"So?" I nudge when he takes too long.

"Knee hockey."

"What, that's it? They give you ice time for a kids' game?"

"What do you mean, that's it? Do you know how much I've played this past month? The skin on my knees is raw!"

I laugh. I can totally believe that Jett's host family's kids have been torturing him with an insane amount of knee hockey. I kind of feel bad, though, too, because he doesn't get much downtime. And now he's spending that time helping me and playing floor hockey on his knees to make it happen.

"Thank you," I say.

Jett nods. "Yeah, sure."

"No, I mean it. I know you don't have a lot of free time."

"I'm basically scheduled down to the minute. It's the only way to make it all happen." Somehow, even when he's complaining, it doesn't sound like he's unhappy with any of his choices.

"You don't have to help me," I say. "You and Dom have already done a lot for my game. You can stop now."

I expect him to be relieved, but he looks at me without even a hint of happiness. "Are you kidding me?"

We stop and stare at each other. "No," I say. "I mean it. You deserve to have some time to just unwind." I cough again, but not as hard as before.

Jett studies me. It feels like he's reading my eyes, as if there are lines written in them that could tell him what I'm really thinking.

"If I need to unwind, I'll tell you." He looks around. "This, this is unwinding. Spending time with the people I need to spend time with. With the people I want to spend time with. Doing stuff that's relaxing. Besides, I don't know if you've noticed, but Marcel adores you. You really see him, past his quirks. And that means a lot to me."

I can't hold his gaze, so I turn and take in the view of the ocean. Two seagulls fly past over the water, undaunted by the late-November cold. Seagulls aren't dainty little birds. They're like sailors or pirates, unafraid to claim their space in the world. They know life isn't easy, and they pluck along anyway, always moving forward to the next opportunity. And then they cry out, long and high-pitched and yearning, and you're reminded all over again that, deep inside, they have to struggle just like the rest of us. Jett's a little like a seagull. I should have realized sooner that there's more to him than I've given him credit for.

Marcel calls us and we race back to Jett's family. Then I take them to Walnut Beach before we head back to Danbury. We walk the small pier that juts over the water. It's not like a boardwalk. There's nothing attached to it. It's just a wooden platform that reaches over the Long Island Sound. The sun is low in the sky as we stand at the edge of the pier and look out at the gently rolling waves. I take pictures for them, and then Jett's mom insists on having me in some, too, and having some of just Jett and me. He slips his arm around my shoulders, the orange sky and blue water behind us.

"How's your breathing?" Jett asks.

"It's easing up."

"Let's race again," Marcel says. "The three of us."

"Ryleigh needs to take a break, Marcel," Jett says. "She has asthma."

"Are you okay?" Jett's mom asks.

"I'm fine, it's mild. I just have to be careful not to get too congested from it or I'll be that way for weeks."

Jett and Marcel go down to the water's edge and race. Jett's mom and stepdad stay with me.

"You're the first girlfriend Jett's had," she says.

"Really?" I can't hide my surprise at this. Jett clearly could have pretty much any girl he wants. Except Peyton. Maybe that's why he wants her?

Jett's mom nods. Then she laughs. "At least that I know of. But I don't think there's been anyone. He was always much too focused on hockey and family."

"Well, that makes sense," I say. When I think about it, it's almost weird that he's wanted Peyton since the beginning of school. But he has his commitment sewn up, so maybe that's the difference from other years.

"I was worried that he was getting burned out on hockey and was looking for a distraction," Jett's mom says. "But it seems more like he found someone who loves it as much as he does."

I smile and look down. Jett and I definitely have that in common.

"You seem really good for him," his stepdad says.

"I don't know about that," I say. "But he's helped me a lot."

"Well, he talks about you all the time," his mom says.

"He does?" I say as his mom nods, but it makes sense. He spends almost as much time with me as with his teammates.

Marcel and Jett come running back, with Marcel crowing that he's beaten Jett again. It should be annoying, but somehow, it's cute, like a duckling bragging about dunking his head underwater. Maybe because it makes Jett so obviously happy, or maybe because Marcel understands that Jett can't help but outshine anyone who stands too close to him.

Afterward, we get a couple of take-out pizzas and go to my house and eat pizza and Thanksgiving leftovers with my family and watch the Canadiens game on our Center Ice subscription. After they leave, Jett texts me the photos from Milford.

My mom wanted you to have these.

When I crawl into bed for the night, I stare at the pictures for a long time. The wind is whipping our hair around, although Jett's is under a beanie. There's a nice one of Jett and Marcel with me in the middle. And one of just Marcel and me as he stands beside me stiffly with an awkward but adorable smile on his face. Then there are several with Jett and me together. For the first few, Jett kept saying, "Don't clown around, Vento," but meanwhile he was making bunny ears behind my head or hugging me as if he's tackling me. But in the last few, he's just holding me from behind, his arms wrapped around me, dimples flashing, eyes crinkled in happiness. And I can't believe I was ever foolish enough to agree to help him be someone else's boyfriend.

Chapter 18

This Was Not Supposed to Happen

WHEN I WAKE UP ON SUNDAY, I KIND OF HATE MYSELF. I KNOW THAT'S not something I should ever say, but it's still how I feel. I've done everything I could to push Jett away since the day I met him. I've worked so hard to keep everyone at a distance over the past couple of years. I say Imani and I don't do things together anymore because she's busy hanging with Lewis and I'm busy with hockey, but that's mostly an excuse. I see everyone at lunch, or Matt and I run into each other at stick time, but I don't spend time with anyone just hanging out. Some of my friends used to try, but after hearing too many times that I was busy with hockey or family, they gave up and let me be.

Imani, my tenacious little Imani, shows up every few months with a couple of sodas or ice cream sandwiches or some hot chocolate and forces a heart-to-heart on me. But mostly, I've hunkered down and dealt with each day as it comes. When my mom was really sick, it was all I could do. I went to bed at night thinking, *Just get through tomorrow. You only have to get through tomorrow.* It made me able to face each morning, but it also became a habit.

When you don't have anything good to share with your friends, you stop sharing anything. I didn't want to talk about my mom burning her fingers because her hands were numb from the chemotherapy drugs, so she couldn't feel the hot pan touching her. Or the comment of the mean guy at the grocery store to his mean friend about the bald lady walking too slowly with her cart. Or the way London cried when she saw the incision for the chemo port the doctors implanted just below my mom's collarbone so they could draw her blood and deliver her medicine easier. I tried to lighten it for them both by joking that it made Mom look like an actor in a sci-fi movie, but the truth was, it made me want to cry, too. And then there was the time I got home from school and found my mom passed out on her bedroom floor and thought she was dead. I couldn't even scream because I didn't want Harps or London to see her like that. So I knelt beside her and called 911. The dispatcher was walking me through the first steps of CPR and that's when I realized my mom was breathing. When I thought about it after, I wasn't sure I'd have been able to do it. I'm still not sure if I could have. I haven't wanted to talk about any of this. Mostly I've just wanted to hang out at home, pretending it was all a movie instead of my life, and soaking up the reality that my mom is still here despite the odds.

Jett barging into my already-complicated life like a hockey mascot on a mission to make me his number one fan seemed like nothing but a huge inconvenience. But maybe I'm the one who is the problem. I've known from the start that he wasn't going to get Peyton to date him, but I went along with this for my own selfish reasons. I've misjudged him and thought badly of him, but I'm the one who doesn't know how to show up anymore.

I scroll through the pictures again, pinching the screen to zoom in on Jett's face. He is beyond. But that's not what makes him irresistible. It's that he doesn't want to use that to get anything in life. Jett makes everything look like it comes easily to him, and he is a natural skater, but he works hard. It's not easy for him to juggle school and elite hockey and his family being so far away. He does his own laundry and takes care of his car and his shopping. He helps me and he calls Marcel every night. Sometimes he helps him with his homework. There's a reason the Jr. Hat Tricks selected him to be their captain.

Now Jett's beautiful dark eyes feel like he's looking right at me in every picture. But he's not. He's seeing the camera, his life, and Peyton. And he's happy with every one of those.

I don't know if I can get him what he wants, or why he even wants it outside of the fact that the girl could be a model for a major lingerie company, but it is what he wants. He's helped me a lot with hockey, especially by roping Dom into coaching me.

I let out a deep breath and commit to helping Jett date

Peyton. For real this time. Not that it wasn't for real before, but this time I will give it my all. I just wish it didn't feel like ripping my own heart out to give it to Peyton Malloy.

My chem nem and my high school nem. A perfect pair. Except that now I wish one of them belonged to me.

Jett, with his always-impeccable timing, lights up my phone with a video call. I wipe a tear from my cheek and plaster on a smile.

"I thought you were taking your family to the airport today," I say.

"I just dropped them off."

"Oh, right."

"Listen, the rink has a tournament this weekend, but it's going to be done by seven o'clock. So my host family says we can have a sheet as long as we want if we skate with their kids until we wear them out."

I laugh. "How hard is that assignment?"

"Mmm, it won't be easy, but I'm taking them running this afternoon to help it along." He smiles devilishly.

"Okay," I say, meeting his smile. "Have you made any progress with Peyton?" I ask. I try to keep smiling.

Jett pulls back, as if he's surprised that I asked. "What made you think about that?"

"I've been thinking I should help you more. You know, make more of a quo for your quid."

Jett's looking at me, his eyebrows raised, his lips furrowed.

"What?" I ask.

"I mean, we talk sometimes." He straightens his shoulders. "I play it cool, you know."

"Right," I say. Jett laughs.

"Anyway, I'll try to come up with a better plan. The TV crew got her full attention, so maybe we can do something with that angle," I add.

Jett nods slightly.

"You seem in a hurry to end your stint as my girlfriend."

I catch his gaze and quickly look away. "I just want to hold up my end of the bargain. You've done a lot for me."

"We're just getting started, Vento," Jett says. "Be at the rink by six-thirty, okay?"

I nod. He gives me a wave, but he's not smiling. And then he disappears as he ends the call.

When I get to the rink, I check the status of the game on the sheet that we're supposed to be on. It's a sixteen-and-under boys' level, but they still have a few minutes in the second period. There's no way we will be on the ice by seven. Being behind schedule is common in hockey, though. I walk through the glass doors to the ice sheet and scan the bleachers. Jett is standing in the top row, watching the game, so I climb the rows to him.

He smiles when he sees me coming toward him. "I thought you'd be rolling in here with five minutes to dress."

"I only do that at five o'clock in the morning. Where are

your minions we need to tire out?" I stand beside him. We're both wearing our team jackets and warm-up pants.

"Oh, they're here somewhere getting in everyone's way. See the kid running the clock for this game? That's the oldest, Kyle. He's fourteen. Rest up because they are ruthless."

"Gotcha."

"So, did you come up with a plan to help me win over Peyton?" he asks as he glances down at me.

I like standing beside him like this. He's moved close, our arms occasionally brushing, and it makes me feel protected. In a world that's a lightning storm, Jett Robitaille is a warm, dry house.

I can't look at him as I answer, so I keep my attention fixed on the game. "Well, I was thinking we could get Matt to clue her in on what a big deal the World Juniors is. Let her know you'll be on the NHL channel and everything. And then, if I wore your jersey to school one day, that might do it."

"Oh, now you want to put your scent on my clothes, like a cat."

"I really don't."

This is a lie. I never thought this was possible for me, but I'd like to be as ridiculous over him as he was at my game over me, even if that wasn't for real. Maybe not with an over-the-top sign like he made, but it would be cool to wear his jersey. There is something seriously wrong with me. I don't even know who I am anymore. If this is lovesickness, then I need some antibiotics.

"Make sure you wash it well," I say. I clear my throat, which is scratchy from my asthma.

Jett laughs. "Now I know why people use dating apps. Matchmakers are way too fussy."

"This whole charade was your idea, not mine."

"Okay, okay, Puck," he says, and turns and wraps me in his arms and sways us on the narrow bench. He smells so nice, like a citrus forest. For one brief instant, I let my head rest against his chest and breathe him in. He has no idea where you are supposed to draw lines. You should not be hugging your fake girlfriend just to thank her for helping you get the girl you really want. I need to give him a lecture on this. Soon.

"That means I should wear your jersey, too," he says.

Maybe it does. I hadn't thought that far.

I pull away, my arms resisting as if they are weighted in place, and the buzzer sounds to end the period.

Chapter 19

I Am the Hero of Meaningless Nothings

JETT WASN'T KIDDING THAT IT WOULD BE HARD TO TIRE OUT HIS host family's kids. By the time we get on the ice, it's seven-thirty, and these three Jett fans have no off button. You'd think they'd be tired after spending all weekend at the rink, especially since two of them played in the tournament.

It's just past nine-thirty when their parents finally come to gather them. Jett introduces me to his host parents, and they tell us not to forget to run the Zamboni and not to get hurt because they don't want to file an insurance claim and to be sure to lock up.

When they're finally gone, Jett looks at me. "Is it too bright in here?"

I nod. It's way too bright this late on a Sunday. When we skate in the mornings, we only ever use half the lights. I love a dark rink. It feels cozy, like a mountain lake below a warm chalet. Jett adjusts the lights. When he comes back, he puts on music, but softer than we usually skate to. "Let's just skate a few minutes," he says.

I fall in next to him and we glide along. He leans his head back. "This is so relaxing, isn't it?"

I laugh. It really is. Just the two of us, in this dimly lit rink, gliding along. No one making us run drills, or telling us what we should be doing, or yelling. But we're still skating. I think hockey players, and probably figure skaters, need the feel of the ice under them the way a mermaid needs the sea.

"I could do this for hours," he says. "It's as good as meditating."

I don't have my glove or blocker on, and Jett chucks his gloves into the net as we go by. Then he takes my hand.

"Do you know," he says, "that I took figure skating lessons for three years?"

"You did not."

"I did. I was sure it was going to help me be a better hockey player. I saw a show once about a wide receiver in the NFL who learned ballet to get better at leaping to catch balls. Figure skating helps a lot with edge work. I think that's why my edges are so good."

"Ah, so all those articles that said you're a natural skater don't know your secret."

Jett shakes his head and smiles. "So you've been reading all those articles about me, hmm?"

"Imani used to figure skate," I say without acknowledging

his comment. "I tried it with her, but I only got as far as a few little spins and jumps. It wasn't as heart-stopping as hockey."

Jett looks at me. "You want to?"

I sputter. "What?"

He goes to his phone and puts on some cheesy, inspirational tunes.

"Come on," he says, and he pulls me to center ice as if we are ice dancers. We must look ridiculous, trying to be graceful in our hockey gear, especially me, who looks like a stick figure someone stuck giant marshmallows on. But we hold hands and spin and laugh. We clown around and do awkward spins and bad, unchoreographed dance routines, and Jett even does some simple jumps. He's pretty graceful for a guy in hockey gear. Jett calls our moves as if he's a figure skating announcer.

"Vento and Robitaille will now do the camel spin," he says, and with my pads I can only raise my leg partway, but we're laughing so hard it doesn't matter.

"Drop to your knee," he says as the music swells, and we slide on one knee and then roll and jump up and he lifts me from behind and spins me as if we're some graceful figure skaters instead of two padded-up bruisers. He sets me down and grabs my hand and continues our improvised, clumsy ice dance for a few more songs. When one of them reaches its high point, we dive onto our knees and spin to a stop. We fall onto our backs and just lie there and catch our breath.

"I think we're ready for competition," he says as he rolls onto his side and looks at me.

I nod. "Definitely." We're both still panting. I start

coughing. Jett jumps up and skates over to where I keep my inhaler on the bench and grabs it. He brings it back to me and drops to his knees.

"I haven't laughed this hard in a long time," he says as I sit up and take a puff.

I haven't, either, which only occurs to me after he says it.

He waits for my wheezing to stop. "So, if you were a figure skater, what would you skate?"

I take a deep breath. "Pairs. For sure. And my partner would be tall, dark, and handsome." I smile, but then my face burns. I just described Jett.

Neither of us says anything as my brain freezes harder than the ice under us.

"Should we put in an hour and call it a night? It's already well past the start of my bedtime routine, and your asthma is in full swing." He gives me a clamped-lip smile.

I nod, and he gets up and gives me a hand, and we start to work for real. Jett sends me slap shots, comes in on breakaways and shoots high, and dangles the puck in cross-net moves until I'm so tired I can barely stand up. He stops every few minutes to check on me, but my breathing is clear even though it's heavy.

"I'm done," I say finally as I yank off my helmet and grab the water bottle on top of the net. My breath fogs in the cold air.

"Okay," he says as he pulls up right in front of me. "You deserve a tap out."

"Well, now I know what I owe you with your host family. You were right. They're a lot."

"I told you it was harder than it sounds," he says as he angles for whatever sympathy he can get.

"Imagine owning a rink, though," I say as I look around. "Every skating kid's dream."

"Ouais, if I ever make a lot of money in the NHL, the only ridiculous thing I want is to build a rink at my house."

"Ooooh, fancy," I say. "What's your model wife getting? A home photo studio? An indoor Zen garden?"

He laughs. "I think they all do Pilates. But that's not my type."

That's exactly his type, though. Peyton is the quintessential tall, Pilates-posing, fashion-setting California dream girl.

"Let's get out of here," I say.

"Do you want to drive the Zamboni?" he asks.

"I don't know how."

"It's easy. Come on, I'll show you."

I drive a Zamboni for the first time, while Jett moves the heavy nets for me, and then he jumps on to help me with it. It takes a couple of extra laps to get all the ice covered, but Jett praises me like I'm a little kid.

"You did an awesome job for your first time," he says as he helps me down from the giant ice-smoothing machine. I waddle and he strides into the lobby to go to our separate locker rooms.

Jett is waiting for me when I come out, and we turn out all

the lights and lock up, and he walks me to my car. The parking lot is empty, but well lit. The night is cold and windy.

"Text me when you get home safely," he says.

"Yes, Dad."

"No detours. It's a school night."

"I know, Dad." I throw my gear into my car. Considering how late it is, I'm not sure where I could detour to.

"You're in Boston this coming weekend, right?"

I have to think about it a moment. "Yes."

"There should be scouts there."

I nod. "Coach says several of the big D3s and at least four Ivies and UMass Amherst. Maybe Boston College or St. Cloud. It's a big draw weekend. Lots of pressure."

"I'll get us ice Tuesday and Thursday and have Dom come. No more clowning around."

He's trying to make sure I'm prepared.

"Okay. And on Wednesday, we'll wear each other's jerseys and put on a show for Peyton, after I have Matt talk you up."

We look at each other. It's a plan. I wish I felt happier about it.

Jett isn't smiling, either.

"It's late, Vento. Get home before your dad calls me."

"He doesn't have your number."

"Ouais, he does," Jett says.

"What? Why?"

"We're buds," Jett says, and he seems proud of this. "Lou is taking me to a batting cage when I get back from World Juniors. He's going to teach me to hit a baseball."

My mouth drops open. I think my dad always wanted a boy. Somehow, I can picture him and Jett hanging out while Jett dates Peyton. Never mind that I will have a broken heart. "So you two are on a first-name basis now?"

Jett smiles.

Oh brother. I open the car door and give him a vague wave.

"Night, Puck," Jett calls as he pivots with his bag and sticks and walks to his Impreza.

As I wait for my car to warm up, I wonder if things might have been different if I'd been nicer to Jett from the start. Maybe he wouldn't have even noticed Peyton then, although she's hard to miss. But it seems like it's Peyton's dad who should be making plans to take Jett to a batting cage. Instead, it's mine, because my dad, my sweet, innocent dad, has no idea that my entire relationship with Jett Robitaille is nothing but lies.

Chapter 20

Sometimes You Sow the Wrong Seed

MY GRANDMA VENTO IS A BIG GARDENER. EVERY SPRING, WE GO over to her house and help her clean up from the fall and get her yard ready for more flowers and herbs. And every year she says that, when she was young, she'd just throw any seeds into the ground and see what came up. But, over the years, she learned it's better to know what plants you are putting where so that you don't end up with tall plants in front of short ones, or get plants that take over, like forsythia and hellebores, or put plants that need sunlight in the shade and ones that need shade in the sun.

"Always know what you are planting before you cover the roots with soil," she says as we begin. "What you sow is what you grow."

I never really took in this advice too much. Not because

I don't like flowers, it's just that I've never been a gardening fan. I don't like the pressure of dirt under my fingernails, or mosquitos nipping me, or the sun beating me into a limp-noodle state. Plus, the humidity is as bad for my asthma as the cold is.

I'm starting to think, though, that my grandmother wasn't just talking about gardening. I thought I was sowing the right seed to train myself into a D1 goalie. Instead, I've sown an invasive weed called unrequited love. I guess this is my punishment for going along with this less-than-smart scheme. Now I get to sit on the bench and watch Jett skate off into the sunset with Peyton Malloy. I have no doubt that she'll find him irresistible, for now, once she sees me in his jersey and realizes what a big deal he is in the world of hockey, especially after the way she chased him out of the cafeteria the day the camera crew was there.

The redeeming element in all this is that I've only hurt myself, and Jett will get the attention of the girl he's been chasing, at least for as long as he can keep it. I'm thinking she'll stay with him through the NHL draft. She'll fill her Instagram with pictures of her and Jett. She never deletes the pictures of her old boyfriends. For Peyton, those photos are a scorecard, showing what she's capable of and what she's unafraid to leave behind for something she thinks is better. So I have no doubt that Peyton will be fine through all this. I don't think Jett is in love, so he should be okay, too, as long as he keeps it that way. Since I've gotten to know him, it seems weird that he'd want to date someone just because she's beautiful. That doesn't seem anything like the Jett I know. But guys are guys, I guess.

On Monday, I try to convince Matt to hype Jett up to Peyton over the World Juniors.

"Why do you want to get Peyton interested in your boyfriend, exactly?" he asks me.

I hadn't thought about this part.

Matt tilts his head at me, his curly dark hair messier than usual. "Ryleigh, are you trying to get back at Peyton by showing off your hotshot boyfriend? That doesn't seem like you."

"It's not that," I say, but I don't have a better answer for him. I stare at him, biting my lip, unable to figure out how to explain the mess I've made. I'm probably going to have to swallow my pride like a gallon of sour milk, but then the warning bell dings. Bless the warning bell. "We need to go. Just trust me, please? It's nothing bad against Peyton, I promise."

"Okay," Matt says, but with enough skepticism in his tone to let me know that, eventually, I'm going to have to explain this to him.

On Wednesday morning, I meet Jett at my locker before classes start so we can exchange our team colors.

"Thanks," I say as he hands me his black-and-orange Jr. Hat Tricks jersey.

"I hope it's not so big that it's a pain," he says.

I slip it on over my T-shirt, but as I raise my arms, Jett notices a bruise I have on my waist.

"Whoa, that's a shiner," he says. "Are you okay?"

I nod and pull his jersey down quickly. It hits me almost mid-thigh and the sleeves go at least five inches past my hands. "Just got clipped with the puck between my pads the other day."

"Here, let me help you," he says. I hold out my arms one at a time and he rolls the sleeves until my hands show. He pulls back and checks me out.

"You look really cute, Puck," he says with a big smile.

I can't hold his gaze, so I grab my jersey and hand it to him. "I hope it fits," he says. He raises his hands over his head to slip it on, and his T-shirt rides up and exposes a strip of his abs. I swallow as my stomach flip-flops. Then he pops his head out and shakes the jersey down. Even though I'm so much smaller, it fits reasonably well on him because it's big to fit over my chest pads, and goalie jerseys have large-cut sleeves to accommodate our arm padding.

"How's it look?" he asks as he pats the fabric into place. "Pretty cool, eh?"

I remind myself that this grin belongs to Peyton. That's what he's happy about. This jersey is going to make her so jealous that she'll finally lower her standards. I almost scoff. She might be Jett's equal in looks, but she's nowhere near the person he is. And her obsession with college guys is creepy.

"It looks good," I say, and force myself to put as much enthusiasm as I can into the words. "It will definitely work." At least that much I can say without showing how I really feel.

I get a lot of comments all morning about wearing Jett's jersey. Things like "Boy, you two went zero to sixty in six point two," or "Ooooh, Ryleigh, so much for your no-dating rule," or, my personal favorite, "Girl, you two hot enough to melt the Antarctic." Yep, I am never living this down if the truth gets out. Heck, even if it doesn't and everyone only thinks that Jett dumped me for Peyton, I am never living this down. I have already mentally scratched off ever going to a class reunion.

I try my hardest to be mature about it, though. The important thing is that I pay Jett back for everything he's done for me. He and Dom nearly killed me yesterday morning, but I feel myself getting stronger with every ice time we have. If I don't end up going D1, it won't be because Jett didn't try hard enough for me.

I am not so mature, however, that I don't get a stab of jealousy over Peyton when Jett meets me at the door to chemistry class. He peppers me with dimples like rapid machine-gun fire, and I regret all over again that I didn't realize just what I was doing when we started this ridiculous scheme.

"We seem to be the biggest event at this school since the Great Fire of '94," Jett says.

I laugh. The Great Fire wasn't really a great fire. It was just a bonfire where the student council tried to roast hot dogs, but the jocks took over and burned them all, which led to a legendary fight between the boys' football and basketball teams over whose fault it was.

"It's an exciting place," I say.

"Oooh, the matching lovebirds," Danny says as he strolls past us into class. Jett smiles and raises his eyebrows at how well this is going, and we take our seats. Our classmates aren't the only ones who notice our jersey shenanigans. Mr. G. also has his gaze fixed on us, more than usual. We've been keeping up with our labs, though, with the help of Danny when Jett is gone, and whichever girl wins the role when I'm absent. Danny told me it's a free-for-all as they compete to be Jett's helper. There's even a rumor that it wasn't an accidental tripping when one girl made a dash for Jett and another sent her flying into the plastic skeleton we call Mr. Withersby.

"Meanwhile, when my lab partner was sick a few weeks ago, all I got was you," Danny had added.

"You're welcome," I'd said.

Now, as the room whispers before the final bell about Jett and me wearing each other's jerseys, I have a sinking feeling that we should have taken them off for this class.

I write a quick note to Jett, who just shrugs.

Mr. G. doesn't say anything right away, but as he wanders around the classroom watching us do our labs, he stops when he's behind us as we stand at our table.

"Mizz Vento, you and Mr. Robitaille seem to be wearing the wrong shirts," he says.

I laugh awkwardly and hope he'll just leave it at that sad joke.

"Mr. Robitaille, you are quite the modern man," he adds.

"In my day, none of us would have been caught dead wearing a shirt from our girlfriend. I guess it's a good thing Mizz Vento isn't on the cheer squad."

Jett turns to look Mr. G. in the eye, although he's still looking down at him. "I wouldn't fit in her uniform, then, Mr. Polachuk, but I wouldn't be ashamed to wear it if I could. Mizz Vento would be just as cool if she were a cheerleader. Besides, while I think hockey is the coolest sport because I love it, that doesn't make any other sport less respectable. There's nothing demeaning about being a cheerleader."

The whole class erupts into "Ooohs," and a few girls on the basketball and cheer teams clap and yell, "Hear, hear!" and "Go, Jett!"

Mr. G. is only about five feet nine, so he stares up at Jett. It could be a scene from an old John Hughes movie, except that Jett isn't the misogynist I once thought he was, but Mr. G. is the misogynist I always thought he was. My heart is pounding as I wonder how much of Jett's speech was meant to protect me, and how much was meant to protect Peyton's cheerleading prowess.

Then Mr. G. blinks. He turns and walks to the next table. "Settle down," he tells everyone. "I forgot how woke your generation is."

Our classmates send furtive glances around the room as we snicker over Mr. G.'s clueless attempt to embarrass Jett and me. Still, you'd think a science teacher wouldn't be so Middle Ages.

"He's such a—" Jett whispers, but I cut him off.

“Shhhh,” I whisper back. I really don’t want Jett pulling detention. For a lot of reasons, but especially not in some sweet but doomed-to-fail mission to bring Mr. G. into the twenty-first century.

After class, Jett walks me to calculus.

“Don’t let that guy bug you,” he says.

I glance up. “I won’t.” Mr. G. isn’t nearly as big of a problem as trying to win over the girl I don’t like for the guy I do.

Jett studies me, but he doesn’t say anything else.

“I’ll see you at lunch,” he says as he squeezes my hand before he lets it go.

I nod and start walking into calc.

“Hey, Vento,” he says, so I turn.

“Yes?”

He gives me his full dimple smile. “You slay in that jersey.” He blows me an air kiss and takes off running for his English class before the bell rings.

He bobs and weaves through the crowd of kids in the hallway. I blink back some tears. I never in my life thought I’d wish to be Peyton Malloy. That’s not it exactly, though. What I’m wishing for right now is a little magic to change Jett’s heart.

Chapter 21

Best-Laid Plans

WHEN JETT AND I ROLL INTO THE CAFETERIA IN OUR HIS-AND-hers jerseys, there's almost as much commotion as there was the day the camera crew followed Jett around. "Woo-hoo, Jett and Ryleigh!" people say, and "Jayleigh in the house." None of it fazes Jett. For just a moment, it's like seeing a premonition of the future, Jett walking into an NHL arena while cameras swirl around him.

I don't look directly at Peyton's table, but I have her in my peripheral vision. She is spending her undivided attention on my fake boyfriend.

Jett tugs me in so he can whisper, "Don't get ketchup on my jersey, Vento."

I laugh as his eyes smile at me.

"Why am I suddenly craving fries?" I say, and look wistfully at the lunch line.

"No, no, no," he says, "I was kidding. Just eat your healthy lunch!"

I turn and pretend I'm heading to the food counter. Jett grabs my waist and pulls me back so quickly that I skid into him, and we go off balance for a second. He wraps his arms around me as we teeter before he steadies us. The whole cafeteria is whistling and banging on the tables.

"Kiss her," someone says.

Our gazes are locked. He looks like he wants to kiss me. That can't be, but still, it feels like it. Or maybe it's because I want to kiss him so much. The moment stretches out, as if time has slowed. Jett doesn't look away. Just like we're in a shoot-out, he seems to be challenging me.

My brain shuts down. I raise myself on tiptoe and I kiss Jett Robitaille, while the kids in the cafeteria meet the full tilt of my carnival-ready heart with their whooping and clapping.

I have no idea how long my lips are on Jett's. It feels like a long time, and yet impossibly only an instant, too. His hand is on the small of my back. His lips are soft, and sweet like fruit-flavored candy chews. And I have officially lost my mind.

I pull away, my face burning. I can't look at him. I stand there, completely paralyzed with shame.

Jett turns and tows me to our table as the cafeteria falls silent. I can't look at anyone. Why are they so quiet? It's what they wanted. If that display doesn't win Peyton over for Jett, nothing will. That's what I'll tell him as soon as I can. I only hope he believes me.

We slide into our places, and I pull out my phone. I text him.

I'm sorry. I just thought it would make Peyton jealous. I didn't mean to do that.

I don't even know what I'm typing.

"You two really put on a show," Imani says. "And I was worried that my little Ryebird would never date again!"

I look up as I hit send and shake my head slightly. The distress on my face must register because she stops laughing. Jett digs his phone from his pocket.

The table gets quiet. I've never felt so awkward in my whole life.

Jett puts his phone away and slips his hand down to rest on my leg. What does that mean? It's okay that I just made a fool of myself, or he believes that my kiss was all in the name of making Peyton jealous? His other hand plops a chocolate protein shake beside my lunch. My heart is pounding so fast that I can't imagine choking down lunch right now. My stomach is spiraling like that ride at the amusement park where the cars go up in the air and spin in loops.

Imani clears her throat. I look up at her.

"Again?" Jett asks. "You'll have to fill me in on all her previous boyfriends."

Imani glances at me. My face feels frozen.

"Hey, you guys," she says as she throws her gaze around the table to make sure everyone is paying attention, "did you watch that latest episode of *The Voice*?"

One of the girls at our table is a die-hard fan. "That guy was unbelievable, wasn't he?" She loves when we dish *The Voice* with her.

"Oh my God, when he hit that high note," Imani says, shaking her head in admiration.

"Was that the guy with the tattoo on his neck?" Lewis asks. He feeds Imani a cucumber from his lunch sandwich.

I tap Imani's leg under the table to tell her thank you and she smiles at me. I am not going to get out of an explanation later, though. Maybe I should just tell her the truth. This seems especially prudent as I catch sight of Peyton heading straight for us like an iceberg looking for a cruise ship to sink.

Beside me, Jett has unpacked his perfectly balanced lunch. He's eating, but slower than usual, or so it seems. He must be shocked that I'd go this far to help him win Peyton over. Or maybe he's wondering if I've become one of his many admirers.

Peyton stops at the head of the table, next to Jett. The conversation dies and everyone looks at her. She's wearing a lime-colored cropped T-shirt and black leggings, her blond hair in a ponytail. She looks like she just left a photo shoot for an athletic clothing brand. I look like a short girl in a ridiculously oversized hockey jersey that smells as if it's been put through the washer three times to make it finally smell almost like detergent.

She smiles at Jett, her lips shimmering from wet lip gloss.

"Can we help you?" Imani says.

I send her a quick glare to tell her to stop.

"Jett, you got Ryleigh to give up her no-dating rule. I'm impressed."

Jett chuckles, but he doesn't take his hand off my thigh.

I should say something. Something smart and savvy to make her want Jett more. But my mind feels stuck, like a car that can't change gears.

"You'd look a lot better in his jersey than I do," I say.

Everyone stares at me, even Jett.

Peyton sputters a laugh. She probably thinks I'm trying to set a trap for her. But I'm not that strategic. Clearly.

"I just mean, you know, that you're tall and—" I look down at myself, swimming in Jett's jersey. Peyton smiles and shrugs her eyebrows.

"It's not really your look," she says, trying her hardest to pretend she means this nicely.

"She's rocking Jett's jersey," Imani says. Lewis elbows her to calm her down. This isn't going at all the way it's supposed to. I'm making Imani mad for me, and my eyes are getting that prickly feeling before you cry.

"I like it," Jett says, so firmly that I glance up. His gaze is settled on me like a raft I can grab on to. I'm barely treading water, but I have to do what I promised.

I nudge Jett's knee with mine. He needs to help me out here. I can't give him any more help than I am. Not without destroying whatever shred of self-respect I still have, not to mention my heart.

"You guys should come to the football game this weekend," Peyton says. She leans her hands on the table so that she's slightly bent over, well aware this makes her bustline bulge right in Jett's face and her butt stick out like a balance ball. I don't know whether to feel grossed out or sorry for her for trying so hard. "It's our big rivalry game of the season, and the cheer squad has a surprise you won't want to miss. We're going all out before playoffs." She smiles at each of us as if she's an ambassador.

Matt mumbles something about going as I say, "I'll be in Boston this weekend, but Jett could come."

"I can?" He swings his gaze from Peyton to me.

"You don't have games on Friday."

"I have practice, though."

"You'll probably miss the first quarter, but you could make the rest of it."

"Come on, Jett," Peyton says, "you're going to love American football. After the game, we're all going for pizza. You're welcome to come. If Ryleigh will let you, that is. You aren't worried, are you, Rye?"

Imani is staring at me. Even Lewis is watching me with his brows crinkled together. Everyone else at the table has suspended their lunch as they watch this train wreck happening in real time. Matt is beside me, so I don't have to deal with whatever face he's making.

"You should go," I say without looking at Jett. "How many senior years do you get? Especially in a foreign country." I take a bite of food to show how unconcerned I am in the whole thing, but it's hard to chew. It's like the sandwich has turned into a wad of paper in my mouth.

"Sorry," Jett tells Peyton. "After practice, I'll be watching Ryleigh's game online."

I cough as some food goes down the wrong pipe. Jett slips his hand from my leg and gently hits my back.

"Are you all right?" he asks.

What just happened here? I literally sacrificed for him, body and soul, and he passed? And now I'm going to have Imani and everyone all over me about it.

I nod to let Jett know I'm okay and grab my water bottle.

"That's too bad." Peyton gives Jett a pouty look, as if he's been completely taken in by me.

"Maybe some other time," Jett says with his dimpled smile. Wait, is he playing hard to get? With Peyton? Whoa, he really is next-level. I can't even imagine walking through life with that much confidence. Although I've never had a guy flaunt his biceps in front of me the way Peyton just flashed Jett her C cups.

Peyton shrugs and gives me a snarky little smile before she takes off back to the cheerleader table, surrounded by the jocks from the football and boys' basketball teams.

When I pull my attention away from Peyton's sashay to her home base, Imani is studying me. In fact, everyone is studying me. Except Jett.

I look down and start attacking my lunch. The period is almost over, and I haven't even cracked the protein shake open. As I munch away silently, choking food down as if I'm starving when my stomach feels like there are rocks in it, the rest of the table falls into their usual chatter. But their gazes keep wandering over me as if they are trying to figure out what creature is possessing me right now.

I should tell them to let me know if they figure it out, because I also have no idea who I am anymore. I'm a girl who swore off dating, who ended up with a fake boyfriend and fell for said fake boyfriend like a building imploding, and who is now trying to push said fake boyfriend out of the fake nest and into the arms of the person she likes least in the world. If that doesn't qualify me for the most ridiculous person in my school, or even in the state of Connecticut, then I can't imagine how much more ridiculous my competition is.

I thought hockey was a tough sport, but it has nothing on the game of love. I don't know if I'm supposed to be guarding my net, shooting on Jett, or taking one for the team. Meanwhile, Jett Robitaille's hand is back on my thigh as I gulp down the last of the chocolate protein shake that he brings me every day, and it's hard to even breathe.

Chapter 22

How Weird Can It Get?

JETT AND I WALK OUT OF THE CAFETERIA AS IF EVERYTHING IS PERfectly normal, but I don't think either of us believes that. Or maybe I am completely imagining how weird it is between us because I am, in fact, a weirdo.

He holds my hand until the hallway intersects, and then we break apart, like we always do. I won't see him again today since he leaves early to go to the gym. The school counts it as his phys ed class.

"I'll text you later." He's standing close to me and looks down like a tall pine tree.

"Oh, okay," I say, in my genius way with words.

He pecks me on the cheek and squeezes my hand before he drops it.

I immediately turn and head for my next class. Imani comes out of nowhere.

"What is going on?" Her dark eyes are lit like a fire.

"Nothing."

She tilts her head. "Ryleigh, you have been acting weirder than usual lately. And you just encouraged your boyfriend to hang out with Peyton? Even if she weren't your rival, that's cursed."

"She is not my rival," I say. "Peyton and apparently you now are the only people who think we have a rivalry going."

"Right," Imani says.

I let out a breath and stop a moment. "It's complicated," I say. "I'll explain it to you, but not at school, okay?" I look around for confirmation that no one else is within hearing distance.

Her eyebrows raise. "I'll video-chat you later."

"I have practice tonight."

"Nice try. That was last night. You don't have it until tomorrow."

Damn, I need to stop telling people my schedule changes. "Oh, right."

The warning bell rings.

"Later," she says in a tone that sounds just like the warning bell.

I nod. "Later."

When I get home, I take Harps to soccer practice. Then we have dinner, and I work on my homework. I need to get ahead in math so that I don't have to worry about it over the weekend, otherwise it feels too overwhelming with travel. I'm sitting on my bedroom floor working, but I've only managed to get halfway through the next assignment due when Imani calls.

In typical Imani fashion, she goes straight for my jugular. "What in the name of names that can't be named is going on with you and Jett?"

I don't know how to even begin to explain this.

"Ryleigh Vento."

I bobble my head. "That is my name."

"Okay, you are scaring me now."

I puff out my cheeks as I exhale. "Same."

"Girl, what have you done?" Her tone shifts from demanding to worried.

"Okay, just don't flip out on me, all right?"

"Ryebird!"

I spill it all out in a word taco that takes my breath and leaves a mess everywhere. By the time I stop, Imani is staring at me with her mouth open, as if I'm a stranger who's regurgitating a complete life history that's way too much information to tell someone you don't know. She blinks several times, and once she opens her mouth to say something, but no words come out.

"Can you please say something?" I ask.

She blinks again.

I've done the impossible. I've made Imani speechless. This is how I know it's worse than I realized.

"And you really like him that much?"

I nod as a tear hits my cheek.

"Well then, forget about Peyton. It's not like she wants him for him. She's just showing Jett attention because it would get her attention."

"That would be a great plan if Jett liked me instead. But he's still all systems go for her."

Imani shakes her head. "I don't get him. He doesn't seem like the shallow type."

He doesn't. And yet, he is. "Maybe it's just a guy thing. Maybe they are all shallow."

"All but Lewis," she corrects me.

I close my eyes and nod. "All but Lewis."

Imani is biting her lip, her eyebrows scrunched together. It's her thinking face. "Are you sure he doesn't like you? He sure puts on a convincing act. And he didn't even bite at Peyton's invitation."

"I'm sure. I think he's playing hard to get."

"Whoa. Next-level. Still, that kiss today in the cafeteria, he was totally into that."

Our eyes meet. I really, really want to believe her. "I mean, just because he doesn't find kissing me repulsive doesn't mean he likes me. It's still Peyton he's doing all this for. And I was the one who kissed him, anyway. He just went along with it."

"Girl, I was so surprised at you. But in a good way."

I groan. "Oh God, when he starts dating Peyton, the whole school is going to think I got dumped. After that display, I should wear a paper bag over my head the rest of the year."

Imani laughs. "I'll put a blond wig on it and lots of blue eye shadow over the eyes."

I laugh a little.

"This," she says, "is the craziest thing you have ever done. But it's not as much of a disaster as you think."

"Right. How so?"

"Broken hearts mend. In the meantime, you said he's helped you with hockey. Maybe at your games this weekend you'll get scouted."

"I hope so. If I've ripped my heart to shreds and embarrassed myself eternally for nothing, I'm really going to hate myself."

"If that happens, I give you permission to sulk for at least two weeks. Then I want you out there finding another Jett Robitaille before prom."

I snort. "There is not another Jett Robitaille out there. Trust me. He is one of a kind."

"Wow. You really do have it bad. I wouldn't even say that about Lewis, and we've been dating for almost two years."

"Mans, what am I going to do?" I lean my head against my dresser and bang it gently.

"You only have two choices."

I look at her. "Which are?"

"Either you pretend like you don't care in the slightest that he's a shallow, Peyton-chasing scuzzball with impeccable hair and a smile that could melt the Arctic, or you let him know that you like him and see what happens."

I shake my head. "No, it's bad enough that the whole school is going to think that Jett dumped me for Peyton. The only things worse would be if everyone knew the truth, or if Jett found out how I feel and didn't feel the same. God, what if he told Peyton that I tried to sabotage them? The two of them laughing at me might kill me."

"What if, and I'm only saying if, he said he likes you, too? I mean, you two have spent a lot of time together. Maybe he's changed his mind and is afraid to tell you because of your no-dating rule."

I think about this. It seems too good to be true, though.

"I don't know," I say.

"Well, Rye, only you can decide if he means enough to you to take the chance. A little eternal shame isn't such a big price to pay for a guy you are this gaga over. And Peyton already despises you. Who cares if she thinks you fell for Jett while using him to get better at hockey? Love happens."

"You're just saying that because you aren't the one who will have to suffer the eternal shame."

Imani laughs. "Maybe. Although, as the best friend of the eternal shame sufferer, I will have my share of eternal shame to carry on your behalf."

"Imagine how many people you would want to beat up for trashing me over it."

We laugh.

"Sleep on it," she says. "But you are going to have to decide pretty soon if you are putting on your big-girl pants and fighting for Jett or if you're just going to let Peyton swoop in and take him." She leans in toward the phone camera and wiggles her shoulders to mimic Peyton flashing Jett.

She's taunting me. She wants me to fight for him.

"I need to get ready for bed," I say. "Jett got us ice tomorrow morning."

Imani purses her lips in a silent whistle.

I make a face at her.

"Okay, okay," she says. "Keep me posted. And, Rye, I'm really proud of you for doing something so colossally immature before you graduate. Just don't do anything like this again. I don't think my heart can take it."

"Mine either. Good night," I say, and click on the X to end the call.

My phone lights up with a text from Imani. Good night, Ice Queen.

Before I can even go brush my teeth, my phone dings again. I wish Imani had an off button. But when I look at my phone, it's Jett.

Are you okay?

I stare at the message. Yes, why?

You seemed not quite yourself today.

Oh, you mean like when I threw myself at you in the middle of the cafeteria? I don't type this, obviously.

I was just afraid that I made things awkward between us.

Jett doesn't reply right away. I wait for the dots to jump. It seems like it takes a very long time.

Not possible, he writes.

I mark his text with a heart. And then I get ready for bed so that I can spend a restless night wondering if I'm willing to put everything on the line for the fake boyfriend I didn't even want, but who, against all odds, has stolen my heart.

Chapter 23

No Pain, No Gain

IMANI WANTS ME TO BE BRAVE, BUT IF I GET REJECTED, EVEN IF Jett and Dom still help me, these morning sessions are going to be unbearably awkward. I can't imagine skating together in all that weirdness. Jett would probably feel bad about making me help him if he knew I was crushing on him hard enough to break my rule. It would be easier to just stop helping me. But if I don't tell him now, I may never get another chance.

I feel like I'm in game seven of the Stanley Cup playoffs, and I have a shot to make a goal on the other team from all the way across the ice, but I could also come out of my net too far and end up losing everything.

This is all my fault. I made a good rule. I should have followed it.

Jett pulls into the lot as I put my car into park. There's no sign of Dom yet. It would be better to shatter my heart after practice, not before. If I can't keep it together, Dom is sure to start asking questions. But Jett and I don't see each other alone after practice. I don't think I could tell him how I really feel on the phone.

I push the button to open the hatch and hop out. Just like in a game, I'll have to see how it plays out.

"Did you sleep here, Vento?" Jett asks as he climbs out of the Impreza.

"Very funny. I just wanted to make the most of the time we have." This is more true than it should be, just not only on the ice.

We grab our bags and head into the rink. Jett has a set of keys to unlock the sliding glass doors.

I try to think of something to talk about, but I'm so nervous that my brain is moving in slow motion. The rink is extra cold. When I get to the locker room, my gear is still damp from my last practice. I should have taken it into the house and spread it out to make sure it dried. There's nothing worse than putting on wet gear when you're already cold. But I'll be sweating again soon enough once Jett and Dom start putting me through their hockey camp.

Jett is already on the ice when I come out of the locker room. Everyone can dress faster than a goalie, because of all the buckled straps on our leg pads.

"Where's Dom?" I ask when I step onto the ice.

"He said he's going to be late, but I told him to make sure he hurries since you have that showcase this weekend."

I nod. "Thanks."

Jett skates up and stops beside me so that our shoulders are aligned but we're facing each other. When I look up, he's smiling.

"You're going to crush it this weekend. I just know it."

It takes me a moment. "I owe you and Dom a lot."

"Non. You are really good, Puck. It's just because you got jerked around last year instead of getting the support you should have that you don't believe in yourself."

Why does he have to believe in me so much?

"Can I tell you something?" he asks as I start moving forward, and he keeps beside me by skating backward.

"Hmm?"

"This, here with you, just the two of us, is my favorite thing about this whole year."

My heart melts so much that I don't know how it's anything but a puddle.

"You haven't gone to World Juniors yet," I say. "Or been drafted."

Jett stops, so I do, too. He just looks at me, no smile on his face. After what feels like minutes, he finally speaks. "You were supposed to say 'Same.' "

I bite my lip and search his eyes.

"Same," I whisper.

Jett pulls off my glove and slips his hand into mine. It's

warm, his palms calloused from so much stick handling. He turns without looking at me and tows me gently. The feel of his hand around mine makes it hard to breathe. Side by side we glide, only the slice of our blades on the clean ice making any sound. My heart is beating as fast as a racehorse's, though, and my brain is on fire. This is my chance. Whether I soar or crash to the ground, this is the time to ask if he's no longer interested in Peyton.

"So," I say. But before I can say another word, we hear a loud "Ahem" from behind us. We both turn.

Dom has arrived.

The closest I come to seeing Jett alone again is in chemistry class. I'm leaving school right before lunch for my hockey trip.

Jett spends most of the period fidgeting, which isn't like him. I'd like to think it's me who is making him jittery, although it could just be how much he has to do before he leaves for World Juniors. I force myself to concentrate on how to balance net ionic equations, but my mind keeps wandering to this morning, and one simple word. "Same."

We're almost at the end of class when Jett leans over to write on my notebook while Mr. G. has his back to us as he scribbles on the board.

Ryleigh, Jett writes, *will you be my girlfriend? For real this time?*

My eyes widen, and I glance at him. It's the first time I've seen him nervous. His eyes are so dark, they're like endless caverns you could get lost inside. Somewhere far away, Mr. G.'s voice is droning on about solubility rules.

What about Peyton? I write underneath.

Jett shakes his head at me, as if that's not even a possibility. Maybe he tried and got definitively rejected.

"Mizz Vento. Mr. Robitaille. Are you with us today? Or has planet Ice Hockey frozen your brains?"

Jett and I turn to look at Mr. G.

"No, Mr. Polachuk," we say in unison.

He tilts his head and nods slightly, but he spends the rest of the period staring at us to make sure we are laser focused on him. Which I guess is good because it's the only way I remember to take any notes, and I don't dare do anything else. The last thing I need is for Mr. G. to walk over here and look at my notebook. He would read what Jett and I wrote in the margins out loud to everyone.

When the bell finally rings, Jett and I pack up our things and scurry out together. But once we reach the hallway, Jett slips his hand around my wrist and stops me.

He raises his eyebrows to ask me again.

I nod. I can't even smile because I'm so nervous. But Jett smiles enough for both of us.

My brain is completely blank, and maybe Jett's is, too, because he doesn't say anything on our way down the hall. He doesn't even chatter like he usually does at my locker when I switch my books out. He takes my backpack and slings it over his shoulder as he walks me to calc, our fingers interlaced the way they always are, but it feels different now, as if his hand really belongs in mine.

It's not like I stole Jett from Peyton, since she doesn't even know that he wanted her instead of me. Her interest may be piqued because she thinks Jett is something to take away from me and because she's realized what a big deal he is in hockey, but otherwise, she wasn't interested in him. You can't miss what you never thought about having in the first place.

When we reach my calc class, Jett hands over my back-pack.

"Let me know when you get to Boston," he says. "I probably won't be able to reply right away, though, because of practice. Coach says we are going over the whiteboard after. He wants to try some new plays in tomorrow's practice."

I nod.

"And maybe we can watch a movie together this weekend."

"I won't be home until pretty late on Sunday."

"I mean together apart. You know, we could video-chat as we watch it. Whatever kind of movie you like. I'm not picky about movies."

I smile.

"And maybe we could—" Jett gets interrupted by the warning bell.

He leans down and kisses me, his lips softly pressing mine. Then he starts running down the hall. "Brick wall in

Beantown, Goalie Girl!" he calls, half turned and almost tripping into the wall.

I stay a moment to watch as he dodges and weaves, telling people "Pardon moi" as he goes. And all at once I find myself grateful to Peyton Malloy, petty rival or not, for her nonsensical decision to only date college guys.

Chapter 24

A New Period

I DIDN'T KNOW I WAS CAPABLE OF FEELING THIS WOOZY ABOUT anything. Or anyone. But the rest of the day seems to float by me, as if it's in another dimension and I'm just orbiting it from outer space. I leave school early, after finding two chocolate protein shakes waiting for me in my locker, and get to the rink in plenty of time to board the bus.

My parents wanted to come on this trip, but I convinced my dad that my mom shouldn't be running around to rinks this close to the holidays, so they're spending the weekend getting the Christmas tree.

"I know that's your favorite part of Christmas preparation," my mom had told me when we talked about the trip. "We can wait and get the tree next weekend."

Even though I hate missing out on tree selection and

decorating, my mom has too much to do with shopping and baking and decorating to lose a weekend to my travel games. If she hadn't been sick, then I wouldn't worry. But she's still so frail. I haven't been much help with all the extra rink time I've been putting in with Jett and Dom. Usually she and I bake cookies every December weekend in between home games. But I've been catching up on sleep and homework then.

I text Harper. Please help Mom with the chores this weekend.

You are such a nag, she replies.

I know. Just do it so I don't have to beat you up when I get home.

Harper knows it's an empty threat. My parents would never condone violence. Plus, I'm not the violent type and Harps is bigger than me. But it lets her know that I'm serious that she needs to help Mom.

Yes, Sister Mary Magdalene.

Whenever Harper refers to me by the nun name she's bestowed on me, it means I've won. I mark her text with a thumbs-up even though it makes me want to kick a soccer ball into her stomach. It's not like I enjoy being a nag. But if I weren't, she'd sit in her room all day watching sports while our mom runs around getting ready for the holidays.

"Are you ready, Ryleigh?" Coach Kaitlyn says as we stow our bags in the baggage compartment.

"Yes, Coach, I've been working hard."

"Alana told me you've been practicing with some of the

boys from the Jr. Hat Tricks." Her blond ponytail swings as she motions for Nina to step forward to put her gear in the bus.

I nod. "They've helped me a lot." I really hope Alana didn't tell her one of them is my boyfriend. I don't want anyone thinking I'm just using Jett. I mean, I was, but it was an even trade, although no one can know that part.

"I like your initiative," she says, and pats me on the shoulder to dismiss me onto the bus.

I slide into a window seat, and Emma, my travel roommate, sits next to me. She grins. She loves away hockey.

"So," she says, "how's the hot BF?"

Before-Jett-and-I-were-for-real me would be extremely annoyed now. After-Jett-and-I-are-for-real me smiles like a five-year-old going to the amusement park.

"He's fine."

"Rye, that was seriously the dorkiest sign I have ever seen," she says, and shakes her head. "But somehow, when you saw the guy holding it, he totally pulled it off. Mad respect."

I laugh. I don't think Jett would care if someone thought he was dorky. At least not someone he didn't know. But maybe when you can pull off the impossible, you don't need to care as much about what other people think.

I dig out my homework and get started. I can't stand to have it hanging over my head. Emma is asleep like a sloth on antihistamines by the time we reach the interstate. A half hour later, Jett sends me a text that's a GIF about champions.

Heading into the gym. I'll text you after practice. He adds a heart emoji with Cupid's arrow. Before me would have said he was being slick. After me says he's just Jett being Jett. He makes people happy just by being him, the way the North Star makes you happy you stopped to look at the night sky.

I mark his text with a heart. I want to message him back, but I should be responsible. He needs to focus on his workout, not on talking to me. And I need to focus on homework. We can't let our feelings distract us from our goals. Not when we are this close. NHL teams are watching what he does to decide if they will draft him and in what round, and I need to get my slot. Then we can make time for us.

I slog through my homework, only checking my phone every half hour or so. But Jett is still as disciplined as always. I don't know if that should make me happy or sad. Would he be this strict with his time if I were Peyton? But that's just being petty. If Jett wanted to keep chasing her, then he would. Even if she shut him down, I don't think he'd turn to me as second best. Not after what his mom said about him never dating before. Unless he has and just didn't tell his mom about it. It would be easy to hide things from your parents if you were living in a different city. But then why would he have told her so much about me when I wasn't even his real girlfriend?

I sigh and look out the window as the trees slip by. I need to spend more time manifesting good things instead of dwelling on the possible negatives of every situation. Reconciling the Jett I know who is capable of scheming with the Jett I know who is about family and doing the right things isn't as easy as I thought it would be when I said yes, though.

Maybe I'm just too used to getting ready for the next

catastrophe. When my mom was sick, I tried to be positive, but everything kept getting worse for such a long time that I had pretty much given up on it ever getting better. People told me how brave I was because I was going forward, but I didn't feel brave. I was a train moving along the tracks it was stuck to. I got up every morning because there really wasn't another choice. The people I love needed me. I did the laundry and made sure Harper and London got fed and to school and to soccer and piano and dance and I reminded my dad which bills needed to be paid and picked up my mom's prescriptions and the groceries because my mom couldn't. I cleaned the house and made sure she had fresh sheets to come home to from the hospital and made sure my sisters had done their homework. But all around me, my life was crashing out. My mom got sicker before she got better. Every day at hockey, Coach Blackmon was nastier to me and the other girls he targeted. I felt totally overwhelmed trying to be my mom's substitute in our family. And I was terrified it might become forever. So everything I'm feeling now is probably me not knowing how to enjoy the good things when they come along. Even though Jett's been showing me since he showed up in my life.

My phone pings with a text. It's my mom.

Are you getting your homework done? Don't forget to sleep as much as you can. And make sure you eat some veggies, even if it's just on a sub sandwich. I put strawberries and kiwi in a container in your bag and those Korean BBQ chickpea snacks you like.

I smile.

Stop feeling guilty about not coming. I'm fine.

I don't mention that Jett has already loaded me up with protein shakes.

I know you're going to play great this weekend! I'm so proud of you no matter what, though. This is followed by a string of emoji. Sometimes my mom and I have entire conversations in emoji.

I know.

We miss you. Don't forget to tell us if your game times change.

Okay.

Love you.

Love you more.

Love you most.

She always wins. But I do think moms probably love the most.

We get to Boston and check into our hotel and grab a team dinner at a pizza-and-pasta place. Then we head to the rink for our first game at nine. I'm scheduled to play tomorrow morning. I hate when we have late games and then early ones the next morning, but it's the luck of the draw.

After warm-ups, we go to our locker room to dress. Everyone is hyped. This weekend is important to more than just me. Everyone wants to go to nationals at the end of the season, and these games count toward it. And almost the whole team wants to keep playing in college at some level. So even the girls who are already committed are locked in. We take turns choosing our pregame playlists. Today is Emma's turn. She has us listening to eighties hard rock and metal like Rush and Iron Maiden. It's not really my thing, so after I get dressed, I grab my phone and headphones and go watch the game on the sheet we will be on. We're the first game of the tournament, so the current game is just a kids' scrimmage, but it's funny to watch how slow they are and try to remember being like that. I'm standing along the boards by myself.

My phone dings. It's Jett.

Good luck tonight.

I'm not playing until tomorrow. But thanks. And for the protein shakes.

I'll watch just in case.

You don't have to. Just get your homework done.

I can do both.

Oh, a new superhero. Everything Man.

Funny. I'll pay more attention to my homework than the game unless you get called in. Then I'll be cheering for you.

Hailey is solid. I won't be going in.

Well, just in case, I'll keep it on in the background.

Just like my parents. They watch even the games I'm not scheduled to play "just in case."

Suit yourself. Just make sure you do chemistry because I'm going to need help with it.

No worries. I can go over it with you when you get home.

One of our assistant coaches comes by and taps me to tell me it's time to go back to the locker room for our coaches' instructions. I nod and follow her.

Gotta go.

Bon chance.

I smile and pull out my headphones and go into the locker room.

"We've seen this team before, so we know what to expect," Coach says. "Keep your passes tight, heads up. Emma, and the rest of you, I don't want any unnecessary penalties, got it?"

We all nod in unison.

"You've been working hard and improving every week. I'm really proud of you. Remember to play as a team, finish every shift, and keep the crease clear. All right, let's hit it!"

The game goes well. I pay attention, because it's my job, but I also let my mind wander to its new favorite topic, Jett Robitaille. My dad always says there's nothing worse than a convert of any kind, whether it's someone who finds religion or stops smoking or drinking. I guess it's true, because I never pictured myself being this gone for a guy, especially not Jett. But my brain has everything about him on repeat like a new favorite song.

I don't even see the puck that Hailey takes to the head. All I see is her down on the ice and our teammates calling for the EMT. I look up at the scoreboard. Sixteen minutes left in the second period. Nina comes over and tells the coaches what's going on.

"She got her bell rung," she says.

I'm worried about Hailey, and I'm worried about how little attention I've been paying. After a few tense minutes, Hailey gets up, and the EMT and Emma help her to the bench. We bang our sticks against the boards to show support. I'm not sure which of their forwards are hot today. What plays have they been trying? And who just clocked Hailey? She's not an easy goalie to hit in the head. Maybe it was deflected?

"Ryleigh, go!" Coach Kaitlyn yells, which shakes me out of my stupor. I jump through the open door to the ice and head for the net.

Just like that, Hailey is out for a concussion-protocol check, and I'm playing.

Chapter 25

Showtime

MY MIND IS MOVING AT THE SPEED OF A SPACE SHUTTLE. I DON'T think Hailey is that hurt because I heard her talking as they brought her to the bench, and she sounded coherent. Her speech wasn't slurred, and she knew what was happening. I should have been paying attention. Wait, which of their players shoot left? Twenty-Three does, but I think there's another. Jett is watching, so I can't go down in flames. Not to mention my family, Coach, and who knows how many scouts who have come to our game. Oh, and my favorite person, Coach Blackmon, has just walked into the rink. I had almost forgotten my old team is playing in this tournament, too. As I scrape the net clean with my stick blade, I see a scout from Hamilton who's been to some of our games talking to a lady wearing a University of Maine jacket.

It's not like I haven't been called in partway through a game before, but this feels bigger than it ever has. So much is riding on this. My future college, Jett's respect for me, my own self-respect. I take a deep breath. *Get it together, Ryleigh.*

The puck drops in my zone. The other team has taken a penalty for roughing our goalie in the scrum that followed Hailey's drop to the ice, so that helps, but it would be less pressure if we were in their end zone or already losing instead of winning.

I make the first save, then the second, and then we take it back to their zone. The pace is ferocious. I don't get a break the rest of the game unless there's a stop in play, and then I'm sucking in air and water as fast as I can before it starts back up. I'm so locked in that I can't think about anything except what's going on in front of me. But my team does a great job of blocking their shots and I don't give up any goals.

Even in the last minute, I don't really get a break until the final twelve seconds of the game, when we're solidly in their zone and tying up the puck against the boards. Still, it's only a one-point game, so I never take my eyes off the action after I check the time.

The buzzer rings and my teammates on the ice fly down to surround me. They tap their gloves on my helmet and yell about what a great job I did filling in, and I feel it deep inside me. This was the first solid game I've had in over a year.

We start to line up, and they push me to the front of the line as they chant my name. We go through the line, and even the other team's coaches tell me what a great job I did taking over on the fly.

As we head off the ice whooping and carrying on, Coach Kaitlyn stops me.

"That's the kind of game I need to see from you, Ryleigh. Can you be consistent with that level?"

I'm still breathing hard, but I nod. "Yes, Coach, I'll do my best. How's Hailey?"

"She's going to have to do protocol, so you're our goalie this weekend. The first game tomorrow should be slower, but I want this intensity and focus."

"I understand." All I'm thinking about now, though, is my inhaler.

She motions me into the locker room, where the rest of my team erupts into cheers as I waddle in.

When we're back on the bus, I finally check my phone. Jett and my family have lit it up.

Rye, you were AMAZING! Jett says. Video-chat me if you have time before bed, but don't stay up just to do that.

Okay, Dad, I reply, but inside I'm squealing like a lovesick girl over her first love. Which is exactly what I am. I've had crushes before, but nothing has come anywhere near to the way Jett makes my heart shiver.

My parents have also texted to tell me how proud they are of me, and my mom is worried that I got rolled on in the third period.

I'm fine, I say. Emma pushed that girl off me.

My parents chat with me about the game until my bus gets to the hotel and I tell them I need to go. We're all starving, and Coach lets us order some Chinese food. I shovel my order in as fast as I can so I can get to my room and call Jett.

I shower quicker than I ever have in my life and call him.

"Puck, you were awesome tonight," he says, his smile illuminating my room like starlight.

"Thanks," I say, my toes scrunching in happiness.

"All that hard work really paid off."

"I owe you and Dom so much."

"We're just rink rats who can never get enough ice time. You don't owe us anything. Wait, is your lip swollen?" He peers into the screen.

"My helmet jammed it when that puck hit my cage in the third. It's okay. No broken teeth, see?" I smile.

Jett smiles back. "Face save. Were there any scouts?"

I nod. "I saw at least two, one from Hamilton and one from Maine."

"D3 and D1. That's good because they are sure to talk about you after the way you played tonight, and then more scouts will come to your games. How's your goalie mate?"

"They don't think it's too serious, but she's got a slight concussion, so she's on protocol."

Jett nods. "You need to dry your hair and get to bed, then. You've got an early game tomorrow."

Mr. Discipline. "Will you be able to watch it?"

"Ouais. I don't have to be at the rink until four o'clock. I'll miss your second game, though, so let me know how it goes.

And just remember what Dom says. Focus on the next shot, not the one you just played."

I nod as Emma comes into the room.

"Pretend I'm not here," she says when she realizes I'm on the phone with Jett.

"I'll try to catch up with you after my game," I say, and wave good night to him.

He blows me a kiss before the screen goes dark, and everything inside me that's been like a glacier for the last two years melts as if it were never anything more than some shaved ice on a sunny day.

Chapter 26

Hope Is the Thing with Feathers

THE REST OF THE WEEKEND IS A BLUR OF GAMES AND MEALS AND bruises and warm-ups and crashing on our bags or back at the hotel. Hailey sits on the bench wearing a helmet and her warm-up suit, but she cheers me on and tells me to make the most of each game. When I'm at the rink, I'm as focused as the zoom lens on a professional photographer's camera. Dom says you have to do a mind ditch before every game.

"I take five minutes and do this meditation to wipe the slate clean," he told me one morning last week as he showed me the app he uses. "No drama, whether it's family, friends, or, you know," he'd said as he indicated Jett, who was standing behind me and resting his chin on my shoulder even though it meant he had to bend. "No worries about your hockey career, nothing. Just let yourself start with a blank canvas and think about how much you love being on the ice and imagine yourself playing the most lit you ever have. You can worry after the game."

"That's pretty good advice for someone who gets hit in the head with pucks all the time," Jett said.

And then Dom yelled, "Elbows up," and the two of them were rolling around on the ice in a mock fight like seven-year-olds.

But Dom's mind ditch has been helping me clear my head before games. It's also helped that Dom and Jett believe in me so much. After all the dragging I took from Coach Blackmon last year, I was a lot more defeated than I realized. It took Jett telling me to knock it off when I would criticize myself to realize how much I'd been doing it. The fact that Coach Kaitlyn is happy with me now is the star on my Christmas tree.

I hear chatter about scouts and what schools have come, and occasionally I see some. They don't always wear their school gear, I guess so that players and parents don't bug them, but you can usually pick them out. I try to forget that any schools are here looking for players so I can keep my slate clean, as Dom says.

I see Coach Blackmon once in the lobby, but it's crowded enough that I don't have to hear his fake platitudes about how happy he is for me. He walked out of the game he was watching me play mid–third period, and I've refused to think about him since. Whatever his issues are, they are his. I'm free of him now.

Jett and I are like two people in completely different time zones, and almost every text is answered hours later. If this were a Ping-Pong game, you'd barely be able to tell the ball was moving. When we do have a few minutes at the same time, our fingers start flying. We give each other stats like we're the team statistician.

How many saves did you make?

33 on 35 shots. One goal was a breakaway and one a rebound deflection.

Your GAA has improved a lot.

Goals against average. It's the mean number of goals you give up per game, and it's one of the most important metrics for a goalie. He must be looking at my stats page.

How many shots did you have? I ask so that I don't become obsessed with my GAA.

He tells me and talks about his last game. I'm going to have to go soon. When are we watching our movie?

When I'm on the bus to come home?

That should work. Pick something out and hit me.

Okay.

Stay lit, Puck.

I smile. Okay, I will.

XO.

XO? Do guys say that? I thought "XO" was something only your aunt and mom wrote, or your besties from elementary school. XO? Is that a declaration of love? I'm not sure how I'm supposed to respond, so I just mark his text with a heart. Then I stare at my phone wondering if I'm being pathetic. Or a chicken. Or too much. I don't know anything about being a girlfriend.

When did I become the kind of girl who stares at her phone and worries about what the boy on the other end is thinking?

Coach Kaitlyn finds me in the back hallway of the rink, where I've been lurking so that I could have a few uninterrupted minutes to text Jett.

"Ryleigh, our final game's been moved up. I need you in the locker room now."

"I'm ready, Coach."

She turns and walks back to the main area with me, a smile on her face.

I don't get to do my clean-slate meditation before the game, but it doesn't seem to matter. I'm so focused on finishing strong and going home to see Jett tomorrow at school that my adrenaline is pumping like a fire hydrant.

This team isn't the toughest we faced this weekend, but it's still competitive. I play well, though. I end the weekend with a shutout when I don't give up a single goal. Our whole team has had a good weekend, with the exception of Hailey and a couple of players who mostly ride the bench, and we're all giddy and ready to be back home as we pack up our gear and head to the bus as tournament champs for our division.

When I walk into the lobby, Coach Kaitlyn motions me over to where she's standing by the door talking with another lady. I go over and drop my bag and hope this is a D1 scout. Although this late in the year, I should be grateful if she's a scout from any school.

Coach Kaitlyn introduces us. She's a scout for the women's team at Cornell. I immediately wonder if that's just a coincidence, or if Jett asked them to talk to me. I hope he didn't because that would mean they're trying to make him happy rather than seeking me out after I played well this weekend.

"I watched a couple of your games this weekend and was quite impressed. Coach Kaitlyn says your grades and SATs are good, too." She has a nice smile and soft brown eyes.

We talk about my academic numbers and what my goals are in life. I don't really have any besides playing D1 and some vague notion of saving the planet from toxic chemicals, but I try to think about what Jett would say in this moment. My brain taps into something my guidance counselor said about Ivies wanting focused students who will make them look good in the future. And then I think about my mom and I'm immediately on autopilot.

"I'd like to do something with conservation to reduce the human-made toxins people are exposed to every day that can lead to cancer and endocrine disruption." I didn't know I could even speak like this. It just rolled out of me as if it were somewhere in my subconscious all along. But it also feels like a good way to spend a life. Helping people. Making the world a little less dark.

"Well, Cornell is a great place for scientific research," she says. "I think you'd be very happy with us."

I smile, not sure how seriously to take her. Plus, I never even looked at Cornell, so I have no idea what it's like. It may not matter, though. I'm in no position to be choosy.

"I know someone who is committed to the men's team," I say, worried about whether I should mention it. "Jett Robitaille."

"Oh," she says, "one of the men's coaches told me to watch for you here, so that must be the connection. We're very excited to have Jett committed. How do you know him?"

"We go to school together. We're chemistry partners."

She smiles. "Well, I had planned to watch the Polar Bears anyway this weekend, so I would have seen you, but it's always nice to hear we have a connection or recommendation from one of our players. We're all expecting big things from Jett, so if he thinks well of you, then that's a great recommendation. We're still looking to fill our last goalie slot for next year. Do you think you'd be interested?"

I stare at her until Coach Kaitlyn nudges me.

"Yes," I say. "Yes!"

She laughs. "Okay, well, we'll keep an eye on you over the next few weeks. I am a little concerned about your size, but you handle yourself very well." She hands me a business card. "Have you filled out our recruiting form yet?"

I shake my head.

"Fill that out and email me your transcripts. If you know what you'd like to major in, please let me know that, too."

"Yes, I will, thank you." I haven't talked to many scouts, so I glance at Coach to see if she seems okay with what I said. She's calm, so I guess it's fine.

"Ryleigh is a very hard worker," Coach says. "She's first on the ice and last off at every practice, and she's put in extra ice time to build up her skills this year."

"That's awesome to hear," the scout says. "We definitely push our student-athletes to be their best while they are with us, so having a good work ethic and discipline is important."

She glances at me as if she's trying to read my face. "Coach Kaitlyn has also told me that you've overcome a lot of personal adversity since last year."

I look at Coach and then back at her. I nod. I hope I don't have to talk about my mom or my abusive narcissist coach from last year.

"We like to see students who have proven they can overcome challenges. It's not easy to be a student-athlete in college. It takes a lot of grit."

"Yes, ma'am," I say. "I understand." I never really thought of myself as gritty, but when I think of everything I've survived in the last two years, and the progress I'm finally making in hockey, maybe Jett is right and it's time to believe in myself. As for Jett, he's disciplined enough to survive anything.

"Ryleigh has plenty of grit," Coach Kaitlyn says, and I smile.

We chat a little more and then the scout leaves.

Coach Kaitlyn smiles at me. "Are you happy?"

I nod. "I just hope it wasn't because of Jett."

"It wasn't," she says. "Trust me. You played great this weekend."

"But no other scouts spoke to you about me?"

"A scout from Colby talked to me about you, so you should fill out a recruiting form for them as well if you're interested."

Colby is a D3 school in Maine. I nod.

"All right," she says, "let's hope for Cornell and get on the bus and get home. Also, I saw Quinnipiac and Union here. Have you contacted them? They both need goalies still. Maybe they just didn't get a chance to approach me. Make sure you mention you were here and send some clips. And then call to follow up."

"Thanks, Coach." My eyes get a little misty. It feels like it's been a long time since I've had a coach this supportive, although it's only been one season. It's amazing how quickly you can let yourself get dragged down when you're someone who is already self-critical. Maybe that's why I'm so hard on others sometimes. Or at least why I have been with Jett.

"I only praise where it's deserved, Ryleigh. You've worked hard and played well. Keep it up, and I think we may just pull off this last-minute grab yet." She gives me a grin.

As I reach down to get my bag, I say, "It may be more of a heist."

Coach Kaitlyn laughs. "That works, too," she says. "Let's stage the biggest heist of the century and get you all the offers we can!"

Chapter 27

Root Beer Float Clouds

WHEN I SLIDE INTO MY WINDOW SEAT ON THE BUS, I'M STILL PROcessing what just happened. I've played five and a half hockey games in less than forty-eight hours, and not one of them was a sleeper. I'm exhausted. My stats have all gone in the right direction, and the only thing I need to worry about before tomorrow is whether I get leg cramps tonight. And I finally have a scout at a D1 program interested in me.

It still feels strange, though, that it's the same school Jett is committed to go to. I mean, Ivies do tend to fill slots later because they cross off a lot of talented players who don't have the academic scores to qualify. But still, I wonder if this is coincidence or fate or just Jett being Jett. Even if this worked out, though, I'd be at school two years before Jett finished juniors. I laugh to myself. He'd be a lowly freshman while I'd be a junior.

Emma plops down beside me. "Why are you so happy?"

The truth would be because I was just thinking about all the ways I could mock bully Jett as his upperclassman, but instead I shake my head. "Just feeling good about this weekend, thanks to you guys. You made me look good."

"You looked great," she says, and smiles. "We also looked good, though."

I laugh.

"I'm going to have a shiner on my ankle from that one blocked shot."

"Sorry," I say. "I did appreciate it, very much. Muchas gracias."

"De nada," she says, and slips her big headphones over her ears as she settles into her seat, pulls her hood on, and closes her eyes. "Wake me up when we stop for food. I am starving with the white-hot hunger of a cheetah that hasn't eaten for at least a week."

"Okay," I say, but Emma is always awake two minutes before Coach says, "Let's stop here." It's like a sixth sense she has.

The door closes and the bus sighs and we're off. Beside me, Emma's face is buried in her Taylor Swift hoodie and wavy blond hair. I pull my phone out and text Jett.

So, I had a scout talk to me after today's last game.

He texts me back immediately, but his last game was done a couple of hours ago. That's awesome, he replies. Which school?

Cornell.

He replies with a string of celebration emoji.

Apparently, someone told your coaches to tell her to check me out.

What a weird coincidence.

That's what I thought.

Look, Puck, all I did was give them a heads-up that you'd be there. It's not like I'm their star player. I don't even go there yet.

Hmmmm.

Honestly. I don't have that much pull.

She said she would have seen the Polar Bears anyway. And Coach said it was my own merit, too.

Well, there you go. I had nothing to do with it. What did she say? Exactly.

We text like this for so long that I don't realize how dark it becomes or that it's time for us to stop to eat until Emma jerks awake and asks if we are stopping yet.

"Coach will announce in two minutes," I say.

Like clockwork, Coach calls out that we're going to stop about a minute later. After we grab our food and get back on the bus, Emma falls asleep while Jett asks what movie I picked.

We can't honestly say we're in a relationship until we've watched Miracle together.

Oh, that fantasy movie where the Americans beat the Canadians?

It's historical fact. Besides, that's not the point. We beat the Russians.

I'm not sure the 1980 Olympics were ever certified. Well, next time we're watching Hockey Night.

Never heard of it.

What!?!

Seriously.

You Americans are so lacking in culture. It's a Canadian film about a girl who fights to play on an all-boys team before that was really a thing. I can't believe you haven't seen it.

I mark his text with a like. Next time, I say. So we both boot up *Miracle* on our computers and then coordinate when we'll start it. Then we text through the whole movie, because we decide there are too many ears on a bus to video-chat.

We're not quite finished when the bus pulls into the parking lot of our home ice.

We're at the rink, I say. We can finish it another time. You still have to call Marcel and get ready for school. I'll see you tomorrow in chem.

Okay, Jett replies.

That's it. No "XO." No "Good night." But I was the one who sent him off to his long bedtime routine. He must be tired, too. He had three games this weekend.

I shuffle off the bus with the others and drag my bag, pads, and sticks from the storage area. I'm so tired, it takes all my energy to walk to my car, which is parked on the side of the building. Everyone mumbles good night to each other as we hobble to our vehicles.

"Great weekend, girls," Coach calls out. "You made me proud."

"Thanks, Coach" reverberates around the parking lot as we spread out like bugs scurrying to our rocks.

I turn the corner and push the button to open the back of my Rogue. Jett's Impreza is parked beside it, and he's standing there waiting for me, a wrapped package in his hands.

He runs over when he sees me and pulls my bag from my shoulder. I don't fight him.

"I thought you were at home."

"No, I've been hotspotting and waiting here since you told me the news." His smile is so dimply.

"I didn't get an offer," I say with a laugh. "Just some solid possible interest." I toss my pads and sticks in and push the button to close the back. Jett wraps me in a hug, and I let myself just stay there a moment and breathe him in, all citrusy and warm. I feel like this is what France would smell like, if it had a single smell. Or at least Montreal.

"I'm so proud of you," he whispers.

"Is that why you brought me a present?" I ask. "That's weirdly shaped like a sub sandwich."

Jett laughs. "It's not a sub sandwich, although you may wish it were."

I shake my head as I reluctantly leave his arms. "I'm still

full," I say. "What have my mad hockey skills earned me?" I hold out my hands and smile.

Jett places the package on my palms, and I unwrap it. It's a red Cornell ice hockey T-shirt.

"Wait, is this yours?"

He nods like a kid. "My signing T-shirt."

"You can't give me this," I say, and hold it out to him.

"I can get another." He doesn't take it.

"Not from your signing."

My phone vibrates and I check it. My dad is looking for a status update.

At the rink almost ready to leave.

"Your buddy Lou is looking for me," I tell Jett as I flash my phone at him.

Jett scrunches his face unhappily at his new best friend's timing. "It's no big deal. You keep it."

"I can't," I say. "You shouldn't be so generous."

"I don't wear it anyway because it feels too show-offish. Keep it until you get your own at least. Then we can wear them together and make everyone barf at our matching cuteness overload."

I laugh and pull the shirt into me like a little hug.

"See?" he says, and wraps me up again. "It's not so hard to say yes to me once in a while. Consider this your first practice."

I laugh some more and tilt my head up and kiss him exactly the way a girl should kiss her first love when he's as generous as Jett is. Even though I'm exhausted, and it's cold out, I could kiss him like this all night under these December stars.

Jett's phone starts buzzing and he pulls away to check it. "Who would be calling me now?" he says under his breath.

His other hand jerks from my waist as if my body just shocked him.

"Ope! Lou might be onto me! Gotta go, Goalie Girl," he says, and waves as he runs to get in his car. "Hey, Lou," I hear him say right before the door closes.

From the safety of inside, Jett motions frantically for me to get in my Rogue. I do, and we pull out of the parking lot one after the other as I watch him chat to my dad on speaker in my rearview mirror. But as we make our turns at the first light, my heart is riding shotgun in the little blue Impreza heading in the opposite direction.

Chapter 28

Un-Explaining What Was Already Explained

BY THE TIME I GET HOME AND FILL MY PARENTS IN ON THE TWO possible prospects in my hunt for a college, I crave my bed. But as I brush my teeth, it occurs to me that I now need to explain these latest developments to Imani. I think, for just a brief, fleeting moment, about letting her think Jett and I are still fake, but that would be (1) impossible to pull off because for the first time in my life I can't stop smiling, and (2) dangerous if she decides Jett is taking the pretending too far. I don't need my boyfriend disfigured by the imprint of a cafeteria tray in his skull.

I put texting her on my to-do list for the morning. Then I text Jett.

Good night, Hotshot.

He already has his notifications silenced, so he's probably asleep, but at least he'll see it in the morning. Then, wearing his Cornell T-shirt, I climb into bed and turn out the lights. As I close my heavy eyelids, the phone vibrates beside me.

Good night, Puck. I can't wait to be at Cornell with you.

The words settle on me softly, with all the generosity this boy with his silky language and smiling soul holds. That's the difference between Jett and me. He dreams big and truly believes it will happen. I dream big and fear it won't. But I summon all my courage and mark his text with a heart. I may have been his second choice, but he seems happy with it now, so I just need to have faith in that. And then I snuggle down and close my eyes and try to imagine what being at college with Jett Robitaille would even be like.

When I see Jett standing by the door of chem class waiting for me, my heart doesn't just somersault, it does a whole floor routine. He wraps his hand around mine and walks into chem with me and we sit at our table, but neither of us lets go until the bell rings.

"Good morning, class," Mr. G. says. "It seems that Mizz Vento and Mr. Robitaille have finally managed to engage quantum gravity to break their hands apart, so it should be safe to begin." He laughs loudly at his joke, but no one joins in. This sours his mood immediately, and his brow creases as he narrows his eyes at Jett and me as if it's our fault his jokes are pointless.

Jett and I spend the rest of the period locked in so that Mr. G. doesn't have anything to criticize us for. There is no way I am getting detention because of this troll wearing human skin. Thankfully, one of the girls who is always giggling near us is nodding off, so after he drops a textbook on the lab table right in front of her and scares her awake, he seems to forget that Jett and I are his sworn enemies.

When we walk out of class, Jett immediately grabs my hand again, and it lights my smile like he flipped on a smile switch I didn't know I had.

"Who do you think hurt that guy?" I ask.

"Polachuk?" Jett asks, and I nod.

Jett shakes his head. "I don't know, but as someone with a fair bit of childhood trauma, I'd guess it started there. Probably everyone."

It is hard to imagine Mr. G. as a boy at all, let alone one who wasn't tortured by the other kids. "Maybe we should feel sorry for him," I say.

"Well, it's okay to feel sorry for someone without excusing them." Jett squeezes my hand. "See, and you think you aren't nice, but here you are, making excuses for Mr. G." He smiles.

"I'm not making excuses for him. I just don't understand how anyone could be so—" I hesitate because I don't even know what word to use. Nothing my mom would approve of.

"Enough about that guy, what do you think about

postponing ice until Wednesday and only doing it once this week? You've got to be beat."

I nod. "Just this week, though. Then you and Dom are on double duty again."

"Aye, aye, Captain!" Jett says as we reach my calc class. He pecks my lips and is gone, but the warmth of that kiss hovers on my lips until lunch period.

On my way to the cafeteria, I realize I still haven't told Imani the latest status in my soap opera love triangle.

Jett is waiting for me in the hallway, leaning against the wall, one leg up against it, head bent over his phone, just like he was that first day we met at the rink. My heart skitters when he looks up and catches my gaze and smiles. He slips his arm around my shoulders as I stop beside him, and we walk into lunch together.

Imani pulls up on my other side and slips her arm through mine. "So, how was the big weekend?"

"She got scouted," Jett says before I can reply.

Imani's mahogany eyes widen. "Details, details," she instructs.

"It's just interest," I say. "Not an offer."

"Not an offer yet," Jett says. We get to our table and sit in our usual seats. Lewis is already there. Matt is in line getting food.

"Let's just wait for Matt," I say. "There's no point in talking about it all lunch period."

"Has she always been this much of a killjoy?" Jett asks Imani.

Imani bobbles her head. "She definitely always had the

tendency, but last year cemented it." Then she bites her lip and stares at me, which is her way of apologizing for bringing up last year.

"I don't think Ryleigh is a killjoy," Lewis says. "She's just cautious about being optimistic."

"Thank you, Lewis."

Lewis shrugs. "I mean, that's the way I see Ryleigh."

"Are you two coming to Lewis's jazz recital Thursday night?" Imani asks.

I nod. "Although I have to leave partway through to get to practice. Sorry, Lewis."

"And I'll be late because of practice," Jett says. "But I'm definitely coming."

Imani smiles. "It's going to be cool."

"What is?" Matt says as he sets his tray down.

"Lewis's recital. Are you coming?" Imani says.

Matt nods. "You guys," he says, "I have big news!" He jumps over the bench into his seat and looks at each of us in turn.

"Spill!" Imani and I say, one right after the other.

"I got early acceptance into Boston University!"

"That's awesome," I say as we all congratulate him.

After we've exhausted Matt's good news, Imani reminds us that I need to give details on my possible potentially good news.

"Which is what?" Matt asks, ready to cheer on everyone.

I fill them in on what happened over the weekend. My friends erupt with so much enthusiasm that the whole cheerleader table turns to stare at us.

"Nothing is for sure," I remind them.

Jett wraps his arm around me. "I'm manifesting it to happen," he says, and I can feel my cheeks growing warm. Jett kisses my temple.

"How cool would that be if you two ended up at the same college playing hockey?" Imani asks. She's always been a romantic, so the sparkle in her eyes as she says this is genuine.

"Just keep your fingers crossed for me." As soon as I get home tonight, I'll fill out the recruiting form.

A shadow crosses the lunch table. I look up and Peyton is standing at the end near Jett.

"What's so exciting over here?" she asks.

Imani wastes no time. "Ryleigh is being scouted by Cornell."

Peyton's eyes get as big as I've ever seen them. "Wow, Cornell. That's not like going to Michigan or BU for hockey, though, right?"

"No, Peyton," I say. "It's not like going to Michigan or BU. But it's still D1." I try not to let her mess with my karma. I don't need to compete with her, and I don't need to have fate decide I'm being too cocky and make it all evaporate. So I just state the facts.

"I think it's better," Jett says.

Peyton smiles at him like he's a sweet little kid. "Well, congrats, Ryleigh." She winks at Jett and saunters away.

Imani starts to get up to go after her, but Lewis pulls her back. "Whoa, whoa," he says.

"Seriously, Mans, don't worry about her. She doesn't bother me anymore."

Imani studies me to see if I'm telling the truth, so I do my best to look like I am. The weird part is, I had completely gotten past all the Peyton middle school and early high school meanness before Jett came into my life. But now, as I sit here beside my boyfriend who used to like her, who used to want to date her so much he was willing to fake date me to lure her in, I wonder if we ever really get over the people who hurt us the most.

Chapter 29

How Do I Love Thee?

WHEN WE LEAVE CHEMISTRY ON TUESDAY, JETT SLIPS A PIECE OF paper into my hands.

"What's this?" I ask.

"We're studying Elizabeth Barrett Browning in English, so I wrote you a poem based on hers," he says. "It's kind of a parody. And kind of not."

"How am I supposed to know which is the parody part?"

Jett shrugs, my hand warm in his. "That's for you to figure out, Goalie Girl."

"Okay," I say with a laugh, and tuck it into my jeans pocket. I don't pull it out again until after dinner when I'm working on my homework. When I read it over, it's so Jett, filled with silliness and joy and, I think, love. Like, anyway. It's filled with like.

> How do I love thee? Let me count the ways.
> I love thee to the height and speed and depth
> A puck can reach when hurtling
> To the back of the net and the ideal grace.
> I love thee with a passion put to use
> In my old hockey sticks, and with my childhood's
>   faith.
> And, if the hockey gods grant,
> I shall but love thee better after
> Cornell and whatever trophies we get.

I laugh when I read it. And then I hug it. I've been doing a deep dive into Cornell, and it looks really pretty. I picture us walking around campus, grabbing hot chocolates at the local coffee spot, and helping each other with hockey and homework, which I will need his help with because these people seem scary smart. Reality would probably be more like now, where I barely see him outside of school, but it's still a beautiful daydream.

I'm lazing away in my daydream when Jett texts.

> So, I checked our schedules and we'll both be done by two o'clock on Sunday. Let's have a date. Like a real date.

I smile so hard I think I pull a muscle. What do you consider a real date?

Anyplace I can be reasonably alone with you. Maybe we could go Christmas shopping (because, honestly, I really need to do that) and then go to the beach and a nice restaurant?

Jett, it's December in Connecticut. Why do you keep wanting to go to the beach?

We don't have beaches in Montreal, so I love them. And they're very romantic.

They are romantic. Just maybe not when it's freezing out. Still, it's for Jett.

Okay.

Really?

Yes. Whatever you want.

He marks my text with a celebration emoji.

You're the best, Ryleigh Vento.

I'm not, but I am not going to argue with him about that. The longer he stays delusional, the better. But I do love him more than Peyton ever could. I'm sure of that much.

On Friday night, my family and I go to Jett's game, which was arranged by Jett and his new bestie, Lou. My dad always said he was going to tell any boys who came around that he's a combat vet, which is true, and that he was a sniper with multiple kills, which isn't true. But Jett has worked his Jett magic on my family, and "scary Lou" has become a teddy bear who texts my boyfriend almost as much as I do. My whole family likes Jett better than they like me. Well, not my mom, she'd always choose me, but I'm convinced the rest of them would choose Jett in a heartbeat.

Our seats are across from the Jr. Hat Tricks bench and toward the goal, and not very far up. "Don't embarrass me," I tell my family.

"What does that mean?" my dad asks.

"It means she doesn't want us screaming for her boyfriend," London says. I've braided her hair the way I do mine when I play and she's wearing a beanie, so she looks her age, even if she sounds like she's twenty.

Jett and his team take the ice for warm-ups, and my family erupts in chaotic cheers, which, maybe, is better than coordinated cheers. I hunker down in my seat as if I'm not with them.

"There's Jett," Harper announces, as if the rest of us wouldn't be able to figure out which one is him. To be fair, my family probably needs his name and number, but I'm so familiar with his skating stance that I could pick him out even if he were wearing an unmarked jersey and a paper bag over his head.

A couple of girls my age come and sit down in the row in front of us. They are dolled up in Peyton Malloy style, clearly here to be seen more than to watch hockey.

Just then, Jett skates by waving at us.

"Did you see that?" one of the girls says. "He was waving at me!"

"He was waving at me," the other one says. "He is cuuuuute." She has lots of blond hair like Peyton.

Harper reaches over to tap on her shoulder, but I slap her arm down and shake my head. Harps frowns at me. My parents, meanwhile, are nudging each other and think this is very funny.

Later in the period, when Jett scores, he celebrates with his team but then skates by and does his best to flash me a heart sign with his gloved hands while holding his stick. It requires a little imagination, but you can tell what he means.

The two girls in front of us jump up and make heart signs with their hands at him.

"Oh brother," London says, laughing.

"Shhh," I say, and elbow her, while Harps and my mom watch my reaction.

At the end of the period, Jett looks back to where we are as he leaves the ice with his team. The girls in front elbow each other and then argue about which of them he was looking back to check out. Dom isn't playing this game, so he's been on the bench, but I don't think he would look for us anyway. It would go against his clean-slate meditation rules.

My dad and London use the intermission to get nachos and miss the first couple minutes of the second period, which includes a second goal by Jett. When they get back, laden with drinks and nachos for Harper and Mom and a pretzel for me, I shake my head at them.

"I'll see the next one," my dad says as he spills nacho cheese on his shirt.

We all laugh, and my mom wipes him clean with a napkin as I munch on my pretzel. It's so weird to sit here watching hockey like this. We're far enough away from the New York teams that we don't get to go to a professional game very often, and my games are nothing like Jett's. These games are like mini NHL games. The seats are stadium seats, and there are concessions, and people are all decked out in Hat Tricks and Jr. Hat Tricks merchandise. The crowd is constantly egging players on to fight each other, which makes me so mad it's hard for me to keep quiet when I hear it around us. Jett's not a fighter. He doesn't have to be because he's got such quick hands and sharp skating skills, but for a lot of these guys who are just trying to make the team, being an enforcer is the way to make it happen. It's the worst part of hockey. When you're a nine-year-old playing, everyone tells you not to fight, but then, for boys anyway, they get to this level and not only is it expected, it's demanded and celebrated.

When a man behind us yells at Jett's travel roommate to fight someone, I turn around. "What's wrong with you?"

"Boys will be boys," the guy says. He's at least forty-five, with a receding hairline and a beard. He's holding a beer, and I doubt it's his first. If he ever had to fight someone, he'd lose, so I guess he's living vicariously.

"This is hockey. If you want to see a fight, go watch MMA!"

"Whoa, whoa," my dad says, maneuvering around my mom and London to reach me.

I turn around as the guy tells my dad he needs to keep "that little bitch" in check, at which point I'm so mad my whole body shudders, but my dad grabs me in a bear hug. "Ignore him," he says. "He's just a blowhard with nothing else in his life to get excited about."

"But they're just kids," I say. "Even twenty is still mostly a kid." I turn around to sit in my seat and the two girls in front of us are looking at me like I'm a weirdo. Meanwhile, they were asking each other what icing is. If they want to come watch cute guys play a great sport without understanding it, fine, but no one should be telling a bunch of kids, or young adults, or whatever, to beat each other up.

My dad shuffles back around London and my mom to the end of the aisle and disappears up the stairs. He comes back a few minutes later with hot dogs for him and London. It's not that I want my dad to cause a scene or get into a fight, but it's hard to picture my Marine Corps dad letting someone call his daughter a name like that. Still, it's better than one of us crawling over the seats and getting into a brawl while I'm upset that there could be a brawl on the ice.

A few minutes later, I catch my dad looking back at the guy who insulted me. I turn around to see why he's watching. Two security guards are talking to the man. I lean forward and glance at my dad, who shrugs innocently. A minute later, the guards are escorting the man out of the building.

My dad smiles at me and taps his temple. He's always told us to fight smart.

I sit back in my seat and laugh.

Jett's team wins easily, five to two. After he's done the handshake line, Jett skates over to us. He yanks off his helmet, his beautiful dark hair plastered to his head, but he still looks amazing. He yells up, "Wait for me," and nods to encourage me to agree.

The two girls in front start pointing to themselves, trying to clarify who he wants to stay, when my dad calls out, "All of us?"

Jett laughs and shakes his head. He skates forward and presses his lips to the space between the glass. "No, Lou, just Ryleigh," he yells. "I'll bring her home, I promise." He pulls back and smiles at me.

The girls turn around and stare at my family. Harper leans over and smiles, her hazel eyes twinkling. "She's his girlfriend," she says, and jerks her thumb toward me.

The two girls give each other a disgusted look and take off up the stairs.

"Ouais?" Jett yells.

Ouais, I mouth.

Jett motions to show me where to wait for him and I wave.

"All right," my mom says, "it's time for the rest of us to go. Have fun, but don't stay out long. You both have games tomorrow."

I cross my heart and wave them goodbye. And then I race Jett to the meeting spot, even though I know he has to go through the after-game coaches' talk and a shower, so it will take a while. We don't have much time together, though, and I don't want to waste a second of it.

Chapter 30

Our Love Is Alive

WHEN JETT WALKS OUT OF THE LOCKER ROOM IN HIS PERFECTLY tailored blue suit with his still-wet hair and his drop-dead smile, my heart floats. His bag is slung over his left shoulder and his sticks are in his left hand, so he snatches my hand with his right and pulls me into him and kisses me.

"Thanks for coming," he says. "I was nervous with you and your family here. I really wanted to impress them."

I laugh. "They already think you're the cat's meow, as my grandmother would say."

"Do you have time to get something to eat with me?"

I nod. "Although my mom did remind me that we both have games tomorrow."

"Come on," Jett says, and tows me down the hallway. "Let's

get out of here before someone tries to latch on. I'm so hungry after a game."

We practically run to his car. He tosses his bag and sticks in the trunk, and we jump in as if we're making an escape. It's only after we've pulled out of the rink parking lot that we decide where to go. "Nowhere near here," Jett says. "I don't want to run into any of the guys. I never get to be alone with you."

This is true. The closest we ever get to being alone is when we're texting, and even then, there is usually a family member or teammate right beside at least one of us.

We find a sandwich shop that's still open for another twenty minutes and far enough from the rink that we won't run into any of his teammates. Jett doesn't let go of my hand until we're seated across from each other. I get half a turkey sub, but it's hard to even eat because my stomach is filled to the brim with the joy of being with Jett with no one we know to watch us, just the guy behind the counter making the sandwiches, who is more concerned with getting the shop ready to close. I can't stop grinning.

Jett stares at me a moment.

"What?"

"I've just never seen you this happy."

My face flushes. I can't remember the last time I was this happy. Long before my mom got her diagnosis.

"It makes me happy," Jett says.

"I thought you liked me scowling at you."

Jett laughs. "I don't mind it."

We smile at each other until I have to look away.

"Ryleigh, I have nine days until I leave for the holidays and World Juniors, and I want to spend every second I can with you."

I glance up at him. I want that, too, but I can't quite say it.

"Yes? No?" he asks.

I look down. "Yes."

I don't need to look at him to see the smile that has just spread across his face. It lights my heart up like a thousand fairy lights.

Jett's hand reaches across the table and takes mine.

"Let's go running tomorrow morning."

Or not.

"I'm not much of a runner because of my asthma."

Jett's face falls.

"We could lift together, but be prepared to have Lou join in."

Jett's smile rebounds. "Okay, and then on Sunday after your game, we could go Christmas shopping and to the beach."

He really loves the beach. I try to imagine the novelty of it if I hadn't grown up around the ocean. "Okay."

Jett leans in and takes a big chomp out of his sandwich, his hair flopping down toward his eyes, his dimples relaxed.

We plan out the rest of our nine days as if we're comparing two corporate executives' schedules, but it's the only way to maximize our time together with school and hockey.

"I've never cared about school activities, you know, like homecoming or prom," Jett says, "but I feel like you're getting shortchanged. I mean, this has been your school for all your high school years. I've had a different school every year, so it wouldn't mean as much to me."

I shrug. "I've never felt like I was missing out."

Jett contemplates me.

"If there's something you want to do and I'm not around, you should go with Imani and Lewis. And if I'm here and can go, then I will."

He's probably thinking about winter formal, which is next Friday night. "I'd rather come to your game."

"Are you sure?"

I nod, smiling.

Jett takes another bite of his sandwich. "I never expected this," he says when he's swallowed. He takes a swig of his water. "I had no intention of falling in love."

Did he really just say that? Maybe I'm hallucinating.

"No," I say. "Me neither."

Jett looks down and laughs. "That first day I saw you, when you walked out, I couldn't believe how pretty you were. Or how much attitude you had. But I did think you were only fifteen."

"Perv."

Jett laughs. "I wouldn't have chased you then. I was so relieved when you said you were seventeen."

"You didn't chase me. You chased Peyton."

Jett's gaze catches mine and holds it. He isn't smiling now. "About that," he says.

My phone starts buzzing. I look at my screen.

"Lou wants to know why you have me out so late," I say as I answer the call.

Jett reaches over and finishes my sandwich, then he wraps up our trash as I promise my dad I'll be home soon. I stand up.

"I'm fine, Dad. I'm with Jett, remember?" I cover the speaker and whisper to Jett, "He has my ETA from every rink in the area down to the millisecond."

Jett laces his fingers in mine, and we head outside as I reassure my dad he can go to bed. "I'm coming home now."

When Jett pulls into my drive, he looks up at the house. "Do you think Lou is watching us?"

I shake my head. "London probably is, though."

Jett laughs and pushes back a lock of my hair behind my ear. "I'll see you in the morning."

The warmth of his words floods through me even though the heater in his old Impreza isn't the best.

Jett and I look at each other. I may not have been his first choice, but the way he looks at me now lets me know that I'm the only one he's thinking of tonight. I lean in and kiss him, determined to keep it that way.

When he pulls away, he clears his throat. "Now I feel like your whole family is probably watching."

I laugh. "It's possible," I say. "But everyone has been worried that I haven't gotten to be a normal teenager, whatever that is, so even if they aren't happy, I'll fight them if they complain. I'll see you tomorrow."

He nods, and I peck him on the cheek and dash from the car through the cold Connecticut night into the house.

I take a deep breath as I hang up my jacket. I'm struggling to remember who I even was four months ago, and that may be the best thing that's happened to me in the past two years. Jett has brought so much light and hope into my life, and he's done it just by being himself.

Jett Robitaille isn't anything I had planned for my senior year, but each passing day is making me less afraid of surprises and more grateful for the crash and burn of my no-dating rule. Instead of making me distracted, being with Jett has made me laser focused on what I really want in my life. I may not end up at Cornell with him, but between now and when Cornell makes its final decision on a goalie, I'm going to do everything I can to be their first choice.

Chapter 31

Why Do Good Times Always Fly

WHEN I WALK OUT OF MY GAME ON SUNDAY, I KNOW I'VE PLAYED well. I'm not just helping us win games, I'm keeping my angles strong, my glove quick, and my five-hole closed. My team's confidence in me has risen as they spend more time in position and less time trying to block shots at any cost, and I'm able to shake off the occasional fail as just part of the process. My stats are soaring.

"Puck, you were awesome," Jett says as I drop my bag when I stop beside him in the lobby, where he's been waiting for me.

"Thanks," I say. He pecks my lips.

"I got some good video you should send to Cornell," he says.

"Okay, thanks."

"And your HAA is soaring."

"Don't you mean my GAA?" I say, referring to the goals-against-average stats we live by.

"Nope, I mean your HAA. Hearts against average."

I laugh. "And what exactly would that be?"

"How many times you drop my heart to my knees in a day."

I shake my head. "You are so corny."

"Does it earn me a kiss?"

I lean up and kiss him.

Some of my teammates flood around us on their way out the door. I introduce Jett to Emma, Alana, and Nina.

"Where's your sign?" Nina asks.

Jett laughs. "Oh, Ryleigh doesn't need that anymore. She believes in herself now."

The girls nod and say I've been on fire lately, but I see Jett in a new way, as if there's no limit to him surprising me. I thought he was just being an embarrassing goof with that sign, taking life as a joke, but he was trying to boost my confidence. He was right that I needed to boost it, even if the sign wasn't quite the best way. It makes my heart melt all over again.

We talk about the game a little, and Alana asks Jett if he likes playing for the Jr. Hat Tricks and living here. "It's the best place I've lived since I left home," Jett says, smiling at me.

"Okay," I say, ready to break up the bonding that's going on with my team. Jett and I don't have much time together before he leaves, and I don't want to spend it chitchatting with my teammates. "We should get going."

We say goodbye, and Jett carries my bag to the Rogue, then he follows me to my house in his Impreza.

My mom is just setting lunch on the table when we walk in, and it feels like the world is in a conspiracy to gobble up the precious time Jett and I have to be alone instead of what it is: lunch.

"Wash your hands," my mom instructs, and Jett and I traipse over to the sink together. He squirts some soap onto his fingers and then playfully swipes some of it onto mine. I laugh and turn the faucet on.

"Who is she?" Harps says from somewhere behind me.

"She's your sister," I say. "The same sister you've always had." Jett and I are looking at each other and giggling.

"You," London says, "are definitely not the same person as our sister."

"Okay, stop teasing Ryleigh," my dad says, but he and my mom are shooting each other looks as if they are about to burst into laughter at me being a nerdy, lovestruck fool.

The lunch conversation is mostly about my game, as everyone provides commentary on my play, including what I can improve on.

"I'm so glad you are all goalie experts," I say when London tells me that I should have come out of the net more on a breakaway.

Jett shakes his head. "No, she played it just right. If she had come out too far, that girl would have amped up her speed and might have beaten her back to the net."

"Thanks," I say. "It's good to know I'm slow."

He laughs. "You aren't slow, but that girl was tall and fast. You're short and skating backward."

I nod to acknowledge his point. Then I nudge him under the table with my foot to tell him to eat faster so we can go.

When we've cleaned up lunch for my mom, I make some hot chocolate and put it in a thermos, and we make our escape.

"I'll have her back before midnight, Lou," Jett says to tease my dad.

"Very funny. It's a school night for both of you. The semester hasn't ended."

My dad doesn't need to worry, though. Nothing, not even love, could make Jett lose his disciplined focus. I would bet my dad money that Jett will be in bed by ten p.m.

We dash to the Impreza and Jett hands me his phone. "Pick a beach," he says.

"I thought you wanted to go Christmas shopping."

"We don't have time to do both. But you can help me choose stuff online and I'll get it delivered to home. That's better anyway—I won't have to worry about packing presents for my family."

I nod and type "Sherwood Island State Park" into the maps app.

I put on Jett's French-pop playlist and scroll the words as I listen to them, and we sing along. Sometimes I ask Jett what the lyrics mean if there's vocabulary I don't know or a way of saying something I can't get.

“So the song says I’ve changed for you so much, but what’s this line mean?” I ask.

“Hmm, he’s saying that people are good at messing things up, sabotaging themselves. When you translate, don’t take the words so literally. Sometimes you have to think about the general idea of them.”

I nod as I start to understand the song. It’s nice to talk to him about something besides our families and hockey. Sometimes I worry that hockey has become my whole identity. Jett reminds me that I have other things in my life, too, even if hockey is what brought us together.

“I have one condition for today,” I say.

“Hmm?”

“No hockey talk. I have so much I want to talk to you about besides hockey.”

“I see. You really just want me for my chemistry brain.”

I laugh. “No chemistry talk, either.”

“Okay, but our topics are dwindling fast.”

I shake my head and start to ask him questions. What’s his favorite color? Blue. His favorite food? Chocolate. His favorite season? Fall. His favorite holiday? Christmas. It’s like we’ve been matched on one of those dating apps that are totally superficial.

We pull into a parking lot, and Jett tugs my beanie into place. “Thank you for doing this cold activity for me.”

I nod and he kisses me.

We follow a small trail that leads to the beach. When we step on the sand, Jett takes in a deep breath. “Wow, this place is beautiful. I feel like I can breathe here. All the stress of the team and travel and school and being away from Marcel, it all seems less crushing."

I smile, seeing this place for the first time through his perspective. The curved beach stretches for what feels like miles because there's no one here. We're the only weirdos who would come when December winds are whipping along the shore. Well, us and the gulls who don't leave for the winter. We feed them unsalted peanuts and apple chunks, and they flock around us, and I take pictures and video of Jett dodging and ducking as the gulls become too aggressive even for his little-boy enthusiasm, although he never stops laughing.

"Save me, Rye," he yells, but I'm too busy trying to land an apple chunk directly on his head.

Jett runs over and grabs me in a hug and spins me around. "Stop that," he says. So, we go back to just throwing the food toward the water, and the gulls chase it until we don't have anything left. I send Marcel some of the video.

Then we walk down the beach hand in hand, and the birds take off when they see we have nothing left to offer except our bubbly personalities. We play keep-away with the little waves rolling in and find a couple of long-empty horseshoe crab shells. We watch the winter-brown seagrass sway in the breeze and jump over large, flat rocks that form a barrier from the tides. We watch the sun crawl toward the horizon, and Jett plops down on the sand and pulls me with him. I sit in front of him and lean my head back, and he kisses my cheek just beside my ear.

He wraps his arms around me to protect me from the breeze. "Are you cold?"

"Not yet," I say. Right now, December feels invigorating, but we've been walking for a while. We pass the thermos of hot chocolate between us and stare at the waves and the sky.

"Will you come here with me when we graduate?" he asks.

"Certainement," I say.

"Bon."

He rocks us a little. "Ryleigh."

"Hmmmm?"

"Je t'aime tellement." I love you so much.

My heart skitters to a stop before it starts back up.

"Je t'aime tellement, aussi," I say. I love you so much, too. Jett squeezes me. I guess I wasn't hallucinating at the sandwich shop.

We talk about all the things we want to do together. He wants to show me Montreal. We want to eat ice cream as we sit on this beach with a summer sunset. We want to play hockey together at Cornell. We want to find treatments for cancer. We want to change the world. We want to remember today forever.

"Can I ask you something?" I nestle into him.

"Ouais."

I turn a little so that I can see his face, but I stay snuggled in his arms. "You don't have to tell me if it's too painful. I've thought about it a lot since you told me about your dad. How did you not become bitter and scared when he died? I would hate the world."

Jett pulls his lips in for a moment and contemplates the horizon. "Because of my dad, I think. He was a big guy, tall and sturdy. Full of light and laughter and love. I always wanted to be like him, from the time I was little."

Jett rolls a tiny bit and takes his phone from his pocket. He unlocks it and opens his camera and shows me pictures of his dad.

"When he knew he wasn't going to make it, he talked a lot about how he wanted me to live after he was gone. 'I don't want you to walk through the world angry or unhappy because of me,' he said. He wanted me to smile whenever I thought of him. He made me promise that I'd give the world all the love he wasn't going to be able to give to it anymore."

My eyes are stinging. "That's really beautiful."

Jett nods and tugs my beanie back over my ears. "How can I be angry at a world that gave me such a dad, when so many people don't even get one?"

Jett brushes a tear from my cheek. "I know how you felt last year. The fear and the anger. The feeling that, any second, everything you rely on in your world could be ripped away from you without warning." He kisses my forehead.

"I just want to feel safe again." I say it so softly, it's practically a whisper.

"Safety is just an illusion, Rye. None of us are safe."

"You're supposed to say you'll protect me."

"I would if I could. You and Marcel and my mom."

"But safety is just an illusion."

"I'm just saying that nothing is certain. When I was fifteen, a kid I played against took a hit, not even a dirty hit, and became paralyzed from his neck down. Just like that. Two summers ago, I went to a hockey camp at Princeton with a kid who was older than me and who was already committed there. A few months later, he ended up hurt enough that he'll never play again. Nothing is for certain in this world."

I search the horizon. I know he's right. I rest my head against him. "I don't know how to live with so much fear."

"No one does, Puck. Some people just haven't learned to fear the world yet like we have."

"So how do you live the way your dad wanted you to? I don't get how you do it. I'm still so angry and scared, and for now my mom is in remission."

"I guess maybe it's a choice. I'm not saying it's an easy choice. Or that I never get mad that he's not here to see what's happening in my life. I wish he could be at World Juniors so much. But when it gets to be too sad, I think about how much time he spent telling me to keep living, and I guess I just think it's how I can honor him. He wasn't bitter, so what right do I have to be?"

My mom would be just like Jett's dad. Even if she relapsed. Even if we lost her. She'd want me to have the best life I could. She'd want me to be fearless and to love and to be loved.

"I've changed because of you." I say this in French. J'ai changé grâce à toi.

"Moi aussi," Jett replies. Me too. He kisses my temple. Or

I should say, my beanie. I know Jett can't keep me safe. He isn't Superman or a shaman holding protective spells. But I believe in his love. In him. And that makes the world a lot less scary.

I take a deep breath. "Do you ever wonder who you'd be if hockey was taken away from you?"

"You said no hockey talk."

I turn and look at him.

He nods. "I love hockey. Every second of it. But I don't want it to be the only thing I ever accomplish in life. You have to stay balanced, or just like on the ice, you'll wipe out."

We sit on the beach together until the sun is low in the sky. Jett shows me more songs he has in French. He shares the playlist he keeps of his dad's favorite songs, a mix of old-school rock, French songs, and the pop we grew up with.

"Your dad was an optimist, I think," I say as we listen to Creed's "Higher" and a cheesy old French song that Jett says is from 1969 that talks about how wonderful it is to walk the Champs-Élysées.

Jett nods. "He was, even when life didn't really give him a reason to be. I feel like he trusted me, though. He trusted me to do the right things, to work hard, to take care of my mom and Marcel, and to love the world for him." He rolls and gets up and pulls me with him. "Your teeth are chattering. Time to go."

I shiver, and then we run back to the little blue Impreza as the sun sets over the water. Jett revs the engine to try to get the car to warm up. I smile at him, and I can't think about fearing the future because the only thought running through my mind is *Je t'aime tellement.* I love Jett so much. I want to love the world for him. I want to love the world with him.

Chapter 32

It's Okay to Miss You

THE LAST WEEK OF SCHOOL BEFORE WINTER BREAK SAILS BY faster than a shooting star. Jett and I make the most of the time we have, but it never feels like enough. I've become a greedy person, always hoping for just a few minutes more with him.

The Sunday before Christmas, I take him to the airport.

We don't say all the pointless things that people say, like "I'll call you later" or "I'll be watching your games," because we've already said them.

"I'd better go," Jett says as we stand outside the security line, his fingers still laced with mine.

I reach up and throw my arms around him and hug him. He squeezes me tight, and we sway like that for a moment.

“I’ll be back in time to torture Mr. G. for the first chem lab after break,” he says.

He really has tortured Mr. G. We’ve gotten solid A’s on every lab, mostly because of Jett, although I get the chemistry once Jett explains it to me. It’s a good thing that labs aren’t subjective like English essays, or Mr. G. would never give us the grade we deserve. Every time he hands our labs back, he makes a comment like “I hope you aren’t using AI to get these answers” or “I’m pleasantly surprised.” He says this last one so dryly that not even the most innocent principal could think he didn’t mean it as a dig.

Jett pulls out a badly wrapped box from his pocket and hands it to me. “It’s for Christmas. You aren’t allowed to open it until then.”

“I have something for you,” I say, “but it’s at my house. I thought I’d give it to you when you get back.”

“We can have our own little Christmas then.”

I nod and kiss Jett one more time and push him into the roped line. I stay and watch until he disappears into the throng of conveyor belts and gray plastic bins. Then I head home and wonder how much I’ll hear from my boyfriend while he’s off on his holiday adventures. I tell myself not to be disappointed if it’s not much. Jett has a lot going on with his family and hockey. I just need to remember that.

I haven’t even pulled out of the airport parking space when my phone lights up with a text from him.

At my gate. Miss you already.

I smile, set my phone down, and put my car into reverse. I may not have been Jett's first choice, but he loves me. Tellement.

In the five days I have before Christmas, I do my best to make up for all the baking, shopping, and decorating I missed out on while I was trying to juggle school, hockey, and having a boyfriend. It's nice to have almost two weeks off from games. My body needs the rest and healing time. I sleep a lot when I'm not talking to Jett or playing Santa's little helper for my mom. I run last-minute errands for her, pick up gifts she hasn't gotten checked off the list, and wrap presents, except for mine from my parents, of course.

My team has a couple of practices over the course of the holiday break, but nothing like what we usually do. Even Coach realizes that we need some time to rest and heal at this point in the season from the constant battering our bodies take. Pucks, sticks, and boards can leave some nasty black-and-blue marks on you. When Nina stripped to her sports bra last game, she looked like a battered girlfriend. I don't know how a game that bruises you so badly can be so much fun, but it is.

My family is glued to the hockey subscription channel as soon as World Juniors starts right after Christmas. London makes a whiteboard of the standings and who Canada will play next and when, which she attaches to the fridge with magnets and updates after every one of Jett's games. We learn the names and numbers of all his teammates, and Harps gets a crush on one of them.

"He could be a total jerk," I say.

"True," she says, "but I'm choosing to believe he's another Jett."

I hate to disappoint her, but there is not another Jett in the world. I should warn her of that, but it's not like she'll meet the guy, so I leave her alone with her crush. He is very cute, whatever his personality is like.

We watch the games, fueled by popcorn and tortilla chips, and my dad has bought us all matching Team Canada jerseys. It's a bit overboard, but even I admit it's easy to go overboard for Jett. And it's nice to spend time with my family and just have fun. We aren't worrying about my mom or planning how to get everything we need to accomplish done in the week. We're just enjoying each other and hockey. That feels like a Christmas present as much as the boxes and bags that were under the tree a few days ago. Even though Jett left my present with me and told me to wait for Christmas, I'm saving it to open until he gets back and I can give him his present, too. I just hope he likes the signed Claude Giroux jersey I got him.

Imani and Lewis come to watch one of Jett's games, and it's the first time Imani and I have done anything outside of school for a long time. It feels really good. I was worried the holiday break would drag with Jett away, but there's so much to look forward to every day that it passes almost more quickly than I want it to.

Team Canada does really well and makes it to the gold medal game, although they come up short in the final by one goal. Mostly because Finland's goalie makes Ilya Sorokin look like an amateur. Even Jett struggles to score on him. It doesn't hurt that the kid is six feet, seven inches tall. He should try guarding the net in my body for a day.

London cries when Jett doesn't get a gold medal, but by the time his team gets to the medal ceremony, Jett is smiling.

"It's okay," I tell her. "I'm not saying Jett's not disappointed, but he played well, and that's what matters when the draft happens in a few months. NHL teams are going to be really impressed."

"I hope they give him MVP," Jett's best friend, Lou, says.

When the announcements for individual awards are made, my whole family erupts even before they call Jett's name. As soon as they say the trophy is going to the captain of Team Canada, my family is out of their seats, jumping up and down and high-fiving each other and screaming with joy. Even my mom is caught up in the excitement. My eyes sting as I watch Jett shake back his sweaty hair and glide over on his right leg to receive the trophy. I'm still ashamed that I ever thought Mr. Discipline didn't work hard enough to deserve everything he's earned in life. The cameras pan to Jett's family, and my dad yells out, "There's Pierre and Ailene!" as if they're lifelong best friends. Marcel is there, too, his face lit with a smile that has forgotten to be shy.

We sing along to the Canadian national anthem as they

raise the flag, except we butcher all the words because we don't usually sing the Canadian anthem. But that just makes us laugh and point fingers at each other as we argue over what we think the words should be.

When the broadcast ends, it's a little like the aftermath of New Year's Eve. My mom says something about having a special dinner for Jett when he gets back to town, but then we all scatter into our own little worlds. I go to my room to text Jett.

You were great.

I could add that I'm sorry he didn't get gold, but that's not going to change anything or tell him something he doesn't already know. I've won and lost enough championship games over the course of playing that I don't tell him the silver medal is still something to be proud of or that he'll probably get another chance.

He won't see my text for a while, as there will be photos to take and interviews to do, so I clean my room and then Harps and I watch a made-for-TV Disney movie with London. I slip away early, though, when my phone pings with a text from Jett.

I really wanted to make you proud of me with a gold medal.

I'm not Peyton. I don't need you to have a gold medal to know your worth.

He doesn't answer me right away. Maybe I said something wrong? Then I see the little dots jumping.

Je t'aime, tellement.

I smile. Je t'aime tellement, aussi. I add a bunch of heart emoji. And then I hit send.

Mon cœur est plein. My heart is full.

Chapter 33

Things Fall Apart

WHEN JETT GETS TO THE BAGGAGE CLAIM AREA, I'M WAITING there with two chocolate protein shakes and a ridiculous sign. He's been a little down about not winning gold, so I figure the best way to counteract that is to be as goofy as he can be.

"Welcome Home, Silver Medalist and World Juniors MVP Jett Robitaille," it says, along with cutout pictures of him in action and a picture of his MVP trophy. Jett laughs when he sees me holding it and waiting for him. He runs over and drops his backpack and swings me around.

"I thought you'd be too embarrassed to do anything like that," he says after he's kissed me and checked out his sign.

"I am but decided to suck it up, as Lou says. Although this doesn't make us even because no one here knows you and everyone at the rink knew me when you brought that hideous sign."

Jett wraps his arms around me and sways us. "I missed you so much, Puck. Tellement, tellement, tellement."

I squeeze him tight. "I missed you, too," I say, although I'm not sure he hears me since he has my face smooshed into his chest. I push myself back to get a breath.

"Did you have any trouble in customs?"

"A little. They made me declare the suitcase of Canadian bacon I brought."

"Very funny."

Jett gives me his full dimple smile and brushes back some hair that's fallen from my clip. "I want to hit the ice with you so bad." That's probably not what most boys would be thinking right now.

I laugh. "Are your MVP legs ready for all that knee hockey?"

Jett groans. "I'll probably have to do ice time with them now, too." He stands with his arm around my shoulders. "Still, it will be worth it to be on the ice with you."

The warmth nestled in my stomach just from being near him again radiates through me.

Jett's bags and sticks come, and we lug everything to my Rogue. My family has planned a welcome-back party. My dad is apparently onto our extended kissing in the airport parking lot because he texts to ask what's taking us so long. I flash the text at Jett.

"Busted," he says, pulling his still-wet lips in and smiling.

My heart spins like one of those playground merry-go-rounds being pushed by someone's big brother.

"Don't forget to act surprised," I say. "My family went all out even though it's too cold for Lou to grill anything, which made him especially sad."

Jett nods. "My next award will be an Oscar. I never want Lou to be sad."

I think about telling him that he probably shouldn't kiss Lou's daughter in a way that makes her barely able to remember to breathe then, but I decide against stoking Jett's ego on this score. We drop his stuff at his host family's house and Jett follows me to my house in his car.

The party includes Imani and Lewis and Matt. Most of my hockey-playing cousins have also shown up, although I told my dad it would be too many people. My mom has made four trays of lasagna, though, and my aunt Satomi has brought sushi rolls, and my aunt Patti has brought a big Greek salad and a fruit tray. Jett is the hero of the hour. Everyone wants to talk to him, and I hear the same stories about the games he's played over and over.

"That was so sick in that game against Sweden when you got the hat trick," Kenji says.

Jett laughs, and I finally see him embarrassed as his cheeks flush. I didn't think anything could do that, but the lavish attention my family is dropping on him is a bit much. He's so cute when he's blushing, though. I have the perfect boyfriend.

"Thanks," he says.

After the others leave, Jett gives my family World Juniors gear he bought them at the tournament as late Christmas presents. We exchange our gifts, and he adds his World Juniors practice jersey.

"I washed it at the hotel, so you should wash it before you wear it," he says.

When I walk him to his car at the end of the night, he takes both my hands as we stand next to the Impreza and let it warm up.

"You, Mizz Ryleigh Vento, are the best thing that has ever happened to me."

"Better than winning MVP at World Juniors?" I believe Jett loves me, but "the best thing that's ever happened to him" seems like a stretch.

"I mean of stuff I haven't worked for."

"Oh, that's right, the great Jett Robitaille didn't have to win me over."

Jett laughs. "You know what I mean. And yes, you made me work very hard to win you over. Harder than you know." His dimples sparkle like the stars watching over us.

I purse my lips. I guess an excessive amount of knee hockey does count, but most of that was in his pursuit of Peyton anyway. I decide to be generous and not mention this, as my heart is bursting, and I don't want to taint what Jett and I have with even an ounce of pettiness.

"I'll see you in chem tomorrow, my beautiful Mizz Vento."

"I can't wait," I say, and plant a kiss to keep him warm on his way back to his host family.

Jett is waiting for me by the door to our chemistry class the next morning. He bites his lip into a smile and slips his hand over mine as we walk in.

"Ice time is confirmed for tomorrow," he says as we slide into our seats and break our hands apart before Mr. G. lays into us. We focus throughout class because, if we don't, Mr. G. will do everything he can to embarrass us. He randomly calls on Jett or me if we even look down at our notebooks. I want to remember everything about this senior year, except Mr. G. I hope to block him out of my memory the day we walk out of here for the last time.

After class, Jett walks me to calculus. "This month is going to suck," Jett says. "There isn't a single weekend when we are both in town."

I smile at him. "But there are two weekends in a row in February when we are."

Jett tugs at my shirt right by my navel. "You've suddenly become a real glass-half-full girl." He's standing close. I look up, and for a moment it's hard to remember that there are people around us. It feels as if Jett and I could be the last two people on the planet.

"Ugh," someone says. "Get a room."

Jett laughs. I turn my head. One of Peyton's cheer friends struts by.

"Why are they all stereotypes?" Jett asks.

I shrug. Then I smile. "They'd probably say the same thing about you, Hotshot."

Jett puts his arm around my shoulders and kisses my temple.

"I will see you at lunch, Mizz Vento," he says as he pecks my lips before he leaves.

I do pay attention in calc, but I also doodle little hearts in the margins of my notes, and more than once I redirect my attention to inverse cotangent functions when my mind strays to daydreaming about spending time with Jett. I don't know if we'll ever end up at Cornell at the same time, or if I'll end up there at all, but we at least have the next five months together. Peyton and her friends can make fun of us all they want. They can't change the next five months.

After calc, I hurry to lunch since Jett will be waiting for me. There's a cleaning crew in the hallway I normally take because someone has thrown up or something.

"These kids skip school all the time, but then when they're sick, they show up!" one of the janitors says.

"They aren't in elementary school anymore," the other says. "They should know better."

The hall smells of a sickly mess of vomit and industrial cleaners, so I turn down a different hallway. When I round the corner to the lunchroom, Jett is standing there with Peyton. His back is to me, and they're deep in conversation.

He's probably telling her to have her minion from this morning back off, but as I approach them, Jett is thanking her.

I stop. I'm not even sure I heard him right, because there's no way he'd be thanking Peyton for anything.

Peyton gives him a flirty shrug. "I'm not all bad, you know," she says. "There was a time when Ryleigh and I could even have been called friends."

"She'd have never given me this chance if you hadn't gone along," Jett says.

My mouth hangs open. What am I even hearing?

"Well, normally I wouldn't be on board to help Ryleigh with anything. I really don't know what you see in her. She used to be okay, but once she started playing hockey, she was always so sure she was better than everyone else. But my friends were totally impressed with that box you got us for the Rangers game, so your bad taste is my gain, as they say."

"I'm glad they had a good time," Jett says, apparently unfazed by her calling me his "bad taste."

"Anytime you need me to make Ryleigh jealous, just say the word. I'm sure we can work a deal." Peyton smiles at him, completely satisfied with herself.

Then her gaze strays from Jett's face to me where I stand just behind them. Her expression morphs into a disdainful laugh. Jett instantly turns around.

I've never seen Jett shocked before. His eyes grow wide and his face flushes.

"Ryleigh," he says, with more surprise than happiness to see me. His smile has evaporated.

"So, what's this deal you and Peyton made?"

Peyton looks at Jett. "This seems like a 'you' problem." She gives him a cutesy little wave before she turns and heads toward the cafeteria.

"Ryleigh, it's not—"

Jett stops himself, apparently unsure for the first time in his life of how to schmooze something over.

"Not what?" I tilt my head and wait.

Jett looks around as if he's wishing a meteor would crash into the ground near us so that he didn't have to explain whatever it is that he needs to explain.

"What it sounds like is that you made a deal with Peyton to make me jealous so that I'd do what, exactly? Date you?"

Jett rubs his palms against his jeans and steps closer to me. "Well, you had that no-dating rule, so I didn't know how to get you to spend time with me."

Do I even know him?

"Wait, so are you saying the whole fake-dating thing you made me do so you could get with Peyton—"

Jett interrupts me, shaking his head. "I never wanted to date Peyton. It was always you, Ryleigh."

I think back on everything that's happened between us, and it all starts to make some sense. All the ways he hesitated to chase Peyton, the times when he flat-out blew her off.

"Why would you go to such extremes? You lied to me!"

Jett grimaces. "I really liked you, Rye. From the very first time we met. I could hardly believe it when I walked into chemistry class and you were there. You were about to go sit with Danny, so I brushed past you to make you choose an empty table."

“Wait, even that was you manipulating me?”

“I mean, not manipulating, just redirecting?” Jett’s words are pleading, which means he knows he was wrong.

“I just wanted to sit with you, get to know you.” He looks down at the floor as he says this. My eyes are stinging. What else has he lied about?

“I was ready to take help from you. We were going to spend time on the ice together no matter what. Why did you have to lie about wanting to fake date so you could impress Peyton? Peyton, of all people!”

“Everyone said there was no way you’d date until you got your D1 slot. *You* said there was no way you would date until you got your slot. I didn’t think spending some time on the ice, with Dom there, was enough. I wanted you to see that I could be a good boyfriend. I wanted to show you how good we could be together.” He slips his hand around mine, but I jerk away.

“Don’t touch me.” I don’t look at him. I know he’s going to look like a wounded animal, and I don’t want to see it. It is not my fault he chose to lie to me. My whole body is trembling.

“Ryleigh, I know I messed up, but I love you so much. You have to believe that.”

I glance up then. Tears fall to my cheeks. “I do believe that. And that’s what makes this even harder to understand. And the fact that you’re running around having secret conversations with Peyton Malloy about how you two duped me into liking you, I can't even—I mean, how do you do that to someone you love?"

"Rye, I'm so sorry, I was so wrong." Jett is standing close enough that his words fall on me like the spray from a waterfall. I take a step back.

"And you just figured this out now? Because I caught you?" I shake my head. "I don't even know who you are."

"I'm still me," Jett says. "I just did something stupid because I liked you so much."

I hold up my hand for him to stop. "I can't do this right now."

I turn and walk away.

"Where are you going?"

I stop so that Jett will hear me, but I don't look at him. "Anyplace where you aren't."

I swivel forward and continue walking.

Behind me, Jett slams his fist into a locker.

I don't know if it hurts, but right now, I hope it does.

Chapter 34

Nothing Is Perfect, Not Even a Kitten

I SLIP INTO THE FIRST GIRLS' BATHROOM I PASS. I'M SHAKING AND crying, but everyone is at lunch or in class. I lean against the wall and try to process what just happened. How the guy I have trusted like I've never trusted anyone completely lied to me and made a fool of me with the girl who hates me the most in the world, because he *likes* me? That's the most fourth-grade, messed-up, bat-crazy excuse I've ever heard.

"Oh, Ryleigh, je t'aime tellement that I had to lie to you and make a joke of you with the girl who thinks she's your rival just to get you to go out with me because, guess what, it's your fault because you won't date anyone until you achieve what you need to achieve." I slap the wall as if it shouldn't be there listening to this ridiculous monologue.

I sniff and look around. What is even happening right now?

I'm arguing with a concrete wall that's painted yellow so that no one notices it's concrete.

I turn around and slide down the wall until I'm sitting and I just cry. I really hope no one comes in right now, but not enough to stop crying. It feels just like when my mom got diagnosed. Everything I thought my life was got hurled into an abyss faster than a tornado rips through a house, and I had to crawl through darkness to reclaim the stuff that mattered. Now Jett wants me to do that all over again? I can't.

I wish I had my inhaler. My lungs are getting congested. It takes me a while, but eventually my breath slows, and I wipe the tears from my face. I haven't had lunch, but I couldn't eat if I tried. I get up and wipe my face with some wet paper towels so that it's not tear streaked. In the mirror, my eyes are red and puffy, but there's nothing I can do about that except keep my head down and avoid making eye contact with anyone. Imani and Matt must be asking where I am. I wonder what Jett told them. Peyton will be in her glory, reigning over the lunchroom when she sees me missing. At least someone is happy my boyfriend is a liar. Ex-boyfriend. Ex–fake boyfriend. Were we ever really together if it all rested on a lie?

The bell must have rung without me noticing because some girls flood into the bathroom. I grab my lunch box from the floor and duck out. I still have history and English to get through this afternoon, and I need to keep my grades up in case Cornell or some other school makes an offer. Cornell. Can I even go there now if they make me an offer? My whole world is imploding.

I scurry to history and keep my face as low as I can all afternoon. I don't worry about seeing Jett, because he'll have left school early to go to practice. No matter what, when you are playing at his level, you show up, no excuses. Even if the girl you supposedly love wants to put your head in a guillotine, his priority is going to be making it to practice on time. Still, just in case, I hang out in my last class, English, long after the bell has rung and the room has emptied.

"Are you okay, Ryleigh?" the teacher asks as she packs up her things.

"I'm fine, Ms. Noel," I say, although the words sound hollow.

She purses her lips a moment and then nods and leaves. I take a deep breath. I sit there until I feel calm. It must be late, because I hear the cleaning crew in the room next to this one. I slide my backpack from the desk and leave.

It's dusky when I get to my car. There's a piece of notebook paper stuck under my windshield wiper. I pull it out and unfold it.

I'm sorry. I really messed up. Je t'amie tellement, tellement, tellement. Jett's carefree print looks just like his voice sounds. I crumple his words, and the only thing that keeps me from throwing his declaration on the ground is my refusal to litter. I shove his note into my backpack and head home.

My parents are in the kitchen when I walk in. My dad smiles. "Puck, do you want to lift with me tonight?"

I shake my head and walk past him to go to my room.

"Whoa," he says, and grabs my arm. "What happened today?"

I look up at him and morph into a sticky, sobbing gelatinous mess. My dad wraps me in his arms. I haven't said a word, but he whispers to himself, "I'm going to kill that kid."

I know he doesn't mean it, so I just sob more. Then I pull away and lug myself up to my room.

A little while later, there's a soft knock on my door.

"Yes?"

The door cracks open. My dad peeks his head in. "Is this a Dad crisis, or a Mom crisis?"

I stare at him. My parents are so methodical.

"Mom thinks it's a Dad thing, but we can switch if it's a Mom thing. She's on standby." He is so awkward. My rough-and-tumble Marine dad trying to figure out how to be an emotional support parent.

I shake my head.

He darts his glance around. "So maybe a Dad thing," he says to himself. He waves off someone in the hall, which must be my mom waiting to see which of them should be the first responder. He comes in and sits beside me on the floor where I'm leaning against my bed.

"What did he do?"

"Do you think it's normal to humiliate and lie to someone you love?"

My dad reaches behind him and pulls a tissue from the box on my dresser. He hands it to me.

"Definitely not."

"Exactly." I blow my nose.

We sit there quietly for a few minutes.

"How did he humiliate you and lie to you?"

I sigh. Then I tell my dad the whole story.

"Wait," he says when I'm all done, "so you two weren't dating for real until after Thanksgiving?"

I nod.

"Wow, you had your mom and me fooled. Like jarhead-level fooled. We totally bought it."

"I'm apparently a master fake dater. But not so great at the real thing."

My dad's jaw drops a little, but he doesn't speak as he contemplates the existence of such a term, and then my mastery of it.

He nods slightly.

I bang my head against my knees.

"Oh, Puck." He puts his arm around my shoulders.

"How could he do this to me?"

My dad pats my shoulder slowly. "Even a kitten isn't perfect."

I turn and look at him. "What?"

There should be a law against ex-Marines becoming emotional support parents.

My dad shrugs. "Nothing, and no one, is perfect, Puck. Not even a kitten. I mean, a kitten comes close. Maybe the closest thing to perfect in the world. They're adorable. But they still scream when they should be quiet and run around like fools and fall into their food. But, when you consider the whole, kittens are basically perfect."

I have no idea what my dad is talking about. I watch him and blink.

He smiles. "You could be a kitten."

When I don't smile back, he gets serious again. "What I'm saying, Puck, is that I think Jett is a good kid who made a really misguided call to spend some time with a girl he liked. I don't think he set out to make a mess or to hurt you. He probably didn't contemplate the full consequences. Kittens are smarter than seventeen-year-old boys."

"Are you seriously taking his side?"

"No, no, no," my dad says, pulling his hand from my shoulder and shaking it for confirmation. "I'm just saying that maybe you're feeling extra hurt because of the whole Peyton rivalry."

"I am not rivals with that girl!" I say this way too loudly for either of us to believe me.

My dad nods and pretends he totally agrees with me.

My life is so messed up. "You think I should just forgive him, as if none of what he did matters?"

"Oh, Puck," he says. "Only you can decide if you can forgive him. Your mom and I will support you no matter what. I like Jett. I finally had a running and grilling buddy. But hurting my little girl is not cool. I can't stand anyone making you cry."

I exhale.

"Honey, Jett is still a boy. I know seventeen seems very

grown up to you, but his frontal lobe isn't going to fully mature for another seven years. If you think about it, he's closer to middle school than he is to being a full-fledged adult."

"So you're taking his side." My dad is starting to tick me off.

"No! I'm not taking any sides. I'm just saying that if he'd come up with this plan in junior high, every boy in his class would have agreed it was solid."

"What is wrong with you people?"

My dad shrugs. "Kittens are a lot smarter than boys."

"And way more perfect," I say.

"Should I go beat him up?"

I give my dad a flatline look.

He clears his throat. "Violence is never the answer."

"If anyone gets to beat him up, it's me."

"That's the spirit," my dad says. "Dinner is just about ready. You'll come down?"

I nod reluctantly. My dad pats my knee and gets up and leaves.

And just like that, my parents have resolved, in their minds, the biggest heartbreak of my life.

Chapter 35

Where Do I Go from Here?

JETT TEXTS AND CALLS ME REPEATEDLY UNTIL I FINALLY TEXT him back.

Stop.

I need some space. I need to process how I feel. He runs through life just letting everything roll off his back, but I can't. Everything feels so huge right now. While my friends are starting to get acceptances to schools and making plans, I'm still desperately chasing the one thing that mattered most to me about going to college. And then to fall in love with Jett and dream about being at school with him, only to have him destroy those dreams—it's too much. He was always too much. Too much to resist. Too much to love. Too much to trust. I'm free-falling, and I don't know how to stop.

I can't avoid him forever, though. He's still my chemistry partner. The thought of being around him for the next five months while I feel this angry scares me. This could be the start of my villain origin story.

The next time I see him, he's sitting at our table in chemistry. When I slide into my seat, he glances up and acknowledges me, but he doesn't try to talk to me. Good. He needs to learn boundaries. He's way too used to getting his way because he's handsome and charming. But I don't dare look at his dimples.

After class, Jett stays back while I leave. I walk to calc without him for the first time in months, except on the days he was traveling for hockey. It feels weird. And lonely. Kids whisper as I go past. I don't know how much they know, but they certainly know enough.

When I reach the cafeteria, Jett isn't waiting for me by the door. I walk in and look at our table. He isn't there, either. I glance around and finally spot him sitting across the room with some boys who play amateur hockey, but nothing like the level he plays. Serves him right.

I've already told Imani what happened. Just like my dad, she took Jett's side. She could have plagiarized her speech from his, it was so similar. "Only you can decide if you can forgive him," she'd said. "Just be sure that what he did is as unforgivable as you seem to think it is."

I don't know if what Jett did is unforgivable. All I know is that I can't find my way to forgive him. I thought I had changed so much with Jett. I thought I was ready to leave behind feeling scared every day. But now I'm right back where I was last year, wondering how to survive when my world has been suddenly turned inside out. This is exactly what my mom's cancer diagnosis felt like. All because he lied to me.

As I slip into my seat at lunch, there are more eyes on me than a celebrity walking into the Met Gala. Not only is my friend group at our table watching me, almost everyone in the cafeteria is staring, even some of the teachers. I guess I deserve that with the public display I made of how gone I was on Jett, although some of that was to help him pursue Peyton. I've made such a fool of myself. I wish we were allowed to wear the hoods of hoodies at school because I would love to hide in mine right now. I pull out my lunch and methodically arrange it in front of me instead, determined not to cry.

"Surely you guys have something to talk about," I say when the table is deathly silent.

I glance at Imani first. She's biting her lip as she contemplates me.

"Lewis got into NYU," she says.

I turn to him. "That's awesome! Congrats." I try to sound upbeat, but it's not as much as he deserves.

"Who knew Lewis was so smart, right?" Matt asks without a hint of sarcasm.

"Thanks, Matt," Lewis says, and then clamps his lips down. "But I didn't get into Berklee," he adds.

"It's okay," Imani says. "You still haven't heard from most of the schools on your list."

We take turns consoling Lewis. Berklee was his first choice.

"What about you, Rye?" Matt asks.

He suddenly dips forward and looks at Imani, so my guess is that she just kicked him under the table.

"Mans, it's okay," I say. "Cornell is still evaluating me and Quinnipiac just sent me a letter to say they'll try to come to one of my games." I got an offer from a D3 school. It's not a serious program, but I guess playing hockey for a scrub program is better than not playing at all.

"I think you'll get an offer," Imani says, and the rest of them agree with her. I glance over at Jett's table. He's watching me but he looks away as soon as our gazes meet.

The next two weeks pass in pretty much the same way. We've stopped having morning ice time. Jett had Dom call me to say we could still have ice time without Jett, but it felt weird thinking that Jett was getting ice for me when I can't even bring myself to talk to him. At school, Jett avoids me except for chemistry, and last week he was away for hockey on our lab day. Danny helped me complete it, and Jett and I just emailed each other about the results.

I keep telling myself it's all fine, and I almost believe it, except when Peyton smirks at me in the hallway or I catch a glimpse of Jett in the cafeteria or the hallway and my heart aches. The worst is when I have to sit beside him in chemistry. That's an hour of hell every time. Jett barely moves after he acknowledges my presence, as if he's afraid of reminding me that he exists, except for taking notes or doodling sad cartoon cat faces in the margins of his notebook. And somehow, even as angry as I am, I still miss him. I still want to be with him.

Every time I'm tempted to talk to him, I remind myself how I felt when I first found out. And I think about Peyton gloating as she saw me in pain. My heart and my head are at war, and all I can do is bleed.

"Mr. Robitaille, is there trouble in paradise?" Mr. G. asks Jett when he notices we aren't holding hands before class. My heart pounds. Our classmates know we broke up, and Mr. G. probably does, too. He just can't stop himself from delighting in our forced-proximity predicament.

"No, Mr. Polachuk," Jett replies. "By its nature, paradise is a place devoid of conflict where every desire is instantly fulfilled, thus creating a space incapable of growth or purpose, which, in turn, creates an endless-summer effect that precludes disharmony or conflict. Trouble, as you call it."

Mr. G. stops pacing and stares at him for a long moment. "We are quite the philosopher today, I see, Mr. Robitaille."

Jett doesn't lower his gaze and eventually Mr. G. blinks and moves on. I want to write "Thank you" on my notebook, but I don't want Jett to think I'm ready to talk to him. I can't open that door. Even though I'm pretty sure he'd be happy if I did.

After we leave class, Imani finds me. "Are you okay?"

I look at her. She does ask me this regularly now, but this feels different.

"You mean generally about my boyfriend lying to me, or is there something new you're worried about?"

Imani contemplates me. "Peyton's been telling everyone how she and Jett played you."

I scoff. "I would expect nothing less from our resident mean girl. I thought maybe she wouldn't want to admit that it was because Jett liked me and not her."

"Well, since she would never be into him anyway, according to her, she seems to be reveling in your misery."

I'm still not convinced that she didn't change her mind about that when the camera crew was following Jett around school, but it doesn't matter. I come out of the whole thing looking like a complete noob, as usual, while Peyton floats above the rest of us in her made-up world.

"Four and a half months," I say, and plaster on a fake smile for Imani. "I have four and a half months until graduation, and then I never have to see any of these people again."

It's not really that long if you think about it. The only problem is that, whether I see him or not, Jett Robitaille is breaking my heart. Every minute of every day. I may be a fool, but I'm not foolish enough to believe that graduation is going to change the ache in my chest from the hotshot who stole my heart like a breakaway goal.

Chapter 36

Dreams Really Do Come True

WHEN I SCHLEP INTO THE KITCHEN AFTER SCHOOL, MY DAD IS standing there talking to my mom.

"Mom, are you okay?" I ask. "What's happening?" My throat constricts and my breath catches.

My mom smiles. "I'm fine, Ryleigh. Your dad just got off a little early today."

My dad almost never gets off early. He's a logistics officer for a company that sells specialized military equipment to the Department of Defense. I dart my gaze from my mom to my dad. They don't usually hide bad news, but something is weird.

My mom comes over and hugs me. "I promise," she says. "I'm perfectly healthy, and so is your dad."

I pull back and search her eyes. My internal polygraph says she is telling the truth.

"Let's have a nice dinner together for once," my dad says. It's rare that we all get to be together for a meal, so I nod. Most of the time, one of us is eating before or after the others because of practice or London's piano lessons or dance class.

"Get your homework done so we can lift together later," he adds.

"Okay," I say. Usually, I like lifting with my dad, but since Jett and I broke up, everything makes me feel tired. It's taken all my energy not to let it show at hockey, although it's helped that Hailey is back. This past weekend was the first since before Christmas that I didn't have to take all our games. It's good to have her playing again, especially now that I'm playing as well as she does. Maybe even better. At least, I was before Jett ripped my heart out and fed it to Peyton. But I'm still playing well enough to compete at the same level as Hailey, and that's something I need to hold on to until my heart stops aching.

It's nice to have all of us around the table for dinner. Every so often, one of them will start to say something about Jett, but then they stop themselves and we all pretend like it hasn't happened. I know they miss him. So do I. But that doesn't make his lying okay.

We're cleaning up the dishes when my phone buzzes. I don't recognize the number.

"Hello?" I answer.

A lady's voice replies. She introduces herself as the head coach at Cornell. I almost drop my phone, and everyone stops what they're doing.

"Who is it?" Harper hisses.

"Is it Jett?" London asks.

I wave my hand to tell them to quiet down and run up to my room.

I come back downstairs a few minutes later. I'm still a little stunned.

"Mom, Dad, Cornell is making me an offer."

There's a momentary silence as they take this in and then a lot of whooping and jumping around. Until my dad stops and looks at me.

"How do you feel about going to Cornell, even if it means Jett might be there in a couple of years?"

How do I feel about getting my dream if it means being around Jett? I mean, two years is a lifetime. Would we even recognize each other? Surely we'd both have moved on. There's no way I could still feel this horrible about our breakup after two years of college, right?

"Yes," I say. "Yes, I want to go to Cornell. I don't care about Jett or anything else." This isn't true. My brain is already creating scenarios where Jett waltzes onto campus with some girl who looks just like Peyton on his arm and I end up in therapy or on the front page of the campus newspaper. But I can't worry about that now. One problem at a time. The important part is that I'm getting an offer.

My dad smiles and balls his hand into a victory fist. "Big Red, here we come!"

I laugh. "Don't get too excited, Dad. It's a very expensive

school and they're only offering me sixty percent now, although she said I may qualify for other grants and financial aid." Everyone thinks that D1 schools give athletes a full ride, and that's true for some of the students. But there are also kids on D1 scholarships that only get a portion of a scholarship, which is split with another student. Sometimes it's not even any money.

"Maybe I won't be able to afford the offer."

My dad shakes his head. "We'll figure it out, if this is what you want. This is a great school. You deserve this. You've worked harder than any kid I've ever seen."

I smile. My dad is always in my corner. Even if he wishes my corner included Jett.

"She says they'd like to spend the first year to two developing my skills since I'm on the small side, but then they see me as a goalie who could take first goalie position when their older goalies graduate. Depending on the speed of my progression, I'll get to play more games my sophomore year, although I may see a little action my first year if I'm playing as well as I am now."

My mom wipes a tear from her eye. "I'm so proud of you for how hard you've worked. I know it wasn't easy because of me."

"Don't ever say that, Mom." I go over and hug her and we're both crying. Then my dad comes and hugs us. Then London.

"Come on, Harps," my dad says, and she grimaces as she piles on.

When we finally break apart, my dad leans against the counter, watching me. "You're sure you're okay with it being Cornell?"

I take a deep breath. Jett is Jett. But hockey is hockey.

"Yes," I say. "Yes, I would love to play at Cornell."

Chapter 37

I Am Skating in Reverse

AS WE BREAK OUT THE ICE CREAM TO CELEBRATE, THE FIRST PERSON I want to tell is Jett. He's also the last person I want to tell.

Still, it's nice to celebrate this with my family. There is one thing that I don't want to lose from my relationship with Jett, and that's how he taught me to be present and appreciate the good things when they happen, because life doesn't wait very long before it throws you more challenges. Even Harps and London are dancing with me.

"We're getting *all* the merch," Harper says.

"You know we are!" my dad says. He whips out his phone and maps our house to Cornell. "Four hours and twenty-two minutes," he declares. "We will be at every game!"

"Well, except when I have a game," Harper says.

My dad nods.

"Or when I have a recital," London says.

"That's okay," I say. "I'll be riding the bench my first year anyway."

"That never stopped us before," my mom says.

I laugh. "No, you're right, it never did."

"The best part," Harper says, "is that I never again have to listen to Ryleigh whine about getting a D1 slot!"

"I was not whining."

"Eh," my dad says, and they all laugh. They are so annoying, but I love them so much.

After we've demolished a half gallon of chocolate pecan caramel hazelnut, I tell them I need to call Imani. They look at me.

"I'm not calling him," I say. "Stop getting your hopes up."

They dart their looks away from me, as if they aren't thinking of Jett all the time. They're so pathetic. Just like me.

Imani is more excited than I am when I tell her over videochat. "Ooh, I can't wait to come visit you! We are going to have so much fun in college."

"I can't believe this is happening," I say.

"So, you're okay with going to Cornell even though you-know-who is also committed there?"

I shrug. "I'd only have to be on campus with him my last two years. Besides, he'll probably be in the NHL by then anyway. He may not even go to college. At least, not in the normal way." I'm kind of proud of myself for how nonchalant I sound, because it's hard not to cry. I really want this opportunity. And I really don't want to have to see Jett moving on with his life. The thought of him with someone else lands like a slap shot on my chest. Without pads.

"Any chance you might forgive him?"

"Forgiveness isn't something I've ever been good at. Peyton can still get to me, after all."

"I get it. But I don't think he's a bad guy at heart. He's giving you the space you asked for, and I can tell it's not easy for him. I know you hate that he lied, but I don't think he ever meant to hurt you."

No, even I don't think he ever meant to hurt me. I'm starting to think it's not just the lying that's made me so mad at Jett. It's the way he could make me free-fall just like my mom's illness did. Because when you're in free fall, there's no telling where you'll land. Jett's right that none of us are safe, but that doesn't mean you should ski down a mountain without a helmet.

"Any word from Savannah?" I ask to change the subject.

She shakes her head. She got rejected from Pratt yesterday.

"I think it will be Savannah. That's far, but when the season ends, I could come down. Or maybe we will have the same spring break."

She smiles. "Well, now that Lewis got into the Manhattan School of Music, I may just go to Drexel. But I don't have to reply yet, so we'll see."

We talk about schools and where everyone is heading.

"I can't believe how fast the year is going," Imani says. "It felt so slow back in the fall. But we're all about to be moving on. I can't wait, but it also makes me sad. I'm going to miss you so much."

I nod. Imani and I know every embarrassing thing the other has done and we're still like sisters.

"It feels huge, doesn't it?" I ask.

"It is huge. We've gone to school together since we were little."

We look at each other and get teary-eyed.

"Let's just hang up," I say. "Before we're both sobbing."

She laughs. "You first."

"No, you." This is what we used to do in sixth grade.

We laugh. "On three," I say. "One, two, three!"

We hang up then and I brush my teeth and wash my face for bed. When I come back and plug my phone in for the night, there's a text from Jett.

> I heard you got an offer from Cornell. That's awesome, congrats! Please don't say no because of me. You should take it. I may never even get there. And I promise not to bother you if I do. I know I'm the one who messed us up.

As always, my first reaction is anger.

I type at least four answers and then erase them before hitting send. They all sound really mean. Everything from *I'm not making decisions because of you* to *You aren't that important to my decision-making process*. They aren't just mean, though—they're also a lie. Only a couple weeks ago, it was my dream to be with him there. Now it terrifies me. What if I'm not over him by then? What if I never get over him?

I already accepted, I finally type, and immediately put my phone on Do Not Disturb.

I see the tiny bubbles pop up but then they stop. He must have gotten the message that I put my notifications on silent. I hold my phone for a couple of minutes, not wanting to let go of the connection to him. I'd be angry if he texted me back, but I'm upset that he doesn't. I need therapy. Or maybe what I really need is to yell at him. I text him.

Let's meet after practice tomorrow. I have some things to say to you.

It takes what seems like a long time, but eventually Jett marks my text with a thumbs-up.

I don't know what I'm going to say to him. I'm not even sure exactly why I want to meet him. All I know is, I feel like I might explode if I never take the chance to tell him how much he's hurt me.

Chapter 38

The End of an Era

JETT AND I MEET UP IN THE PARKING LOT OF THE JR. HAT TRICKS' rink because it's the only time that works. I'm waiting for him when he comes out of practice, my Rogue parked beside his Impreza one last time. In my rearview mirror, Jett strides out of the rink and walks over. He pops the passenger door to my Rogue. It's no different from sitting beside him in class, I tell myself. Except that it's dark out and we're alone.

He smells like tea tree shampoo and citrus aftershave. My heart is beating faster than a hummingbird's. If I hate him, it shouldn't do that.

"Salut, Rye," he says. His voice is gravelly, and he clears his throat.

I turn my gaze from him. From the perfect layering of his

hair. From his dark eyes and soft dimples and strong jaw. From the boy who reminded me how to believe in myself again.

It no longer seems like a good idea to confront Jett with how hurt I am. I rub my index finger over my thumb and wish it were a magic lamp.

He doesn't say anything. He just slowly brushes his hands along his thighs.

All the words I had sitting in my head waiting to be unloaded on him are now jumbled and incoherent.

"About Cornell," I finally say. The words come out like a whiff, not a slap shot. "I'm taking it because it's a great school and a good offer, not because you're committed there, too."

He nods.

We sit there silently. I don't want him to stay. I don't want him to leave. I miss him. I miss us.

"Ryleigh, I know I hurt you. Et je suis désolé. Truly, truly sorry. I wish I could have another chance at meeting you for the first time." His voice is shaky. Repentant.

"I believe you. I just don't know how I could ever trust you again." My hair clip brushes against the headrest. The orange glow of the parking lot lights reveals a slight snow drifting down, although it melts as soon as it touches the cars or the ground.

Jett turns to me then. "What would change how you feel? What can I do to prove to you that I never meant to let things get so messed up?"

I don't look at him. "How could you lie to me like that?"

"It didn't seem like a lie. Not at first. I wanted to spend time with you. I wanted to help you with hockey. I didn't think I'd fall in love with you. I just knew I wanted to be around you, as much as I could. I guess that was always a form of love, but I didn't know it then. At first, it just seemed like a harmless way to be near you."

"Messing with my feelings just seemed like a game to you?"

"That's not what I mean. Spending time with you by letting you think I liked someone else seemed like I was the one taking the risk."

"But I asked you to help me! I was going to be on the ice with you, whenever you got us time. Why did you have to escalate it to pretending you wanted Peyton?" A tear slides down my cheek, and I hate myself for letting it show.

Jett stares out the window for a long moment. "I thought you'd never break your rule. When I knew that you and Peyton didn't like each other, I hoped you might be competitive enough to let me get close. I never expected you to take me wanting Peyton so seriously. And when you did, I got scared that you'd stop spending time with me if you knew that you were the one I wanted. When the camera crew came to school, Peyton told me that she'd consider lowering her standards for me. After I explained the truth to her, she offered to go along."

"Of course she did."

"I should have thought about that more. It seemed like she was just doing it to get attention, maybe save some face. I didn't really get how much she enjoyed pulling a fast one on you until it was too late. You said you didn't see her as a rival. But she sees you as one. I shouldn't have misjudged her the way I did."

"I always wondered what you saw in her, besides the obvious."

"She is definitely not for me. The way she acted that first day, about her summer in France and 'Cali,' I thought you'd catch on. I almost told you so many times, but then I'd get interrupted or chicken out. I know you're angry with me and I deserve it. I just don't know how to make it better."

I turn to look at him. "I trusted you!"

"I should never have lied to you, Rye, I get that. But it was you. Doesn't that count for anything?"

"How do you think we can ever go back to the way we were?"

"Because I love you?" he asks.

"And you expect me to put my faith in that? I don't know how to do that, Jett." I pick at a ring on my finger. I don't know how to put faith in him if I could just lose him anyway.

"What I can't understand is why you won't even try."

I wipe a tear off my cheek.

"I had finally crawled out of the hole I was in from the worst year of my life. Between my mom's cancer and Coach Blackmon bullying me, there were days I went to bed hoping I didn't wake up in the morning. And you changed all that. You made me believe that good things could happen for me. You made me believe in myself. In life. In you. But the whole time, it was a lie."

"That's just not true, Ryleigh. Every moment I spent with you was the truth."

“Maybe. But it’s also true that you thanked Peyton for playing along. It’s true that you gave her Rangers tickets you schmoozed from somewhere. And it’s true that, sooner or later, she was going to drop that bomb on me so that she could end the rivalry she thinks we have on a high note. Every time I see you now, I think of that. The whole school thinks I’m a joke. Peyton’s joke.”

Jett pulls back in his seat and clears his throat again. Even in this dim light, I can see that his eyes are red. He looks at me for a long moment, as if he’s trying to commit my face to memory. “If I knew how to make this better, Ryleigh, I would. Je t’aime. Tellement.”

He sniffs and gets out of the car and into his Impreza. He pulls out of the parking space without looking at me again, and I sit there and cry until I have to use my inhaler just to breathe.

Chapter 39

It's Always Darkest

WHEN I WALK INTO MY NEXT CHEMISTRY CLASS, DANNY IS SITTING in Jett's seat. I slip into the seat beside him and stare.

"Don't ask me how he did it. All I know is Mr. G. told me to start sitting here," Danny says.

Jett walks by and takes Danny's old seat. The whole class is looking at each other. Only Jett and I face forward, determined to seem like we haven't noticed the change.

"Mr. Robitaille," Mr. G. says.

"Yes, sir?"

Mr. G. smiles. "Can you explain the reaction that we witnessed in last week's lab?"

"Yes," Jett says. He launches into a succinct and erudite explanation without any of his usual swagger.

"Do you think Mizz Vento was able to understand that explanation?"

Jett looks down. "Yes, Ms. Vento is very smart." Jett defends me, but he's no longer challenging Mr. G. as he does it, or mocking Mr. G. by calling me Mizz. Mr. G. has won. Just like Jett bought us ice time with knee hockey, he bought me a new lab partner by offering subservience to Mr. G.

My stomach turns. But I didn't ask Jett to do that. He shouldn't have done that. Mr. G. doesn't deserve it.

Danny glances over at me, so I look at my notes and pretend I haven't noticed anything. I blink back some tears and refocus.

"You okay?" Danny whispers.

"Perfectly fine," I say, and plaster on a fake smile.

I don't see Jett again, outside of lunch. There, we are like two people who don't really know each other as we sit at different tables. I feel his gaze as I go to the vending machine, but when I turn, he's staring out the windows that line the back wall. He doesn't seem to be engaged much with the conversation at the table, although he glances at one of the boys and nods slightly before he goes back to his vacant staring.

Whispers follow me down the hall and into the girls' bathroom. They linger by the cafeteria doors and the library.

By the time the last bell rings, school has become suffocating. I grab my books and my sister and rush home. I should feel better about ending things now before Jett can hurt me any more than he already has. But all I feel is grief.

January rolls on whether I want it to or not. I'm busy with my signing and hockey and school, but when I wander around the rink now before practice or a game, my mind is like a scab that keeps getting torn open. All I can think about is Jett. I miss him in every quiet moment. I miss laughing. I miss being on the ice with him and Dom. But I keep working on everything they taught me, and my game is getting stronger shift by shift.

I should be happy. My mom is healthy. I have a D1 commitment. My grades are fine. My coach and my team are thrilled with me. This year is nothing like last year. But somehow, I still feel like a hollow shell going through the motions. They're just different motions than they were when my mom was in crisis and my coach hated me.

When I come downstairs on a Saturday morning, I stop just before I get to the kitchen.

"You can't wear that, Lou," my mom says.

"But—" My dad stops before he finishes.

"I know, dear, you 'paid good money for it.'"

"It's not even that," my dad replies. "We were going to go to the batting cages."

My mother exhales. "I swear, you are taking this harder than Ryleigh is."

"I'll go change," my dad says. "But you saw him play the other night. He's brokenhearted."

I clear my throat and walk into the kitchen. My dad has on his World Juniors Team Canada shirt.

"You can wear the shirt, Dad." I don't tell him that he shouldn't be watching Jett's games. That's his business. I tried to watch one, but it just made me miss Mr. Miracle more.

My dad stares at me, a coffee mug in his hand. "Are you sure?"

I nod.

"You wouldn't want—"

"Yes, Dad," I interrupt. "I'll go to the batting cage with you. But I'm not calling you Lou." Sometimes he's like a toddler.

My dad comes over and hugs me. But the next time I see him, he's wearing one of his old Marine Corps T-shirts.

By the end of the first week of February, the chatter at school has died down. A couple of weeks ago, it seemed so important what everyone thought. Now it's just exhausting and pointless.

"None of these people really matter to your life," Imani says when we catch a snippet of someone in the hall saying I think I'm too good for a future NHLer now that I'm committed.

I'm finally starting to see that. "They didn't show up at my house with food when my mom was sick last year like you did. They don't try to cheer me up like you and Lewis and Matt do. And they won't be at Cornell with me or calling to catch up when I come home for winter break. I don't care anymore what they think."

"Have you talked to Jett?" she asks.

"No," I say. I don't tell Imani the real reason I can't forgive him. She wouldn't be proud of what a coward I am. I thought I had overcome being afraid of fear, but I guess I'm really no different than I was last year. I can't lose Jett tomorrow if I give him up today.

Imani gives me the "come here" look and hugs me.

"Maybe you should think about the reason more and the facts less," she says.

I pull away and study her face. She's in my corner no matter what, even if she thinks I'm doing the wrong thing.

"Okay, I just have to say this one thing, and then I'll stop," she adds.

I exhale and wait. Stopping her at this point would require a Marine battalion.

"If the reason you can't forgive him is your pride, then Peyton has won. You just admitted that you don't even care what these people think. But you're fixated on Jett lying about liking someone else just to get your attention."

When she puts it like that, I sound pathetic.

"A lie is a lie," I say, not sure I believe myself.

"Even Prince Charming needed a slipper to recognize Cinderella," she says before we part ways.

Chapter 40

Never Say Never

THE WEEK OF VALENTINE'S DAY, I DON'T HAVE THURSDAY-NIGHT practice. Normally a change of routine is refreshing, but today I wish I had to be busy. Today, I wish I had my team expecting me to be me.

Five minutes after I retreat to my room, though, Harper and London show up.

"We need to talk to you," London says. She's definitely going to be a girlboss someday.

"If this is about Jett, then I don't want to hear it." How am I supposed to let him go when no one else will?

My sisters exchange a glance.

"Too bad," Harps says.

I groan. "Fine, get it over with."

"Jett might not be perfect, but he's the best thing that's ever happened to you," Harper says.

I stare at them. "That's it?" I really expected a full-on assault.

"You and Jett balance each other," London says. "He's reckless and free-spirited and you're cautious and controlled. But, Rye, underneath, you two are exactly the same. You both have hearts that are overflowing."

I blink. Why does my twelve-year-old sister sound like a thirty-year-old therapist?

Harper nods.

"Harps and I talked about it, and we know we made you take on too much since Mom got sick. Some of this is our fault. If you hadn't felt so pressured with everything, then maybe you wouldn't have had that ridiculous no-dating rule and none of this would have happened. You and Jett could have just met like normal people."

I laugh. *Like normal people.* What does that even mean? Maybe no one is normal. Maybe we're all just kittens trying to find our way. Imperfect animals stumbling around in a world that's too big and unknown. Some kittens are just cuter than others.

"I don't blame you guys. I'm not even sure I blame Jett anymore."

"Well then, what's keeping you from forgiving him?" London asks.

I shake my head. Maybe it is my pride. At least, I think I'd prefer that to the real reason. If it were just my pride, would't that mean I didn't care that much in the first place? Instead of being too scared to lose because it would be completely reckless to ever trust him with my heart again? Maybe it's because I'm nothing but a coward terrified of this free fall. Somehow, that doesn't seem to stop it, though.

"Don't lose Jett over this silly mistake," Harper says. "Mom should have taught you how precious and rare love is."

I look up and stare. Harper has never even hinted that she's been as traumatized by Mom's illness as I have. She's never hinted that she understands what a miracle it is that we still have the precious and rare love of our mom. My phone vibrates. I exhale and turn it over. It's Dom.

I didn't expect to hear from him again, but maybe he's calling to plead Jett's case, too. I hold my finger up to my sisters to tell them to wait. "Hello?"

"Ryleigh, this is Dom."

"I know."

He must be outside the rink, because I hear cars going by and a crow in the background.

"Look," Dom says. "I'm not trying to get between you and Jett, but there's something you should know."

Let me guess: Jett is heartbroken. That makes two of us.

"I don't know what he told you," I say.

"He hasn't told me anything about what went wrong with you two."

"Oh."

"We're getting on the bus soon. We're heading to Johnstown this weekend."

I nod, forgetting he can't see me.

"I don't know if you care, Ryleigh, but Jett is going to ask for a trade this weekend."

I sit up. "What?"

"He says his presence is making you miserable, so he's going to ask Coach to be traded. He's going to wait until he can be alone with him, because Coach isn't going to be happy about it, even though Jett has played like total garbage since you two had your fight."

"I don't understand. Why would they trade him?"

"I don't know that they will. They're going to be ticked off. But if they think he's going to blow it if he stays here, then they might."

I stare at the floor as I process this information. Jett is trying to leave. Because of me. My eyes prickle.

"Look, Ryleigh, I'm sorry for whatever he did that's made you miserable around him, but if there is some way for you to forgive him enough to coexist until the end of the school year, I'm asking you to do it. This is bigger than you and Jett. Our team needs him. He brings attention to all of us, not just himself. Every guy on this team is trying to get somewhere, and we need the exposure he brings. We're so close to making playoffs, but if we lose Jett, there's no way that will happen. He's our captain for a reason, even when he plays like trash. If the team agrees to trade him, they're going to send him to one of the worst teams to punish him. You know how hard he's worked to get here. Can you please forgive him? Just enough to get him to stay until the end of the season and his school year."

My brain is on fire trying to understand what Dom is

telling me. Jett wants to leave, because of me. That would mean a new host family, school, and team for him. With less than half a year left of his senior year and only a couple months in the season before playoffs. While he should be getting ready for playoffs and the draft. Because he liked me and was imperfect about it.

A voice in the background yells, "Dom, Coach says get on the bus."

This isn't something I can fix with a text or a video-chat. Maybe I can't fix it at all.

"Dom," I say, "can you stall?"

"What?"

"Stall the bus. Can you keep it from leaving? I'll be there in thirteen minutes. Eleven if I hit some lights." My sisters are grinning at each other.

"I'll do my best, Ryleigh. Thanks."

"I'm not making any promises," I say as I run downstairs and grab my keys.

"I don't need promises. I just need you to tell him to stay."

I click my phone off and throw it into the passenger seat as I start the Rogue. I don't know if I have it in me to tell Jett to stay. But I know I don't have it in me to let him go.

I swing into the rink lot like a Formula 1 driver. The doors of the baggage compartments on Jett's bus are closed. The bus exhales and drops as the driver closes the main door and rolls out of a spot spanning several parking spaces. I'm still about thirty feet away from the bus, so I turn my car to block its path and jump out. I run to the bus.

As I reach the door, the driver opens it.

"What are you doing?" he yells.

Inside the bus, I hear Jett's coaches asking the same thing, and then a ripple of guys saying, "It's Jett's girlfriend."

Coach Mike comes to the door. He doesn't know me, but I recognize him.

"Please," I say, "I know you need to go, but I need to talk to Jett. Just for thirty seconds, please?"

Jett appears behind his coach. "Ryleigh, what are you doing?"

"Don't go, Jett. Don't ask for the trade."

Jett's eyes dart from me to his coach.

"What the hell is going on?" Coach Mike asks. "What's she talking about a trade for?"

"That's my girlfriend," Jett says. "My ex-girlfriend, I mean."

Jett's coach groans. "Is this why you're suddenly playing like you belong in Tier Three Alaska?"

Jett nods as he looks at the floor. "Sorry, Coach."

"And you want a trade?" Coach Mike asks.

"No," I say. "He doesn't. He doesn't want a trade."

Coach Mike motions him to get off the bus. "Make it quick," he says.

Jett jumps down the steps and stands before me, his mouth open.

"How'd you know?"

"That doesn't matter. Just don't go."

"Ryleigh, I know how painful I'm making things for you. I can't stay."

"Why don't you let me worry about my heart, and you worry about yours." I'm still mad, but now it's at myself instead of him.

Jett stares at me. On the bus, windows are sliding open as his whole team invests in our drama.

"I love you too much to do that to you. It's better if I go."

The tears that have been threatening burst from my eyes and roll down my cheeks.

I can be mad and hurt and scared all I want. The truth is that I love Jett with all my heart and the idea of him leaving Danbury, leaving me, is unbearable. Harper is right. Love is precious, and even if we end up losing it, at least I'll have taken the chance.

"Jett, I'm not good at shifting my emotions suddenly," I say.

"I know, that's why it's better if I go."

I shake my head. "Can't you just give me some time to process all this?"

Jett's eyes widen. "Seriously?"

Shouts of "Forgive him" come from the bus, and Jett waves his hand at his teammates to tell them to shut up.

"I'm really mad at you."

"Ouais. And I deserve it."

"It scared me. As much as last year did. I felt like I was losing myself all over again."

Jett shakes his head. "I never meant to hurt you like this."

I look away and bite my lip. "But I don't want to lose you. To lose us."

Jett tilts his head down to catch my gaze as if I might change my mind and bolt.

"Are you sure about this?"

I nod.

"Je t'aime. Tellement." I say it without a smile, because I'm still a little scared. But there's no telling what tomorrow can bring. Jett can't protect me. He can only love me, if I'm willing to let him. Somewhere inside me, I want to kiss him like it's the last kiss at the end of the world. The boy standing in front of me isn't perfect, he's just waiting for me to love him. A kitten who came to me out of nowhere. And really, I'm just a kitten myself. Full of imperfect rules and expectations and fears and doubts.

Jett's face slowly transforms into a smile, as if he can't really believe I've just admitted how much I love him.

"Je t'aime, tellement," he says, and pulls me into a hug.

The whole bus erupts into cheers. There's so much yelling that it rocks the bus side to side.

"Okay, can we go now?" Coach Mike asks. "We're at least ten minutes behind schedule, which means there better not be a wait at the Jersey Mike's on the turnpike or my team is going to be starving during the game tonight."

Jett and I laugh.

"We'll go hungry, Coach!" someone yells, and the whole team cheers again.

Jett wipes a tear off his cheek. Any lingering resentment I had evaporates with that tear.

"Just ten seconds more," I say. I jump up on my toes and pull Jett's face down to mine. I kiss him with all the love I felt before I ever learned that he liked me enough to lie to me. The guys on the bus sound like middle schoolers with their whistling.

When we finally pull away from each other, I scrunch my face up. "Don't you *ever* lie to me again."

"Jamais," Jett says, and crosses his heart. Never. "Jamais, jamais, jamais!"

I step back and let go of his hand. The guys on the bus are still cheering, and Jett's coach is still annoyed. But when I look into Jett's eyes, it's as if we're floating alone on a sheet of ice that's all ours for as long as we want it to be.

He goes to step on the bus, but he's looking at me and almost trips.

We laugh. "Go, before you hurt yourself," I say. "And play great tonight! Don't embarrass me!"

Jett nods and stumbles onto the bus. We're both crying.

"You'd better play well now," his coach says, "and no more nonsense about a trade."

"Yes, Coach, sorry about all this," Jett says, and then makes his way back to his seat.

I run to my car and move it so the bus can leave. Then I jump out and wave as Jett's bus swings onto the road that leads from the rink to the main street that will take them to the highway. Jett and all the guys on his side of the bus are waving back.

I wipe the tears from my cheeks and get in my car.

My phone dings with a text from Jett.

I promise I'll never lie again. No matter what storms we hit, no matter what I want, I'll tell you the truth and live with the consequences. The only thing better than being your fake boyfriend is being your real one, but I won't ever lie again to make it happen.

I close my eyes a minute, the late-afternoon sun warm on my face. My phone dings.

It was supposed to be a fib, not a lie.

Too soon, I text.

Jett marks my text with a thumbs-up.

Want to watch a movie? he asks.

I laugh. I want to do everything with him.

Ouais, I text back. Give me fifteen minutes to get home.

I love you, Ryleigh Vento.

I take a deep breath. Jett and I may not be perfect, but somehow, just like a kitten, our love is as close as you can get.

Je t'aime, aussi, Jett Robitaille. Tellement.

ACKNOWLEDGMENTS

I am so grateful to have written this book, which was a true labor of love. I'm grateful to my three kids, who made me spend ridiculous amounts of time and money chasing their love of hockey around the country. When I would sit in those cold rinks with my toes frozen and my teeth chattering, I never knew how much I would miss getting to just be there for them, cheering them on. Now I only get to do that from afar.

I'm also grateful to my writing group: Sally Alexander, Heidi Brayer, Dave Crawley, Amanda Hooper, Alan Irvine, Linda "Casey" Kustra, and Cristina Rouvalis. Thank you all for always pushing me to be a little better, and for understanding why I'm always behind schedule. Thank you to my friends and family who support my writing dreams. You are too many to name, but I love you all.

Thank you to my dear Wyatt, who brightened every day as I was on deadline for this manuscript. I miss you more than words can express.

Thank you to my agent, Michelle Hauck, for supporting me no matter how unstable my life gets, and thank you to the best editor a romance writer could have, Wendy Loggia. Thank you, too, to my imprint-mates, who are always super kind, especially Katrina Emmel, Kristy Boyce, and Becky Dean. I'm very grateful for everyone at PRH who helps to make my books, from my publicist team to the PRH Audio team to the cover team and everyone along the way. I'm so grateful for all you do to enable me to have my books see the light of day.

And, for the big finale, I'd like to thank everyone who reads my work. I'm especially grateful to everyone who lets me know that it meant something to them. Those are the words that keep me going when I get discouraged or feel overwhelmed. Books are more than words on pages. They are conversations between friends, fellow readers, and future friends. I'm grateful for all of you.

ABOUT THE AUTHOR

SABRINA FEDEL is an environmental attorney, writer, and fully credentialed hockey mom. Sabrina's hometown is Pittsburgh, and she holds her MFA in creative writing from Lesley University. She believes chocolate is a love language, the beach is the most likely place to find magic, and that someday she'll outsmart her deaf dog. She is the author of *All Roads Lead to Rome* and *All Paths Lead to Paris*.

SABRINAFEDEL.COM
@sabrinafedel

IT'S A LOVE STORY.